iKill

iKill

A NOVEL

MURALI VENUGOPALAN

authorHOUSE®

AuthorHouse™ LLC
1663 Liberty Drive
Bloomington, IN 47403
www.authorhouse.com
Phone: 1-800-839-8640

This book is a work of fiction. Names, characters, places, and incidents either are
products of the author's imagination or are used fictitiously. Any resemblance to
actual events or locales or persons, living or dead, is entirely coincidental.

Published by AuthorHouse   11/22/2013

ISBN: 978-1-4918-3715-3 (sc)
ISBN: 978-1-4918-3714-6 (hc)
ISBN: 978-1-4918-3716-0 (e)

Library of Congress Control Number: 2013921075

Any people depicted in stock imagery provided by Thinkstock are models,
and such images are being used for illustrative purposes only.
Certain stock imagery © Thinkstock.

This book is printed on acid-free paper.

This book is dedicated to my parents, Mundiyath and
Johanna Venugopalan, who showed me the world.

*T*he end of November brings an onslaught of death. All the leaves fall from trees as a precursor to dying. They die every year; we die only once. And I'm in the middle of my death. Today is the Sunday following Thanksgiving break, the worst day of life, and cloudbursts of blood leave me thinking of death.

We're always dying, ever since we're born. If there were a God, He wouldn't let us die. He wouldn't let me die. I would know what to do about these cancerous thoughts drowning my mind in a sea of red.

"Dead." The word sends my imagination reeling. Now I'm thinking about "Death Round the World." Time to bring the rest of the crew in for a sound check. Is that Death knocking inside my head again? It's a bloodthirsty drink.

I should have known Death would follow me down to quiet Blackwood. Some days I wake up to see Death burning a CD—the greatest hits of dying.

"Kill," it says. I can't control my thoughts anymore. Got to set them loose even if it means wiping out the whole campus. Let them burn beyond eternity.

Ever since I can remember, I've been doing my tour of duty. Now it's time to act.

Not a peep, not out of me, I'm invisible.

Not quite, but I'm working on the formula. Love = Girl + Sledgehammer.

"iKill . . ." Anybody listening? Does anyone hear that sound? What is that?

That's the sound of me. Everybody ready for the Death Dance?

Got me in a trance and I can't get out of it. Save the last death for me.

Chapter One

A round eleven Sunday night, Jenny Curtis got off the bus and smiled as she walked up the steps to the lobby of Edgar Hall. Thanksgiving break was over, and while she loathed the onset of finals and papers, she looked forward to seeing her friends—all relatively new friends, this being her first semester at Blackwood College. She wondered how Mindy, George, and Jackie were doing . . . but she hoped she could avoid Chip, who also lived in Edgar Hall.

A fortnight before Thanksgiving, Jenny had found out about Chip's infidelities and, goaded by her sister and Jackie, decided to break up with him. Breaking free from an unhealthy relationship felt right, Jenny thought, and yet she still was troubled by a looming sense of doom. Her mind was tattooing disaster all over a heart she had listened to for eighteen years.

Jenny passed the front desk and greeted Charlie White. He always had a smile waiting for her. This evening, he and Abby Jones, a student worker, were handing out donuts.

"Welcome back, Jenny," Charlie said. He appreciated the purity of Jenny's appearance, simple yet refined. He thought she possessed an uncomplicated beauty that many college-age men found appealing. "Abby and I got a couple dozen donuts, knowing that all you students would be returning this evening," he told her. "There's still a bunch of different ones you can choose from."

"Thanks," Jenny said. She set her suitcase down and grabbed a glazed chocolate donut. She was always impressed with Charlie's kindness and good humor toward the students and staff at Blackwood. He stood about six feet tall and had short, thin brown hair that was beginning to gray at the temples. Though very skinny, Jenny thought Charlie was in good shape for someone she guessed must be around fifty years old.

Abby, Charlie's long-legged blonde graduate assistant who got a lot of attention from the guys on campus, also had a friendly disposition but somewhat of a selfish streak. She was at least as good a flirt as Sheila, another Edgar Hall resident.

"Most of the students got back a few hours ago," Abby said. "How was break? Get to spend some quality time with family?"

Jenny beamed. "Got to spend lots of time with my folks and older sister, and of course I did a little homework, but not as much as I should have. You know how that goes. Best of all was hanging out with all my dogs and cats. I really miss them down here and can't wait till I can have my own apartment next year and can bring them down. Just wait till you meet Chestnut—he's the cutest little cocker spaniel in the world."

Charlie and Abby remembered that Jenny was a preveterinary major and fond of animals.

Jenny continued, "And guess what? I got an internship approved with the Humane Society for next summer."

"That's great news, Jenny," Charlie said. He shook her hand to congratulate her. Jenny laughed at his trademark formality.

Abby gave her a big hug. "Awesome," she said. "I've been looking for an internship myself, but nothing's come up yet. Watch me get stuck with nothing but classes in the summer."

"You never know," Charlie said. "You have to hang in there and good things might happen, like for Jenny here."

Jenny leaned toward Abby and whispered, "You haven't seen you-know-who?"

Abby coughed. "Chip? He's here all right, got in around three p.m. to catch the football games on TV with the rest of the guys. I think he came in on the afternoon train from DC with Tyler, Chainsaw, and George."

"That's too bad."

Abby's curiosity was overflowing. "Have you guys talked things out yet?"

"Not a word," Jenny said.

"Not even an e-mail?"

"Nothing. It's the only black mark on an otherwise perfect semester. I don't want to even see him, but at the same time, I wouldn't mind if he came back begging, you know? Isn't that awful? Like I don't want him, but I want him to still want me."

Abby said, "You made the right choice. Don't wait for a man to change his ways. Change your ways and watch him weep. That's what I say."

"You girls are rough," Charlie said. "In my day, women followed men. Now it looks like we're the followers. All you girls are just plain mean."

"And don't forget it," Jenny said, winking at Abby and Charlie. "I better unpack and catch up on some reading before the big speech tomorrow night. You guys going?"

"I have to—my political-science professor made us go and write a two-page paper on his speech," Abby replied. "What's the guy's name, anyway?"

"Thomas Malkin," Charlie said. "He's achieved so much for being only about 45 years old. He is a Blackwood alumnus—got his bachelor's here about twenty years ago—but since then he's gone far. The press release on him—it's around here somewhere, but you can find it online too—said he served in the Gulf War, Iraq War, and from what I hear is brilliant. Now he's one of the leaders in Homeland Security."

"That's right," Jenny said. "My dad said this is one speech I don't want to miss. He almost came down with me just to listen to his talk! I guess Malkin's big claim to fame is tracking down that anthrax poisoning case in the DC area about ten years ago. And wasn't he also involved in arresting those two coconspirators plotting a terrorist attack in Houston?"

"I think so," Charlie said, raising his eyes to the ceiling to jog his memory. "He's definitely respected in the field of counterterrorism—bad news for al-Qaeda."

"Wish we could line all of them up for public hangings. I'd be the first in line for tickets," Abby said.

"That's a bit harsh, don't you think?" Charlie asked.

"Still, we're lucky to have such a distinguished alum," Abby said, as Jenny enjoyed her donut.

"If someone can cover for us," Charlie added, "I think I'll run over to the Grand Ballroom and catch the speech as well."

Jenny took the elevator up to the third floor. At least most of the construction was over. Edgar Hall, the oldest residence hall on campus, had undergone massive renovation over the last two years. It had gone from archaic to including such modern facilities as Wi-Fi throughout the building, a recreation center, a lounge with a new sixty-five-inch flat-screen high-definition TV, and a new computer lab and cafeteria, as well as a few new meeting rooms and a conference center.

Though Edgar Hall had six floors, all of the students living there currently had single rooms on the third floor because of the renovation. It felt weird having only sixteen students living in such a large residence hall, but Jenny was used to it and had come to appreciate the more intimate atmosphere. She had made good friends and was enjoying her classes. Now she just wanted to avoid Chip, at least for the time being.

Jenny got out of the elevator and turned right. She heard voices at the other end of the hall—male voices—and it sounded like they were watching a late football game. Jenny thought she would avoid that side of the building today and go straight to her room, unpack, get started on homework, and then catch up with friends later. All except Chip, of course.

She entered her room and unpacked her suitcase. She was happy that everyone in Edgar Hall had a single room so she could decorate hers as she pleased. She loved her room—the World Wildlife Fund poster on her closet, the light blue and yellow pillows strewn across a red bed cover, and the small desk with a computer and printer and large reading lamp. The lamp reminder her of the reading she had to do for next week.

She sat at her desk and opened her biology textbook. She yawned and stared at a picture of her family on the bookshelf. She missed them already. She wished her dad had come down with her for tomorrow's speech. Just two more weeks, she sighed, and she'd be back together with family.

* * *

A couple hours passed. Jenny had dozed off, tired from the bus ride. She awoke in a panic—it was almost 1:00 a.m., and she had to prepare for finals.

Jenny found it hard to concentrate, so she decided to check her e-mail. Maybe Chip had . . . no, better not to think that way. She still wanted nothing to do with that boy—not till he came back begging on his knees for forgiveness and admitted that what he did was wrong.

She clicked on "Inbox" and swept her hair away from her forehead. She looked outside and yawned at the darkness that had descended like doom on Blackwood.

There were two new messages in her inbox. Suddenly her eyes widened. Each was from a sender named iKill. Who on earth could that be? Jenny was sure it was some sort of joke and clicked on the first message, titled "I Missed You." It had to be from Chip, she thought, but why would he use such a ridiculous user ID?

The message had been sent on Thursday afternoon and read:

Dear Jenny,

>   *I've missed you all week. Thought you might send an e-mail or even call me but never heard from you. Shame on you. You should know better. You know my life depends on you. What have you been up to? Give me a call or reply to this e-mail or else . . . Love, iKill*

Jenny dug her nails into her palms. Who would be so sick as to send such a message? Only Chip. Of course, it could have been someone from back home, but who would write this kind of message? It didn't make sense. She was afraid to open the second message, titled "See You Soon," but she did so anyway.

This message was sent yesterday afternoon and read:

Dear Jenny,

>   *I still haven't heard back from you. Are you afraid? You've got nothing to be afraid of . . . if you don't disobey me. Call me or reply to this e-mail or else I will get revenge. Who the hell do you think you are? I'm starting to lose my patience with you. You better do as I say. I'm sure you'll come to your senses soon. You're a smart girl, Jenny. I want to see you and kiss you. I can't wait . . . Love, iKill.*

Jenny froze and stared at the monitor. She reread the message and shuddered at the thought of Chip losing his mind over her, but that's obviously what was happening. This was a threat, and Jenny didn't respond well to threats. Her mind started racing. It would be just like Chip to make up some strange identity to scare her—he had done weirder things in the last two months, in between cheating on her and breaking promises. Jenny sank in her chair and felt lonely and afraid. What was going on?

She logged off and decided to peek outside her door. There was no one standing in the dull-green-painted hallway, but she heard the guys down the hall shouting over the television. She felt at once like confronting and avoiding Chip. Why was she always so conflicted? Jenny looked round her room one more time, grabbed her keys, and darted two doors down to Jackie's room. Surely her best friend would be able to help her. She knocked on Jackie's door and felt a rush of relief as the ever-empathetic Jackie, standing the same height in socks and sporting short raven hair that contrasted sweetly with the gleam of her teeth, welcomed Jenny with open arms.

*   *   *

Monday evening, and the big speech had finally arrived. Blackwood College president Dr. Arnold Keyes greeted Thomas Malkin outside the entrance to the Grand Ballroom. President Keyes was clearly happy that Blackwood College's most famous alum had accepted his invitation. There were other college leaders admiring Thomas Malkin, including Joe Flanagan, vice president for public relations; provost Ann Lewis; and various deans and chairs.

"Thanks for having me," Malkin said. He sported his usual olive-green suit with solid charcoal tie and exchanged firm handshakes with the men. "Just arrived around noon and had a nice lunch at the old Sycamore Barn with a few former professors. You might remember Ben Michaels from law enforcement?"

"Of course," President Keyes said. "See him on the golf course every so often. Been retired about ten years now but keeps in good shape."

"Then after lunch, I took a long walk around campus—down Nostalgia Avenue, you might say—and enjoyed the flood of memories that came back to me. A lot has changed since I left about twenty years ago. There are more cars and parking lots; Edgar Hall, my old dorm, is in the process of renovation; all the new restaurants and coffee shops, the Lighthouse and so forth; and of course, just about every student was walking around campus talking and sending texts on their cell phones!"

Provost Lewis laughed. "And they say supply doesn't create demand! Amazing how technology has changed this campus over the last ten years. Computer labs, online courses, and now many textbooks are on CDs or e-books. It appears the days of lugging a backpack full of heavy books are soon past us."

"It's going to turn us into a nation of wimps," Malkin said.

As they entered the ballroom, Malkin straightened his tie. It was a full house, with a pack of about seventy-five students standing in the back of the ballroom.

"Looks like publicity did a fine job," Malkin said to Flanagan.

He mingled with a few alumni and university representatives and discussed topics ranging from Blackwood College concerns to Washington politics. Following dinner, President Keyes introduced Malkin, whose speech focused on fighting domestic and international terrorism. He gave examples from his own recent experiences dealing with al-Qaeda operatives in Houston and cautioned against taking a passive stance toward what he considered a mounting threat to civilization. The speech reached its most sobering note when Malkin referred to America's duty to "fight World War III wherever the battles lead us."

He received a standing ovation and then answered questions from the audience. Malkin was relieved to finally step down from the podium, and he once again took in the atmosphere of the ballroom. Though large, it seemed much smaller to him now, and his mind drifted back to receptions and speeches he had attended in his own college days.

President Keyes interrupted his drive down Memory Lane. "Thanks again for coming, Tom. I think they really enjoyed your talk. Well done."

After Keyes, Flanagan, and many other dignitaries left, Malkin noticed a few patient students waiting for autographs. He always felt strange about signing them but understood that attaining slight celebrity status through recent cases obligated him to appease young autograph-seekers.

"My name is George Young," one student said. "I've read all about you online. Keep up the good work. I'm also an LEJA major, and I'm here on a baseball scholarship. I play third base." His voice was more eager than professional, but Malkin had come to expect that from undergraduates.

"Baseball—one of my favorite sports," Malkin said. "Best of luck with your batting average, and don't forget your academics. Remember to play hard and study hard. If you don't do the latter, you can't have the former."

George shook his hand and felt like he had just been handed a million dollars.

Behind George stood a stolid Jenny Curtis. It was obvious she was trying to act as if nothing was bothering her. For a couple hours, Jenny had been pretending everything was all right and the mysterious iKill e-mail writer did not exist. She offered Malkin a few words of praise, indicated that her father wished he could have attended the speech, and thanked Malkin for his autograph with a hesitant smile. Her mind was paused on the iKill e-mails.

After Jenny and George left the ballroom, a couple dozen students flocked around Malkin to ask him questions on topics ranging from international politics to time management and school mascots. He offered brief answers and signed more autographs. A thin, unassuming girl with light blonde hair and a pointed nose approached him next.

"My name's Mindy Adams, and my older brother works in Washington and told me all about your exploits out there," she said. "Must be tiresome tracking down international terrorists day in and day out."

"It's a team effort," Malkin said, "and I'm just one link. International terrorism will be the greatest challenge of the twenty-first century, but we've also got to keep an eye out for domestic terrorism. Nothing the outsiders would like more than to see Americans committing acts of treason to satisfy the evil whims of fanatics, such as suicide bombers."

Mindy thanked Malkin, but she wasn't interested in the finer points of fighting terrorism. Behind her, Charlie stood waiting with a humble grin.

"It's an honor to meet you in person," he said. "We're glad you haven't forgotten your roots and that you came here, even with your hectic schedule and everything that's going on."

"This is where it all started for me," Malkin said.

"Me too. Though I never got to go to college. I've been working as a front-desk manager for almost thirty years. The last twenty years or so, I've been assigned to work in various places around Blackwood College, and now in Edgar Hall."

"My old residence hall," Malkin said. "Must have missed each other by about five years. Nice to see that it's in good hands, and I like the renovation efforts . . . finally accepting the twenty-first century is upon us."

"It's getting there," Charlie said. "Right now, only sixteen students live here, but about two hundred more will be moving into Edgar next spring."

Charlie introduced his graduate assistant, Abby, who was starstruck despite not having a clue about Malkin's speech. She was happy that at least she got an autograph from someone famous.

"You've got a long way to go, but you'll get there," Malkin said to Abby. "Make the best of what you have." Abby wasn't sure what he meant but nodded in approval.

Tired after approximately three hours of socializing, Malkin shook a few more hands and decided to call it a night. He went back to his hotel room and showered, fixed himself a drink from the mini-fridge, and turned on the television. The local station had breaking news about a fourteen-year old mother from Blackwood who left her three-month-old baby girl to die in a dumpster. Apparently water rats and raccoons had gotten pieces of the daughter before officials found her. The mother was not found at her residence and had been reported as missing.

"It's an evil world we live in," Malkin said, finishing his drink. He got up and stared at the full moon. "Those kids have no idea how much evil lurks out there, but they'll learn soon enough."

* * *

George walked into Chip's room and joined the gang in time to catch the second half of the Ravens-Patriots Sunday-night game. He sat next to Chip, to whose right was Tyler Mitchell, a well-built, brilliant, crew-cut information-tech major of medium height, and Hank Kilger (affectionately nicknamed "Chainsaw" by his friends), a linebacker-proportioned first-year student taking mostly general-education courses and known equally for his notorious temper and his disregard for proper study habits; Gottlieb Heiner, a lanky and querulous German exchange student studying political science; and Branford Smith, a tall, thin techie with short black hair and a freshman computer-science major.

"Pats are up 14-7 at the half," Chip told George.

Chainsaw laughed. "It don't matter. Just like the Redskins, the Patriots' defense will find a way to lose. Just watch! And besides, it's like the Ravens always play better when it's cold out. Glad I picked them this week."

Chip ignored Chainsaw's comments and asked George, "So how was that big speech of yours?"

"Excellent," George said. "You should have come."

Chip frowned. "Nah—bunch of nonsense . . . unless Jenny was there."

"Yeah."

"That chick is really messed up. I mean, breaking up with me just a week before break—piece of trash. She'll get hers in the end."

"Ah, get over it," Gottlieb said, speaking with a strong German accent. "In my country, the way we forget about a girl is to drink a lot of beer and find other girl. We can do that tonight if you like."

"Drink Nazi brew?" Chip asked. "No way. If I'm going to get drunk, I'll do it with good old Jack Daniels sour mash—nothing else."

Chip followed through with his idea and poured himself a Jack and Coke. He offered the same or beers to everyone else, and everyone except Branford accepted.

"I'll just take a Coke, Chip," he said.

"Aw," Chainsaw chuckled, "would you like a lemon with that, Branford?"

Everyone laughed, and Tyler recalled the first week of the semester when Edgar Hall students put themselves through a low-scale hazing, part of which included proving one could handle a substantial amount of alcohol. Branford ended up passed out in the bushes adjacent to the lake across the street. In fact, he may well have fallen into the lake had a stone bench not impeded his downward roll.

Branford flipped Chainsaw off. "Got a twelve-page Java program to write up for tomorrow and plan on spending most of the night on it," he said. "Then again, I could just ask Chainsaw to write it for me, given his awesome academic prowess."

Chainsaw ignored Branford's sarcasm and focused instead on the game.

Tyler said he felt hungry and suggested ordering pizzas.

"To hell with pizza," Chip growled. He put his hands between his knees and then covered his head with crossed arms.

"I think he needs another drink," Gottlieb said.

"She just broke up with me," Chip said. "What a damn bitch!"

"What? You mean Jenny dumped *you*?" Tyler asked. "I thought it was the other way around."

"Hey that's pretty sharp thinking there, Tyler. You must be a scholarship student. Or maybe Denise's brains are finally rubbing off on you."

Gottlieb told Chip to have a beer.

Chip was in no mood to be happy or to entertain humor in his own room. "Hitler Heiner, I'm sure beer is the remedy for just about any ailment in your country."

The pale-faced Gottlieb got along well with most of the guys in Edgar Hall but resented being called "Hitler Heiner." Gottleib smacked Chip across the head and warned him that the next time he used that slur, he would be pulverized into a heap of bone-crushing bruises and shoved down a toilet. Chip shoved Gottlieb against the door.

"Like to see you try," Chip said. "Go ahead, and I'll snap your neck in half so fast you'd paralyze in slow-motion."

"All right, girls," Chainsaw said, "stop your whining." Chainsaw, who could bench 350 pounds with the flu and had a habit of watching girls across the courtyard through binoculars in the evening, was still searching for his first successful date at Blackwood. He was also still looking for his first decent test score. His frustration led to his often sparring with floormates because of his short temper—even worse than Chip's.

"It's no use," Chip said. "I might as well walk down to that witch's room and smack some sense into her with her broom. Maybe a few right hooks would do the trick."

Tyler laughed. "Witch's broom? What, you're going to swing at her with a broomstick?"

"Bitch's room—I said *bitch's* room, you moron. Get your ears checked at the Health Center. They do free screenings for seniors, but they might make an exception in your case."

Tyler suggested Chip get his blood-alcohol level checked before he tried flying out the window on a broomstick.

Chip thought he had no chance of winning Jenny back, and he was determined to make her pay a price. "Here I am at the bottom of the sewer eating all the crap she's spoon-fed me over the last couple months. One good turn deserves another, and that tart will get hers. Everyone's gonna find out sooner or later." He walked out of his own room and into the bathroom.

"Who cares?" Chainsaw said. "He's wastin' his time; Chip don't know what he's doin'. Let's just watch the damn game and drink up. Besides, now one of *us* can date Jenny. If it's a real man that she wants, give her a week with me." He envisioned sweeping Jenny off her feet and kissing her in front of Chip just to spite him.

Gottlieb laughed. "Ya, maybe if she suddenly becomes blind then she will do that. But really, you know, it is the German man that every woman wants. Because we can give her the good cars, good beer." He paused and then added, "Chip should just take her out of his brain and have a few beers; it's what the doctor prescribed."

"Prescribed," Tyler corrected.

Suddenly a tall, lean, mysterious brunette stopped in the doorway and threw a reproachful glance at Tyler.

"Hi, Denise," he said. None of the other guys said a word; Denise had an irate expression on her face aimed in Tyler's direction. This was one of those moments when he knew he had forgotten to do something for his new girlfriend but forgot what it was he had forgotten.

"So, Tyler, what are *you* up to?" she asked with an insolent tone.

"We're just hanging out, watching football."

"That's a good use of time," she said. "Don't call me in the middle of the night asking how to write your economics report just because you spent most of the day playing Wii and watching football." She crossed her arms and said, "Can I talk to you for a minute?" It was more of a statement than a question.

Talk about catty. The cat's not having a good day, Tyler thought. He got up and walked with Denise to her room. She was good-looking enough, he thought, that some damage control on his part was necessary in order to prevent their relationship from bleeding all over the place like Chip's had.

On the way to Denise's room, they passed by Rhoda Remlinger's. It looked as if she was busy unpacking and discussing sorority information with her neighbor and friend, Sheila Underwood.

Once they had entered Denise's room, she said, "Stupid women! Neither one of them could string two sentences together. All they ever talk about are boys and rushing that damn sorority."

"What's wrong?"

"Wrong? You promised you would study at the library with me, and you completely forgot about it. Is this the first time? No. Will it be the last? Somehow, I doubt it. So what do you say, Mr. Genius? Are you going to blow me off and make me pull a Jenny on you, or are you going to stick by your woman and keep your promises like a real man? What's more important—finals or Sunday-night football?"

Tyler knew the answer to that question, but instead he said he'd meet her in his room in ten minutes.

*   *   *

Stacy "Head Case" Nutter sat alone in her room wearing an oversized black silk robe and admiring the Moroccan scarves draped around a pale light in the corner. There was a sociology textbook and another book on black magic. Next to the desk was a black light shining on a burning incense stick. A few feet to the left was Nellie, her pet parakeet, in a cage. Stacy watched the smoke waft up toward the window and bounce off it, distributing its aroma across the room.

She wondered what Nellie was thinking. She welcomed Nellie's advice, and from time to time she even conversed with Nellie, whose bright red, blue, and yellow feathers made the room glow. In truth, Stacy held far more conversations with her pet bird than with all her fellow Edgar Hall residents put together, a fact of which she was proud.

Stacy was barely five feet two inches tall, and her floormates agreed she looked like an obese weirdo. She opened the bottom drawer of her desk and took out a crystal ball the size of a mini-basketball. She smiled at its beauty and placed it on a small table next to the bed. She laughed in a sadistic manner and wrapped a scarf around her rotund head. Stacy lit a cigarette and smoked for a few minutes, admiring all the strange thoughts crossing the energy panels of her small room as she made sure to exhale out the window.

She thought of possibilities. She imagined ruin and ecstasy. She put the cigarette out and turned toward the crystal ball. She rubbed her thick hands and smiled. Her green eyes dilated in the amusement of the moment and twinkled with joy.

"Tell me what I need to know," she spoke to the crystal ball. "What is going on that is wicked and wonderful in the world tonight?" Stacy's face gleamed in the psychic glow of Mr. Wizard.

She stared into the crystal ball. Tinges of smoke and malice blew from its epicenter. She studied the various images being sent to her. She saw faces both known and unknown. She saw one face in particular and shuddered. Could it be? How strange. The patterns were not entirely clear, and Stacy shielded her eyes against the dim light emanating from the corner of the room to enhance the picture forming in her best friend.

"Looks like me, lost in a crowd, and there is trouble," she said. "But there is more . . . come to me, Wizard . . . let the pictures come . . ."

She studied the crystal ball for a few minutes and watched its center fade from colorless to faint red. Stacy jumped to the edge of her seat and moved as close to the Wizard as possible.

"This I've never seen before," she said. "And to think, most people don't believe this is real science." She opined that the energy she felt was at times more accurate than many of the plunders performed in the name of authentic science.

"This is more authentic and more real," she said to Nellie. "And check this out. Looks like trouble on the horizon . . . I think I recognize that face . . . yes, it's coming in clearer . . . I can see it. But I wonder . . . dear Wizard . . . what are you trying to tell me?"

The Wizard shifted colors and moods. A storm was on the horizon? Stacy was convinced something was amiss.

Danger, she thought. Danger.

"Well, that makes things easier. We must get those tarot cards out, don't you think so, Nellie?"

*   *   *

Zach Gillett, with a mop of dirty brown hair piled upon a mop of stained clothes hanging off his bones, had a terrible Thanksgiving break and was happy to return to Edgar Hall. He felt much better here. Back home, he had to put up with his parents admonishing him for poor grades. Zach thought it was better they found out now than as a bad surprise during Christmas vacation.

Still, Zach wasn't in the mood for academics. He wanted to be a musician, to form his own band and write songs. This was his first priority in life, so he thought nothing of skipping more than half his classes this semester. He thought having a sexy female lead singer would be a good draw for his band and was in love with many of the good-looking women in bands today.

He'd slept four hours since arriving back on campus, and his parents' last words of advice still echoed in his brain: Don't waste your education. Don't waste your education. Don't waste . . .

What do parents know? he thought. It was his life, his dream, his talent. If he didn't put this to use, he'd never make it big. Probably end up a loser anyway.

He was depressed and obsessed with the idea of death. He called Malcolm's room, but there was no answer. He could hear some of the guys on the floor having fun and watching football, but he wasn't interested in either football or fun.

He tried calling Jenny, the girl with the golden voice and golden hair. She was soft and sweet and sensitive. And she had a good voice—a blonde version of Shirley Manson, one of his idols. Jenny would be the ideal vocalist for his group. He even had a name picked out: End of Life.

But Jenny did not answer. He thought about leaving a message but didn't. Zach did not quite understand himself. He was a born musician, and yet he was plagued by strange thoughts. He considered suicide. He considered murder. He thought about killing his parents, just as many teens in most states had; he heard all about it on TV. Not a bad idea—they were irrational and didn't even try to understand him.

Some mornings Zach would wake up and wish life were over. He wondered what was before the beginning and what would come after the end. He thought about the gift and torture of life. He was confused, and his head felt heavy. He debated the merit of death and questioned the merit of the debate, considering its inevitability.

Zach thought about turning the lights on and then thought of a better idea. He grabbed his guitar from the closet where he'd thrown it a few hours ago and dusted it off. He loved this guitar—a brown acoustic Gibson with expensive strings. He liked his electric Telecaster too, but he preferred playing the acoustic in his room. That way he could keep away from the poison of the crowd.

"I've got to come up with a great song," he said. He looked for a lyric sheet he had started writing during break. He found it stuffed into the pocket of his guitar case. It was all about Jenny. He read the lyrics over and over again:

Went to sleep alone last night
And thought of you
The feeling put me on a cloud
Without a clue
I wonder what you're thinking
I wonder where you are
Wish I could just whisk you away
In my brand new car
Then we could drive away
From this evil place
And settle in the white hills of wherever
As long as you're in lace
Come save me tonight, little angel
And tell me who you are
Come save me tonight, little angel
Or I'll leave you with a scar
The nights sometimes torture me
Into believing you're a ghost
Stitched into my bleeding heart
Nailed into a wooden post
Come save me tonight, little angel
And tell me who you are
Come save me tonight, little angel
Or I'll leave you with a scar
Don't make me mistreat you
Don't make me abuse you
But I would never forgive you
For not offering your wing
So please show your face tonight
And show me so much more
Or I'll slice and dice you
To even up the score

Zach studied the lyric sheet and smiled. Perhaps not his best lyrics, but good enough for now. He was still waiting for his angel, every night in every dream. Could be Jenny. Jenny had not really noticed him, but he felt they had made a connection.

He obsessed about her. He definitely preferred blondes. Maybe he should call her again. This time, if she still wasn't home, he could leave a message. He resisted the temptation for the moment.

He had imagined going to Jenny's room when Chip was out drinking with the guys or on a date with another girl—poor, sweet Jenny found out about that too late—and kissing her and telling her that he was in love with her. Jenny Curtis. Jenny. Sweet, little Jenny. She would be the answer to all his prayers and all his dreams. But he needed time. "I'll get her in the end," he declared. "I'll get Jenny to like me by Christmas." He thought about Shirley Manson and her voice, and focused again on Jenny.

Jenny was ready to make a change, Zach thought. He was certain Jenny had dumped Chip to give Zach a chance. It was about time she came to her senses. Zach was determined to knock some sense into her.

"Damn it all to hell," he said. "Her loss if she doesn't let me date her. I'll get her attention one way or another." His mind spun into another set of thoughts, and possibly another song. He decided against giving her time. It's better to hit women when they least expect it—sweep them off their feet and surprise the heck out of them, that's how they like it. No time to waste. Tonight called for drastic action, and Zach was determined to get Jenny. She had to understand his desires.

He needed a plan of attack. Suddenly another tune came to mind, and selfish brown eyes squinted in sinister pleasure.

Chapter Two

Jenny managed to stay away from the inevitable—a confrontation with Chip. She wished he would transfer to another college.

There were still issues, however. This had been a valuable lesson in Life 101, for the romantic side of Jenny yearned for reconciliation, forgiveness, and the satisfaction of undeterred eternal bliss with her first true confidante since high school.

Maybe he had e-mailed her—that would solve all her problems. Then she could reply, forgive, force him to adopt a new attitude, and offer ultimatums. But had Chip sent those weird iKill e-mails? Jenny opened her inbox and found one new message; it had been sent this evening while she was studying, at 11:22 p.m. late Monday, about three hours after the speech.

She clicked on the message subject—"A Tasty Breakfast"—and read the message:

Dear Jenny,

> *You mystify me. I still haven't heard from you and wonder if you've even read these e-mails. But I'm sure you'll check e-mail this evening before going to bed—it's your habit. Now be a good little girl and meet me for breakfast tomorrow morning in the Student Commons about 9 a.m. Hope it's not too early. Don't disappoint me by not showing up. If you're not there, I'll find you . . . you can be sure of that . . . so be an angel and everything will be OK. Love, iKill*

This time, however, iKill had included an attachment. Should she open it? She hesitated, knowing how many attachments turned out to be viruses. But curiosity got the best of her, and she clicked on the file. It took two seconds to load, and Jenny could not believe her eyes.

The picture showed a dead cat seemingly run over by a car. It was white with patches of dried-up blood smeared all over its insect—and bird-pecked fur. Jenny felt a sudden urge to vomit and reached for her wastepaper basket just in time. Three dry heaves were followed by that night's supper, a yellow and brown mix of Chinese food from the Red Dragon.

Jenny looked at the picture again. She saw the cat's eyes bulging out of their sockets, with pus all over the pupils. Tire tracks were tattooed on its flattened torso. This was obviously someone's pet that had been run over by a car, and a lunatic named iKill cared enough to snap a picture of a dead cat and e-mail it to her.

What was going on? Jenny's love for animals was by no means a secret, and she preferred their company to that of people. Only an insane and heartless savage could have sent this e-mail and picture.

Jenny closed the message and almost deleted the three she had received, but then she thought again. Suppose this got serious and went to the police, she thought. She would want some sort of proof that a deviant had been harassing her.

Stalking. Isn't that what it all amounted to? This was twenty-first-century online stalking. Jenny winced at the thought that someone might want to do her harm. She thought a moment and couldn't come up with a single enemy she had in life, other than Chip. He wouldn't do this . . . or would he?

There were a lot of crazy people around, she thought, that's for sure. You can't count on most people, her mother had once warned her. Look out for number one. Jenny had followed her mom's advice and taken that a step further by caring for numerous animals over the past several years.

That poor kitty . . . Jenny cried for a few minutes and held back another regurgitation session with Mr. Wastepaper Basket.

It must be Chip trying to get some sort of devious revenge. Or it could be one of her floormates—even though she was on good terms with all of them, even Head Case and Chainsaw, whom she had come to have very little respect for. All those rumors about Chainsaw being a puppy and kitten torturer could have been fabricated; she wouldn't put it past someone on the floor playing some sort of e-mail prank on her.

But why Jenny and why now, right after Thanksgiving break? That didn't make sense. Maybe Mindy would be able to help her. Jenny reflected on her conversation with Jackie the night before the talk in the ballroom, and she locked her door and closed her blinds before falling into bed with her biology textbook. She had to catch up on reading and not allow a couple weird e-mails to derail her studies. She alternated between reading a few pages and reflecting back on the e-mails. Maybe this was just someone's sick idea of having fun with her emotions.

*   *   *

It was almost 2:00 a.m. Jenny had slept off and on since opening her biology textbook—mostly off, as she had enjoyed avoiding Chip and listening to the orchestra play. It was a strange time for classical music, she thought, and she couldn't figure out why she had brought her textbooks and notes to the opera. She examined her clothing and was amazed to find she was dressed like an angel—all in white, but with strange red splotches all over her blouse and pants. She couldn't quite see who was onstage, for her seat was in the nosebleed section. But she loved the music nonetheless. It made her feel like she was floating in heaven.

Jenny had a feeling of utmost bliss. She couldn't remember the last time she had felt so good. The music transported her from the opera house into a white Sequoia and past some large building into the bright lights of a white-walled corridor. Her mind drifted from cellos and flutes to squeaky wheels and fluorescent lights.

"We'll be there in no time, Jenny," a woman with a light green shirt and white cap said. "Just keep breathing deeply. We're almost there . . ."

Jenny wasn't sure where "there" was, but she felt as if the earth was moving beneath her feet. In fact, she'd just realized she wasn't sitting but lying down, and a tall, dark figure above her upside-down field of vision was wheeling her away. All she saw were lights and light gray ceiling tiles. She heard frequent announcements on the PA, but they mixed in with the tiles and lights into a mass of gray confusion.

Jenny was pale. She was covered in a white sheet and pushing hard. A man was holding her hand and coaching her along.

"Whatever you do, don't choke on the oxygen tube," he said. "You might miss all the fun!"

Jenny laughed and smiled the way only a mother-to-be could beam. Sweat was pouring down her forehead. The nurse wiped her face with a red cloth. It looked like a flat tomato but smelled like blood.

"Keep pushing," the doctor ordered. "Looks like we have a boy."

Jenny realized three helpers surrounded her: a doctor, a nurse, and Chip, all dressed in typical green surgical gowns and visibly excited. Jenny kept pushing and breathing hard. This was to be their first day as a family. Jenny would make a great mom. She was beautiful. She was all his. She was ready and she wasn't, but there would be no looking back. She looked like an angel. His angel. Everything was perfect, as it should be.

Jenny pushed and squeezed Chip's hand with a viselike grip for what felt like days but actually was about a half hour. She felt uncomfortable and on the verge of passing out. The nurse wiped her head with an ice pack to invigorate her. She felt a needle slide into her forearm. She missed home. Memories of the salt and pepper shakers placed in the center of the dining room table and of dinner being served . . . good times.

The doctor pulled something out from between her legs, and Jenny heard it screaming like crazy. It was crying, but it was an unusual cry. In a moment of sheer anxiety and vexation, Jenny sat up to watch the doctor pull the baby out. Chip sat next to the bed and lit a cigar; he had gotten exactly what he wanted.

"Look at our baby, Jenny," Chip said. He had never sounded happier. He walked slowly over to her with glazed eyes and sweat pouring down his face.

The doctor froze for a moment. He cut the umbilical cord, which was unusually thick and furry, and held the baby in his arms. Jenny stared as his mouth flinched behind his white mask. The doctor's eyes looked grim as he handed the baby over to the new mother.

Inside Jenny's arms was a dead cat. Not just any cat, Jenny observed, but the cat she had seen in the picture not long ago. Jenny held the cat in her arms and cuddled him. The cat's body was flattened and had tire tracks stamped onto its side. Its eyes sprung out of their sockets, and Jenny noticed a sticky yellow film of pus behind both eyes. Dried blood formed a second layer of dark red fur atop its white coat. Jenny kissed its eyes and walked toward Chip, who put out his cigar and took the baby from the proud new mother.

"Should have known you'd mess this up too," he said.

Jenny was furious at Chip. She felt her lungs collapse; her chest tightened, and she heard a hissing sound that accompanied a difficulty to breathe. Her heart raced to 150 beats per minute as she grabbed the dead cat back and held it in her arms. She felt like throwing it back at the nurses, who were busy putting utensils away and tossing bottles and syringes at one another.

Jenny screamed in pain. Suddenly her eyes popped out of their sockets and stuck out by at least an inch. Chip stepped back and glanced down at the cat. The cat's eyes and Jenny's eyes were exactly alike.

Chip stood frozen still. "You're a loser, Jenny. I should have picked another girl."

"I'm sorry, Chip."

"Swine . . ." He lit a cigarette and exhaled angry puffs of smoke in her direction.

"It's not good for the baby, Chip."

"It's dead . . ."

"Look into my eyes," she said. She stuck out her thick blood-soaked tongue to lick each yellow-pus eye as it drooped lower and lower toward her chin.

"Shut up," he said. Chip was raging with fury and began hitting Jenny. The nurses jabbed syringes into Jenny's arms to calm her down. "Any more, and she'll take that flight upstairs in a hurry," one fat nurse said.

"Stop that!" Jenny shouted. Chip looked like he was enjoying the show.

The nurses laughed. They looked demonic. Four eyes burned holes into Jenny's thoughts; she doubted she would get out of the hospital alive. She went through several corroded convulsions.

Chip whistled one of his favorite songs and grabbed an ax from a nearby bench.

"Time to go to the Homecoming Dance, Jenny dear," he said with a laugh that would have made Satan jealous. "Who's the lucky guy this year? Gonna dump me for that sissy Zach? Or will it be the tech wizard Branford? Or that addition-challenged lumberjack Chainsaw?"

Jenny was still holding the cat and mothering it like it was a live baby of her own. She opened her hospital gown to expose a breast and lifted the cat's dead mouth toward her chest.

Jenny had no energy left. She lay down to die. Chip sat down on her delivery bed. Chip could see Jenny's heart beat ever slower. After a few moments, it stopped.

Was she dead? How did this happen? And how did she come to be in a hospital when all she had planned for was a late-night biology study session and snacks to keep her awake?

The doctor reached down to the bed, picked up Jenny, and threw her at Chip. He slipped on her blood and fell to the ground. By now there was about a gallon of dark red blood covering the tiles. Is this how the opera ends?

Jenny's death ended and her shallow breathing resumed. She was surrounded by blood. She could feel blood soaking her clothes and washing through her hair. She wanted to get out of the room and find out what was going on. No one was around; an eerie silence pervaded the room. She wasn't sure if she had to register the names of still-births or if . . .

Jenny reached up and looked out the window. She rubbed her eyes and found no blood on her hands. The biology textbook had fallen on the floor. It was a beautiful night, and a full moon shone through the trees. She was looking out of her own window in Edgar Hall. She was sweating but fine. It had all been a terrible nightmare.

Her T-shirt matched the color of the doctor's smock. She flinched at the memory and switched her train of thought to the possessions staring at her in her room.

Alarm clock. 2:24 a.m. World Wildlife poster. Teddy bears and pillows scattered around the room. A computer—a gift from her Dad. If she earned good grades this year, he had promised a new car for her sophomore year. What would Dad do had he received e-mails from a psycho like iKill? Following the nightmare, she was now more afraid than ever of Chip. Or was she going crazy? Jenny felt like crying but repressed her tears.

Jenny put on her bathrobe, opened her door, and looked into the hallway. No one was around. It was dark. She was happy that she was awake and everyone was asleep. She walked past four doors to the middle of the hallway where there was a drinking fountain and drank some cold water. She felt better.

She returned to her room but couldn't sleep. Jenny thought she heard another door open, and that noise made her jump. Her heart began racing again. She took a few deep breaths and tried to calm herself down.

Jenny wondered what Chip was doing. Had she not broken up with him, she would have called him after such a nightmare, and he would have come to her room at once. She could count on him. Or could she? Jenny felt as if Chip was a little too dangerous

She didn't want to think about that now. If she did, she might not sleep. Jenny reasoned that she wouldn't be able to return to sleep as it was, and she looked around her room for something to do. She picked up her biology textbook and a highlighter and made a few marks. Her hands were shaking. It was no use. She was frightened, but she knew that being scared would solve nothing. She had to be strong.

Jenny considered calling Zach. He would calm her down, perhaps even play a song on his guitar or hum her a tune to sleep. Maybe Zach had no idea Jenny knew . . .

After biting her nails for a few minutes, Jenny decided to do laundry. She had been so busy all week worrying about Chip that she'd neglected to wash her clothes at her parents' house. She got her white laundry basket with wheels out of her closet and grabbed some detergent, a couple of textbooks, her ID, and her keys and locked her door.

She walked to the elevator. As she stepped in it, Jenny had the strange feeling that someone was watching her. She looked around and saw no one. It felt as if she had walked into a mobile futuristic coffin with buttons designating heaven and hell. No good feeling paranoid, she thought—just do the laundry and forget about everything. She might grab a snack from the vending machines too. A little chocolate wouldn't hurt.

She turned right and walked into the laundry room. The light was on, but the room was empty. No one was pulling a late-night laundry session. *Of course not*, she thought, since everyone had done it at home. Everyone except Jenny—because of Chip, she reminded herself.

Chip. She had to put him out of her mind. Zach. Would he make a good boyfriend? She thought about sending him a text, but it was the middle of the night. More her type than Chip; she had dated Chip mostly because of his insistence. He always had to get his way. Would Zach be the same?

She began sorting clothes and putting them into three washing machines. After a few minutes, she swiped her ID, and the machines began the wash cycle. She sat at a table and opened one of her textbooks, but she couldn't concentrate. She thought a soda and a candy bar would do the trick.

Jenny got up and reached into her bathrobe pocket for a few quarters. She counted them, and figuring she had more than enough for some snacks, she walked toward the door. She thought she heard someone whistling in the hallway; then again, these older washing machines make strange high-pitched noises . . .

Suddenly the door opened, and Jenny was surprised to see a ghost-white face staring at her. The man was walking funny and held an ax in his right hand. He smiled at her; Jenny's arms froze as she struggled to rub her fingers against her shoulders. Her throat and stomach knotted up.

She smiled with a nervous grin. She thought she was dreaming again. She squeezed the quarters and looked up at the figure standing in front of her, still smiling. Jenny felt her heart shrink into a hole and quelled a silent scream.

She felt like running, but her feet were cemented to the floor, and there was no escape route. Her knees wouldn't listen to her brain.

She thought, if only *this* were a dream . . .

*   *   *

I walked into the laundry room and saw her pretty face. White as snow, innocent as a lamb, and frightened like a kitten high-tailing it in a tornado.

I looked at her and smiled. "You got nothing to be afraid of, Jenny." She raised her arms up to her cute blonde hair and stepped back.

"Don't be afraid, little girl . . . Daddy's come downstairs to give you a little midnight snack. Couldn't wait till breakfast."

"I don't, uh, need, er . . . don't need a . . ." she said, her mouth quivering. Her voice was drowned out by the washing machine. "What are you doing down here?" she asked.

"Not hungry? Well, that's okay. I can see you brought your books with you. Thought we might have a little private study session. Just you and me, Jenny—what do you think of that?"

"Okay, okay," she said. Her eyes shone with fear and horror. Jenny covered her eyes with both palms and wished me away. She was hoping this was a nightmare, but I was all too real. She opened her eyes and almost fainted.

I closed the door and took out a new stainless-steel ax. Bought it on sale.

"Can you see the edge on this?" I asked. "Pretty sharp, it is, just like you, my darling."

"What are you doing down here?" she asked, moving back one row of washing machines. "How come you're not sleeping?" She looked like she'd never felt so frightened in her life. "So it was you who sent me those e-mails and that stupid picture? Damn you."

"It's called art, my dear. Let's just say I was a little concerned. Well, I couldn't get to sleep and thought I'd do a little laundry myself. Just got one big load to do, then I'll call it a night."

Jenny tried to scream, but I punched her in the face. She fell to the ground, and I hit her again. She started crying. She better not get anyone's attention before I'm through with her.

"Shut up, you sick bitch!" I said. "Stay quiet, and this will only take a second . . ."

Jenny squirmed beneath me as I forced my knees onto her thighs. I hit her one more time. Her eye was bleeding.

She struggled to break free, so I kicked her in the stomach. She bent over, and there was blood dripping from her mouth and nose like a leaky faucet.

I pushed her against the washing machine and grabbed my ax. I raised it above my head and slammed it into her neck. She fell to the ground. I think it knocked her out, but you can never tell these days. Blood gushed out of her like a geyser.

I took three more hacks at her face, chest, and legs. Blood was coming out of everywhere. It's nice to get a reaction out of people.

I could still see Jenny's heart beating. It made a soft rhythm in the blood-soaked white-walled white-floored laundry room. She got what she deserved—a one-way ticket to death.

Time to do the dirty laundry.

I picked her up and tossed her into the dryer. Thought about giving it a whirl, but that might be too cruel. No need to spill her blood and dry her up all in the same day.

I couldn't help but laugh.

I had a quarter on me and put it in the slot—what the hell. The dryer started spinning Jenny's body round and round. Her head faced the window of the dryer, and she looked so peaceful. Fifteen minutes of merry-go-round fun.

I looked into the dryer one more time. She was warped. Her pink bathrobe and blonde hair mingled well with her own blood splattering against the window.

I looked around for fabric softener but saw none. Just like liquid embalming.

There was blood all over the eight washing machines in the center of the room and on the dryer being used, as well as all over the floor. Her clothes were still in the washing machines.

I stuck the ax inside one of the washing machines full of hot water and soaked it for a while. Good to get any blood and prints off the ax, then I could just leave it in the washing machine and not worry about hiding the weapon.

The cops won't know what hit them. She was dead before she could say my name.

I looked around one more time before leaving the room. The basement was empty. Lucky thing no one wanted to do laundry tonight.

I walked upstairs whistling a tune from long ago.

*   *   *

Around seven in the morning, Chip—who hadn't slept much and looked like a nervous, somnambulant zombie—knocked on George's door to see if he wanted to go down to breakfast. The latter thought that was a good idea but needed a couple minutes to get his book bag and personal items ready. "Get her out of your mind yet?" George asked.

Chip grunted. "She's history. Can't stand the thought of her, so I just deleted her from my memory. Talk about going from ecstasy to misery in two weeks."

"Time to meet someone new," George said, whistling to a tune he heard yesterday and could not get out of his head.

"Right now, I think I could go for a laid-back, purely physical relationship without all the commitment and emotional crap."

"If only it were that easy, we men would have it made. But women make it difficult for us, don't they?"

"They make it so we can't be savages. But I like being a savage. Leave it to a woman to mess things up."

George zipped his book bag and grabbed a sports magazine. "Maybe that's why you're single again," he said.

Chip thought that last remark needed no rebuttal. They met up with Mindy in her room; Chip avoided looking down the hallway at Jenny's door. Mindy and George waited for Chip, who seemed lost in the not-so-distant past.

George suggested Chip knock on Jenny's door to see if she'd like to join them. Chip thought there was no use.

Mindy said, "Jackie told me that Jenny was pretty upset last night. She got back from that speech after eight p.m., and I don't think she would want company today. Or the company of *some* people." She shot Chip a look. "Maybe we should just leave her alone."

Chip suddenly punched the wall and blurted out something along the lines of "her damn loss." He then told Mindy and George he was determined to get her back or else get back at her. He had an evil, twisted look in his eyes.

Mindy stepped between the door and him, but Chip pushed her aside. "Let me handle this," he said.

"Are you nuts?" George asked. "She'll call you if she's interested. If you don't hear from her, just let it go."

Mindy agreed. "Punching walls will only convince her she made the right choice."

Chip stared at George. "Don't think I'll hear from her . . ."

"What you have to do is stay calm and cool," George said. "Only then do you stand a chance of getting her back."

Chip had grown tired of all this unsolicited advice and pounded on Jenny's door, no doubt waking up half the students on the floor.

"Get the hell out of your room this minute, Jenny Curtis! Do you hear me? Get your ugly animal-rights ass out of bed or else I'll smash the damn door down."

There was no answer.

"She may already be downstairs," George said. "Or in the library."

"To hell with it," Chip said. "Good riddance!" He looked like a man bent on revenge. Mindy had never heard him talk this way.

They walked toward the elevator and ran into a red-eyed Malcolm Huntington dashing toward the stairs.

"Haven't seen much of you lately," George said. "Been hanging out at Webster a lot?"

Malcolm—a tall, lean 25-year-old African American student from Baltimore who was using his admission into Blackwood College's School of Business as a third chance at beginning a worthy life—was the least-seen resident of Edgar Hall. Students could only speculate based on rumors of Malcolm's past. They had heard various stories of a girlfriend back home, a child or two, some trouble with the police, possibly armed robbery. He was a very furtive character.

"Yeah," he said. "You know it! Got me some group presentations and a paper to finish by the end of the week. I tell you, these next couple weeks are gonna be mean ones."

"Nothing but fun going down the home stretch," George said. He remembered that he had not yet seen Jerry Fowler, another Edgar Hall resident and a good friend of Malcolm's. "Hey Malcolm, seen Jerry around? Don't think he came back from break."

"Uh," Malcolm hesitated as he spoke. "I—I got no idea. He might be coming back today I guess. You'll know it when you see him!" Malcolm left to meet up with friends.

The three students took the elevator down to the basement. They got out and turned left toward the brand-new cafeteria. Since the completion of the basement renovation, Edgar Hall was the only residence hall on campus featuring various entrees as well as a hot breakfast buffet set up in the middle of the cafeteria. Whereas the previous cafeteria had cheap, foldable picnic-style tables, students could now sit at any of thirty round oak tables with comfortable chairs.

They scanned their IDs and picked up trays at the buffet. Rhoda and Tyler were the only other students in the cafeteria; George wondered why Denise wasn't with Tyler. A few of the cafeteria staff were eating breakfast during their break in the far left-hand corner.

Chip, still immersed in thoughts of Jenny, didn't even notice Rhoda and Tyler. He had tunnel-vision depression. Everything in his field of vision was a darkening spiral of madness and disbelief.

At the other end of the mood spectrum, Mindy had temporarily forgotten about the Chip-and-Jenny drama and decided she would have a good day. Hers was a gentle and positive spirit. She smiled at the smell of food. "They have French-toast sticks today. Cool! I love them. I haven't had those in a while."

She nearly dropped her plate as a horrific scream shook the foundation of Edgar Hall. George walked toward the right to look out the door and noticed that the scream must have come from the laundry-facility entrance, where Sammy "Shaggy" Miller, the bald and brawny fifty-five-year-old building service worker with a devil-may-care attitude, was standing.

The scream was sufficiently alarming that the five students and a few staff all got up. George and Mindy entered the hallway. Chip, still lost in his thoughts, wasn't sure if the scream had come from within his brain or from another source.

"Oh my Lord! What in God's name?" Shaggy said.

"What's wrong?" George asked.

Shaggy doffed his hat and threw it. He covered his eyes and belted out a guttural groan. He screamed for help.

Rhoda and Tyler joined the crowd. "What's going on?" Tyler asked.

"Oh dear God." Shaggy began to cry. "Get some help. Someone call 911."

Chip stared down at the floor, lost in his own world.

"What's the matter?" Rhoda asked.

"Don't think you wanna know, kid," Shaggy said in a low, furtive voice. His eyes darted left to right and up and down, checking the surroundings.

A wave of panic swept through Chip, and he was filled with an explosive sense of doom. He covered his face with both hands as Mindy began to speak.

"What is it?" she asked with a sense of calm the others lacked.

"Lord almighty, kids," said Shaggy. He looked at the students with a sullen expression. "I'm really sorry, man, but it looks like Jenny."

"What?" Mindy asked.

Chip and Mindy looked into the laundry room at the same time. The stench coming out was nauseating; it smelled like roasted human limbs marinated in type A blood. They saw dried brown-red bloodstains all over the otherwise clean white tile floor and on many of the washing machines and one dryer. The door was open.

"Don't touch a thing till the police get here," Shaggy warned them. "You can go over there if you got the stomach. It's bad, kids. I ain't lookin' again."

George and Chip stepped to the left of the row of washing machines in the center of the room and glanced inside the opened dryer. Mindy, Rhoda, and Tyler joined them. Everyone was speechless. Except for Chip's heavy breathing, no one made a sound. Alarms rang in their minds at the sight of . . .

The figure in the dryer was mutilated. The students could barely make out Jenny's face—everything was out of place. Her pink bathrobe barely covered strikes to her entire body, likely with a blunt instrument. She was a mass of broken limbs smothered in dried scabs of tumbled blood. Her eyes stuck out as if she'd gone into shock shortly after being struck. Those eyes that once embodied caring and sympathy now stared into another world—a place of shock and horror.

"I'll stay here with the body," Shaggy said. "Could one of you go up to the front desk and see if Charlie or Abby is here yet? Get someone down here and have one of them call the cops right away."

Tyler volunteered to fetch Charlie and give him the tragic news.

That couldn't be Jenny, George said to himself. He felt like throwing up. He made a fist and shoved it into his mouth.

Chip stared in disbelief. He was certain that his mind was suffering from some sort of comical delusion. He shook like a clothes dryer. Jenny had left him, he thought . . .

Mindy broke down crying on George's shoulder. She was hysterical. George tried to calm her down but failed. He was in a state of shock. He thought his heart had stopped beating, but it was just numb with fright.

A few minutes later, Tyler returned with Charlie, and said an officer was on the way. Shaggy told Charlie that they had found Jenny's dead body chopped up in the laundry room.

Charlie stepped back in disbelief and covered his face. He saw Mindy hunched over sobbing as Chip stared into space. Chip moved back against the wall rubbing his chin and blurted out, "Hope they send a cop with half a brain."

Shaggy put his arm around Chip. "Do you know anything about this?" he asked. In a macabre way, he was having fun with this. There's nothing like making the best out of a dour situation.

Chip was too frozen to talk. He managed to shake his head in slow motion.

Mindy lifted hers to whisper between sobs, "We had no idea where she was. She—"

Mindy couldn't finish her sentence before breaking down again. George was livid and banged his hand against the wall.

Tyler and Rhoda stood motionless as they tried to understand what they had walked into.

Rhoda spoke: "I hadn't seen her since before break." She added, "Well, I saw her for like a couple seconds in the hallway yesterday, but that was it. I didn't talk to her." She shuddered at the memory. Her eyes felt like they would freeze.

"Let's wait till the cops get here before we go any further," Shaggy said, composed and pragmatic. "Let's everybody just have a seat and wait this one out a few minutes."

Shaggy took out a cigarette and started smoking, despite the fact that it was a nonsmoking building. No one was in the mood to stop him.

Shaggy puffed on his Marlboro. "She's in the damn dryer," he said slowly. "Chopped dead."

Rhoda gasped. Tyler held on to her as she lost her balance. He sat her down, and a cafeteria worker brought a glass of water for her.

"I want to know exactly what the hell is going on here," Tyler said.

No one answered. By then, a small crowd of student workers and food-service staff had gathered around the cafeteria's entrance. Among them was Denise. She looked around for a few minutes before finding Tyler holding Rhoda. Denise's face was whiter than white.

She gave Rhoda a bad look and then dealt with Tyler. "So here you are. I'm glad you've got some entertainment for the wee morning hours. I suppose she's breakfast, I'm lunch, and you have a third girl lined up for dinner?"

Tyler snapped at her. "Shut up and listen. Something terrible happened, not that you'd care." He gave his girlfriend, who was burning with jealousy, a spiteful look of condemnation.

Chip broke the silence. "I . . . I . . . had no idea . . . what I was doing. This is my fault. I shouldn't have . . . I don't know what I'm saying . . . It's a damn . . . ." Charlie noticed Chip's hands were shaking.

"Take it easy, Chip," Charlie said. "You can tell the police everything once they get here."

Shaggy put his cigarette out and exhaled one last lungful of smoke. "Looks like someone cut her up pretty bad and just left her here."

Denise, by this time standing between George and Mindy to avoid Tyler, winced at that. "Can't you be a little less melodramatic?" she asked.

"Just stating the facts, kid. Cops will tell you the same."

Chip's facial expression said that he didn't care for the facts; he just wanted to make sure his mind didn't drift too far. At the moment, he was still lost somewhere between one of Jupiter's moons and an asteroid.

At that moment, Frank Tanner, head of the campus Office of Public Safety—a stout and proud officer sporting his usual tan shirt with dark brown slacks and black tie—appeared on the scene. He asked for a summary of the morning's events and then called the Eller County sheriff's office, state police, and Blackwood city police to send officers.

Harry Sampson, a lean, seasoned law-enforcement officer with thinning white hair who was serving his thirtieth year with the Virginia state police, was among the first to arrive. Tanner called upon him to help unload Jenny's body parts onto a white sheet Shaggy had rounded up for the purpose. They spread the sheet out next to the dryer.

"If anyone is squeamish," Tanner said, "turn away. This isn't going to be easy. But I will need one of you to identify the body, if you are able to."

Tanner noted that one of Jenny's fingers was missing—the index digit on the right hand. Though some of the blood looked moist, most of it had become crusty.

Rhoda fainted into Tyler's arms. Denise thought it was a good act. Tanner called OPS and asked for several medical personnel to come at once.

"Did anyone at any time touch the body?" he asked.

Everyone said no.

"Good. I know this is a rude awakening for all of you. I am very sorry. But I will need each of you to tell me exactly what happened this morning and what you did since you got up. I need you guys to stay strong here. We've got to get to the bottom of this. More officers are on their way."

Tanner wrote down everyone's name and then asked for details.

Chip spoke first and explained what happened; he had returned from his mental voyage round the solar system. George and Mindy followed with identical stories. Next, Shaggy and Charlie confirmed their testimonies. Shaggy admitted to opening the dryer but insisted he did not touch the body. He claimed too that no one had touched the body till Tanner had taken it out of the dryer.

Tanner listened to Rhoda and Tyler's stories. They had come down for breakfast just before the others had entered the cafeteria. Then came Shaggy's wail. Tyler reiterated his assumption that a student must have left his or her clothes unattended in the dryer.

"They left a whopper," Tanner said.

He looked at everyone as he said, "This isn't going to be easy, but can someone positively identify this body for me?"

Chip looked down and swallowed hard. He stuttered and said, "It . . . it's my girlfriend, Jenny Curtis."

He couldn't bring himself to say "ex-girlfriend."

"Thanks," Tanner said. "Did she live here?"

This time Mindy spoke. "On the third floor of this dorm. All of us live on the third floor. She's—was—my neighbor."

By the time medics arrived, Rhoda was feeling a little better, though her face was still pallid. They gave her smelling salts and some orange juice to bring her out of her fainting spell and shock.

Mindy pointed out that she had a class to attend at 8:00 a.m. but was not going to go.

"I think your professor will understand," Tanner said. "In fact, if you all feel up to it, we're going to need more in-depth statements from you later today. You can go to your classes if you can handle it, in which case we could . . ."

None of the students had any interest in going to class.

A short, lean man with gray hair and a thick gray moustache introduced himself as officer Vernon Gull from the Virginia State Police Department. Standing next to him was a tall and trim man in his midfifties who looked confident and resilient and introduced himself as Terence Foster, Eller County Sheriff. To his right stood an officer in his thirties who acted like a rookie taking orders learning the job. He introduced himself as officer Peter Morgan of the Blackwood Police Department.

Tanner filled them in on what had happened since he'd appeared on the scene. He said the students present had been helpful but that they were understandably in a state of shock.

Sheriff Foster reassured the students that they would be well taken care of and that counselors would soon arrive. Meanwhile, he ordered a few more sheets to cover the body and hoist it onto a gurney.

Foster added, "Get labs on everything—prints, blood, etc.—ASAP."

Tanner ordered Charlie to shut down the cafeteria till lunch and to lock all entries from outside Edgar Hall. Charlie followed orders.

Suddenly, Denise turned to Tyler with an expression of anger and grief. "I need to talk to you. It's important. I know you're having breakfast with your new fling, but . . ."

"She's not my new fling," Tyler said, looking with sympathy at a recovering Rhoda. "For God's sake, Denise, we were just having breakfast before going to class, and then all this happened."

"Come up to my room right now," Denise said. "I—I can't bear it anymore. I have to tell someone. I don't trust anyone, but you'll have to do."

They received permission from Sheriff Foster to go to Denise's room provided they returned within thirty minutes for questioning. Denise didn't say a word while they were in the elevator. Tyler was unsure of Denise's motives. She was usually of strong character, but now she appeared on the verge of a nervous breakdown.

They approached her door, and she asked him to be quiet.

"Good God, Denise, everyone's up by now," Tyler complained.

"Not everyone," Denise said. "A lot of them are still sleeping." Tyler realized he hadn't seen Branford, Jerry, Jackie, or Chainsaw downstairs.

Denise's hands were shaking as she turned the key to open her door. Tyler was losing patience with his part-time girlfriend and demanded to know why she had brought him up here.

Denise started crying. She sat on her bed and sobbed. Tyler was speechless and had no idea what to do.

"I'm going back downstairs," Tyler said. "Why don't you just get some rest, Denise? Your eyes look like they haven't seen much sleep."

Denise turned on her computer and asked Tyler to wait. He was growing impatient with her antics and was anxious to see how Rhoda was doing downstairs. He thought about last night; there was a full moon, and someone with an ax to grind ground it deep into Jenny's body—several times. The memory made him want to throw up.

"I have something to show you," Denise said.

Tyler hoped it wasn't another friendly family picture taken last week in front of the turkey of the year. Denise had all her pictures sorted by date and event and saved in iPhoto.

Hurry up, for God's sake, Tyler thought. The usually quick Denise was a fumbling fool this morning. Perhaps she knows something, he guessed. It wasn't typical of her to act so neurotic.

It took Denise three attempts to log on to her e-mail, but she finally prevailed. She clicked on the top message, titled "Cleanliness is next to Godliness."

"Check this out. Did you send this to me?"

Tyler read the e-mail from a sender named iKill:

Dear Denise,

> *How are you doing? It's been a while since I heard from you. I was wondering if you were still interested in going out. My treat. Maybe we could meet this week. Don't make me come looking for you or you might end up like poor Jenny. You're so pretty, and gentle like a baby lamb. I want to sit in your lap and purr all day. What do you say? Enjoy the pictures and see you soon. Love, iKill.*

Tyler looked at Denise, who had been watching as he read every word. She was still trembling, and her eyes looked like messy blotches of green putty above a quivering mouth.

"Did you send this to me, Tyler Mitchell?"

Tyler moved back from Denise. "Are you crazy? Of course I didn't send it to you. That's not my e-mail address."

"Then who did? Anyone can create an e-mail account in two minutes."

"I have no idea. Must be a joke. Or did you meet some guy last week who wanted to take you out?"

"No."

Tyler reread the message. "That part about ending up 'like poor Jenny' sounds ominous. Don't you think? Help me here."

Denise didn't want to think. Her first instinct was to kick Tyler out of her room and sleep all day.

"What are those pictures this guy's referring to? Did you open the attachments?"

Denise's face expressed utter death. She clicked on the attachment and began to breathe in spiked gasps. Tears flooded her face and ran down her neckline.

She scrolled down to view the photos. Tyler couldn't believe his eyes. There were two pictures of Jenny's body in the dryer.

"Better tell the police," Denise said between attempts to resist throwing up.

Tyler raised his voice. "Damn straight. I'll let them know what you received and they will probably want to talk with you."

He gave her a pretentious hug. Denise felt cold. Nothing was right this morning.

Chapter Three

Tanner turned to Foster and insisted on contacting Joe Flanagan. He got the number from OPS and dialed through to Flanagan's cell.

"Hi Frank," Flanagan said. "How are you doing? I'm here at the hotel to see Malkin off. He's about to drive back to Washington."

Malkin was thinking he should come back to his alma mater more often. Nice place. Good people—but too small. Roxanne and the kids would tolerate Blackwood for at least a couple hours, he thought, and then die from boredom.

"What's that? Are you sure?" Flanagan asked. "Damn, I'll be right there."

Flanagan's appearance was suddenly ghostly. "You're not going to believe this," he told Malkin, "but that was Officer Tanner from Public Safety. They just found a girl killed in Edgar Hall—one of our residence halls."

Malkin set his suitcase down. "Killed? In Edgar Hall? That's where I lived my first two years here—I walked past there just last night. When did this happen?"

"Late Monday or in the early hours this morning," Flanagan said. "I need to meet with some officers and talk to the president about this. This is terrible. I've got to get out of here. Listen, Tom, thanks for everything and . . ."

Malkin interrupted him: "Killed? You mean murdered? Remarkable. I'd have never thought it . . . and yet I'm not surprised either. Always expect the worst."

38

Malkin thought for a moment and turned to Flanagan. "Let's check it out, Joe," he said. "Let's head over."

Flanagan objected. "That's very nice of you, Tom," he said, "but we have excellent law enforcement, and we wouldn't want you to miss your trip just because of this."

"Nonsense," Malkin said. "Murder in Blackwood . . . that's not supposed to happen in a town like this. I want to get help you guys get to the bottom of this—I mean, if you don't mind."

Flanagan was at a loss for words. He wanted Malkin to remain on the scene and help out, but he didn't want to impose. Flanagan wasn't the type to make quick decisions.

Malkin continued, "Tell you what—I'll remain behind the scenes and help out where I can. Otherwise, it's up to the university and city to deal with. I'm an unofficial private detective. How does that sound?"

"That would be great." Flanagan smiled and, upon reflection, realized that Blackwood law enforcement would probably need all the help they could get.

"I have an obligation, Joe," Malkin said. "It would be ridiculous for me to leave now."

Flanagan agreed. Malkin looked far into the distance, as far as when he was a student at Blackwood.

* * *

Flanagan informed President Keyes, and the director of housing, Tammy Smith, of the murder. Afterward, he and Malkin introduced themselves to the officers and students who had stayed together and been joined by a few others. The president had ordered Edgar Hall closed till law-enforcement officials could conduct tests and interviews, all of which would take most of the day.

During the remainder of the morning, Morgan and Tanner ordered twenty officers to inspect Edgar Hall and the surrounding areas. Ten officers combed through the residence hall and nearby buildings but noticed nothing out of the ordinary. The other officers patrolled a wider area off campus and had news to show and tell.

"Look at what the building service worker dragged out of the washing machine," one of Tanner's OPS assistants said as he held up an ax.

Malkin said, "Wicked business. Looks like he hacked her up and down, and then soaked the murder weapon in her own dirty laundry." He had seen worse, but not in Virginia, and he'd never expected to wake up to anything like this in Blackwood.

Tanner said, "No use getting labs on that, but label it as evidence." The assistant left on his duty.

President Keyes appeared shortly thereafter and listened to comments made by Foster and Tanner, with which he was impressed. The president spoke with Malkin and all the officers and students. He had issued an all-campus bulletin concerning the murder and cancelled classes.

"We'll get to the bottom of this," he told the group, which by now consisted not only of students residing in Edgar Hall but also some friends of friends and other hangers-on who'd made their way into the residence hall before it was officially closed to the public.

Malkin realized he had met the victim last night following his speech and signed an autograph for her. Jenny Curtis—she was the one who had mentioned her father. Malkin also remembered Charlie and Abby. They all looked tired and distraught. He also recognized George Young, the baseball scholarship student.

Mindy spoke up. "It's like we've lost one of our family. We're all still in a state of shock. At least I am." Her pulse was rapid and her breathing shallow; a vulgar vertigo hit her like a fervent funnel cloud spinning confusion round her brain.

"I understand." Joe Flanagan spoke this time. "And once this gets out to the rest of the university and community, not to mention the media, it's going to become a zoo. But take my word for it: I'm going to try to make this as painless for all of you as I can."

President Keyes added, "I'd like to commend you on your courage. As for now, I would like to ask everyone to follow officers' orders. Sheriff Foster and officers Tanner, Morgan, and Gull have quite a monster on their hands, and they will appreciate your continued cooperation."

The president spoke briefly with Malkin, whom he thanked for staying in town to help, and Charlie White, and then left Edgar Hall to return to his office.

Sheriff Foster's cell phone rang. He spoke for a few minutes before announcing to everyone that Jenny's parents had been notified and were on their way down from Fairfax.

"What the hell are they going to think?" he asked. No one had an answer. No one cared to answer. Chip feared Jenny's father would suspect he had lost his temper one last time and left Jenny with a lethal dose of fury.

"Are there any other students who live in Edgar Hall who are not present at this time?" Tanner asked.

George looked around. "Sheila, Branford, Head Case Stacy, Chainsaw, and Jackie aren't down yet. And I haven't seen Jerry since before Thanksgiving break."

Shaggy said, "Probably upstairs still sleeping." He volunteered to bring them down for questioning. He returned fifteen minutes later with five of the six students.

"Had to shake some of them lazy bastards out of bed," he said. "They don't get up early like they used to. No idea where that Jerry Fowler is. He didn't answer his door."

Mindy suddenly remembered how Chip had angrily knocked on Jenny's door this morning and assumed she hadn't opened it because she didn't want to see him. How silly their little breakup seemed now. She wondered what he was thinking. She wanted to dull her senses before returning to the misery of contemplation.

The students who had just come down from their rooms all looked sleepy. Foster provided a summary of the morning's events to them. The other students didn't want to hear the details and went into the hallway.

Head Case Stacy held her head up with her hands and tried to keep her bloodshot eyes open; she appeared indifferent about what had happened. Her facial expression seemed to say, "I saw danger coming all along, and now I'm the only one in this room who isn't surprised this happened."

Foster, the Eller County Sheriff, suggested that the students return to their rooms and remain there till further notice. No one was to leave or enter the building. Officers would split up and interview each student individually. Malkin, quiet until now, had been trained to rule nothing out. He offered to help interview the students and staff.

"Wouldn't bother me a bit," Tanner said. "It's a pleasure having you around, Mr. Malkin, and we welcome your input."

George smiled in mourning as he saw Malkin would be involved, and he went over to shake the man's hand.

"Good to see you again," Malkin told him. "Though I wish it were under better circumstances. Go rest up in your room. We'll handle this."

Charlie stared into the cloudy morning sky and shivered. Shaggy lowered his voice and said, "I think one of them kids must have had themselves one hell of a good time last night. Suppose that's the way things go these days."

Back inside the building, Vernon Gull looked over his notes. "This isn't going to be easy," Gull said. "Girl found cut up in a dryer in the laundry room in the basement of a residence hall? I sure hope there is some madman worker or crazy bum who we can find and lock up."

Malkin straightened his tie. "It's been my experience that things never quite work out that easily."

"Mine too," Gull said.

"And there's one other thing," Malkin said.

"What's that?"

"Where is this Fowler character?"

Gull removed his cap and swept his short hair back. "He's the only student living in this building who was not around this morning."

"That's right."

"Think it means something?"

Malkin cleared his throat. "No idea," he said. "But whenever there is one person missing, it's usually not a good sign."

*   *   *

Officer Morgan had already taken out his notebook and started questioning Charlie and Abby at the front desk. His discussion with them did not take long.

"I see," Morgan said after he received information he already had. "And have you noticed anything unusual or peculiar the past few days?"

"Not really," Abby said. "I'm just learning this job, so I haven't had much time to get to know students or faces. But there is one thing I remember . . ."

"What's that?"

"The day before Thanksgiving break, I think it was Thursday, some guy came up to the desk at night and asked for one of the students."

"What do you mean?"

"He was black and tall—about six-foot-two at least—and big. I mean, about two hundred pounds. Anyway, I hadn't seen him before, and he was trying to get in touch with someone fast."

"With whom?"

Abby looked at Charlie. "I think it was Malcolm. Yeah, he wanted Malcolm to come down. See, we can't just let them up without permission from the student. And Malcolm wasn't around at that time; he hangs out in Webster Hall, just up the road, a lot—has a lot of friends there and I see him there pretty often. So we didn't let this visitor up."

Abby explained that she had never seen him before and he didn't leave a name or message. If not for the murder, she added, she would not have thought twice about it. "It's not like it was that big a deal," she said.

"Perhaps," Morgan said, "but a girl bludgeoned and left in a dryer downstairs is a big deal—a very big deal. So I just want you to know that any detail, however small, must be mentioned. I've heard stories of how the most insignificant clues eventually became monumental in solving a murder investigation. Is there anything else you can think of?" he asked.

Charlie and Abby shook their heads.

Morgan recalled the James River Killer case from about a decade ago . . .

*   *   *

Officer Gull, Sheriff Foster, OPS Officer Tanner, and Malkin introduced themselves to Tammy Smith, director of housing at Blackwood College, and Teresa Martinez, director of Blackwood's counseling center. Tammy and Teresa had been contacted by Joe Flanagan and immediately made their way down to Edgar Hall. Teresa was visibly upset and fought her emotions in order to communicate in a professional manner with the officers.

Malkin checked out the ladies and noticed how much they were opposites. Tammy was somewhat oval shaped and loquacious. She had a small head that carried a lot of weight—mostly cheeks and two auxiliary chins—and dull brown hair. Two small feet supported what Malkin guessed to be a two-hundred-pound frame that was widest at the hips. She was wearing a thick brown coat and carried an oversized black organizer in her left hand.

Teresa, on the other hand, was an eye-catching woman with a pleasant smile. She had short reddish-brown hair and was thin and stood tall, around five-foot-ten. She had a welcoming nature about her and was a good listener—and no doubt a good counselor.

The officers briefed Tammy and Teresa about the situation and explained what had been done as well as what still needed to happen.

"How are the students doing?" Teresa asked.

"Not so great," Tanner replied. He said that Jackie and Mindy, Jenny's good friends, were having a hard time.

"They'll pull through," Teresa said. "I just wanted to let you know that we're ready and willing to talk with any students who might need assistance. I'm available, and we have several good, qualified counselors who can be called in at any time."

Malkin thought of his mother as he watched Teresa explain her willingness to help. She possessed a warm, generous heart.

Tammy indicated the housing department's willingness to help as well. "We'll do whatever we're asked," she said. "I know the dormitory's been closed to the public for now, but we're willing to get the cafeteria open so the kids can eat. I know some of them must be getting hungry." She spoke with her hands as much as her mouth.

"Perhaps not, but that would still be appreciated," Foster told her.

Malkin said, "Let's get prints and look for trace blood specimens down by the entrance," he said. "They can sweep in less than an hour. Doubt they'll find much of anything, but who knows . . ."

"We'll get right on that," Gull said. "It's almost noon now. Our next step is to interview students, see if anything turns up. And we'll have to examine the victim's room as well. Might find some clues there."

Tammy said, "If a situation arises in which a student indicates he or she would like to change rooms or dorms, we can accommodate that as well. Just ask them to give us a call, or if one of you or Charlie wants to call us, that's fine."

Tammy returned to her office while Teresa indicated she preferred to remain on the premises for a while. "I've been through some pretty traumatic cases like this one—murder, rape—on other campuses before I started working here," she explained. "I know how a situation can suddenly blow up."

Malkin thanked Teresa for her patience and willingness to help. She replied by saying it was just her job.

"If only 10 percent of workers were as conscientious as you," Malkin said with a wry grin.

Gull cleared his throat and looked over at Teresa. He commended her for her stoic behavior. "If any students express interest in counseling, we'll certainly send them to you."

On that note, Teresa left the officers to fulfill their duties.

* * *

The officers relocated to the new lounge on the fourth floor of Edgar Hall, in its final stages of renovation, to discuss details of the case. Morgan informed them of Abby's story regarding the visitor who had wanted to see Malcolm Huntington during Thanksgiving break. Malkin said they would need to learn more about the case before judging whether that was an important piece of evidence.

Gull downed a quick cup of black coffee and spoke to his colleagues in a stern voice. "All right, men, we've got to determine some facts in this investigation. First, I think we should just do a quick run-through of all the students living in Edgar Hall. It should be relatively easy to question each one and check through their rooms because they all have singles in this building—lucky bastards."

He continued, "We need to get names, majors, room numbers, and what they were doing between, say, ten p.m. last night and early this morning. No excuses. Note any hesitation or questionable behavior—especially avoidance."

Tanner interjected, "But we don't even know if one of these students was responsible."

"True," Foster said. "But we can't assume anything. I personally think this was the work of some crazed madman who must have picked Jenny up and sliced her up good and dropped her off here for kicks."

Malkin said, "That may be. Or it could have been a student living in another building."

"Yeah, that's true."

Malkin continued, "Or he or she could have been a professor or an administrator or a front desk manager or a student worker."

Everyone was silent for a moment.

"No professor would do this," Tanner said.

"I disagree," Malkin said. He described Jenny Curtis's body to remind the officers that they were not dealing with a squeamish killer.

"Good point," Gull said. "It's one thing to shoot someone in the head; it's another to cut her up like a butcher."

The officers separated and agreed to meet back later. Malkin invited Foster to breakfast, and the latter accepted. They were about to take the elevator up when Shaggy, the building service worker busy cleaning on the fourth floor—perhaps conveniently so—poked his head into the lounge and expressed an opinion.

"You know, guys, I knew Jenny pretty well. She was a straightforward, honest sort of girl," he said. "Know what I'm saying? She wouldn't do anything to provoke such a murder. She never made anyone angry. She never pissed her friends off, is what I'm trying to tell you people. And I don't think she made no one else angry either. So I don't get it. Because if I wanted to cut someone up real good like they did to her," he continued, "I'd have to hate someone pretty bad. Know what I'm saying here? They would have had to cut through my nerves so bad that I'd be counting the minutes till I could cut through theirs. But I didn't hurt her. Never would. Least not Jenny."

The officers were not sure what to make of Shaggy's comments. He seemed to be a lonely man in need of female companionship in his already-past-prime life.

The dangerous sort, Malkin thought to himself.

"So Jenny was well known to all the students?" Tanner asked.

"You got that right," Shaggy answered. "I'm sure she's looking down on me now and is happy. Not because she is dead, but that I am here to look after her things for her."

Foster was surprised. "She asked you to look after her things?"

"Yes," Shaggy said.

"And what about her boyfriend?"

"He had a temper, wouldn't want him to be my son."

Malkin brought the conversation to a halt. "If we don't start thinking and do our work, we'll never find out."

Shaggy obviously had problems, Malkin thought. The man reminded Malkin of a deluded, quiet alcoholic—or of a loner capable of killing to stave off unbearable boredom.

*   *   *

The medical examiner informed Malkin and Gull that Jenny had been dead at least three hours but no more than seven. This meant the murder must have occurred between roughly midnight and 4:00 a.m.

"Not a bad time frame in which to work," Malkin said. "Let's get down to business."

They interviewed each student individually, and approximately two hours later, Malkin read a summary of his notes to the officers.

"Four students—George, Jenny, Mindy, and Abby—attended my speech. I remember talking to them, so they've got alibis from about six to nine p.m. last night, which doesn't coincide with estimated time of death. They all claim to have hung out afterward—playing video games, watching football, doing homework, checking e-mail, and going online—and then gone to sleep relatively early. Sheila said she and Rhoda caught up on local gossip and ordered out for pizza, and afterward they did homework and were in their beds before midnight.

"Branford said he watched part of a football game in George's room and then stayed up most of the night writing a computer program; he said he didn't go to sleep till around three a.m. Hank Kilger—or 'Chainsaw,' as they call him, a dubious nickname if you ask me—was watching football and then played pool, then went to bed around midnight, perhaps a little later. Stacy Nutter—she's an odd one, 'Head Case Stacy' they call her—says she drove back to campus in early afternoon and stayed in her room the whole day and night. Says she was reading the entire time and playing with some pet parakeet named Nellie. And they say colleges don't know how to recruit! Find that hard to believe. Apparently went to sleep around two a.m.

"Though every student here has a computer—at least one—some don't have printers, so they use the color laser printer in the second-floor lab. A few students mentioned stopping by the computer lab—let's see, Branford, Zach (who just stayed in his room all night playing guitar and writing songs), and Chip and Chainsaw. And then there's also Gottlieb. Each saw the other at one time or another, so there seems to be no problem there.

"Malcolm Huntington claims he got back from D.C. around five p.m. Sunday evening, talked briefly with his hallmates—George says he saw him while they were watching the Patriots game—and then decided to visit friends in Webster Hall and insists that he got back after midnight but didn't see or hear anything unusual. The German, Gottlieb, says he was in the computer lab after the football game—Branford vows he saw him as well—and then went to his room to do homework. Says he fell asleep after the late edition of *Sports Center*—that would be about one a.m. Probably stayed up to check on scores from late games on the west coast. Maybe there was a riot . . .

"Finally, Zach Gillett, a music major, says he returned from home in the early afternoon and spent most of the day in his room. He writes music and said he was trying to play guitar and write some songs. This guy might be bright but definitely is way too introverted and depressed for his own good. And I don't trust these people who claim they just stayed in their rooms all day—this includes Stacy, Branford, and Zach. It's not normal human behavior."

Malkin took a sip of coffee and continued.

"Now we get to the five interesting cases. First, Jenny's best friends on campus live in this residence hall: Mindy Adams, George Young, and Jackie Lowell. The latter claims Jenny Curtis came to her room in tears after receiving a couple suspicious e-mails yesterday. Strange. If there is a link between the e-mail and the killer, then we're definitely dealing with someone who's playing with half a deck at most.

"Next, Chip Patrick apparently got dumped by the victim just before Thanksgiving break. This makes him the obvious suspect, at least for now. Screaming and loud arguments between Chip and Jenny were heard by many of the students throughout the semester. He might have planned this whole thing out during Thanksgiving break.

"Speaking of those e-mails, Denise received an e-mail from a sender named 'iKill' who—get this—sent pictures of Jenny's body in the dryer. And here's the real kicker: Denise was afraid to convey this information, why we don't know.

"Tyler Mitchell's testimony is consistent with Denise's, except he makes no mention of the e-mail she received." Malkin shook his head.

Foster said, "Maybe she sent the e-mails to herself to try and cast blame on Tyler."

"That we can check out easily enough," Malkin said. He continued, "Finally, where the hell is Jerry Fowler? Classes were to resume today. Maybe he just took an extra day off and will arrive tonight."

Morgan nodded approval. "A very well-organized summary, Malkin. No wonder you worked your way up to a Ph.D."

Malkin ignored the compliment—he ignored most compliments—and, after taking a sip of coffee, mentioned a few more relevant items:

"First," he said, "it is fair to presume this was the work of a man, not a woman."

All the officers agreed.

"Second, it is possible that some local madman could have slipped through the exit that is close to the laundry, but typically used for supplies and equipment only, and is usually unlocked, walked into the laundry room, and killed her in seconds. This is an option to consider if we can find that madman. If not, we're probably facing a madman from within these walls."

Gull and Morgan shivered at the thought.

"Third, we still have no motive. In the next few days, we will probably learn more so that we can establish some sort of motive. We need to understand the psychology of the killer through learning the psyche of the victim. Then again, if she was killed out of some sick moron's need to impress . . ."

Foster and Morgan added, "The only things we came across of any interest were pornographic magazines found in the closet of Jerry Fowler, still unaccounted for, and several pictures—digital printouts—of Jenny Curtis in various places in Zach's and Branford's rooms."

"True romance," Malkin laughed.

A forensics lab located approximately fifty miles northeast of Blackwood informed Sheriff Foster that no prints had been found on the victim's clothing. Malkin was not surprised; however, Foster and Gull expressed severe disappointment on this point.

"It's as if a damn ghost did her in," Gull said.

"A powerful and wily ghost," Foster said.

"We've got our work cut out for us, men," Malkin said. "Looks like several guys in this building had a crush on this Curtis girl, and it just might be one of them who in turn hacked her to death. While we consider that, let's have lunch."

"Where can we take you, Tom?" Foster asked. "There are many nice restaurants around town. Do you prefer barbecue, buffet, seafood, or steak?"

"I usually prefer a little food and no other people around, but today I think I'll go for the sinister basement cafeteria of Edgar Hall."

*   *   *

They were provided free meal tickets and ate a late lunch among the mourners of Edgar Hall. Malkin scanned the lunch clientele and noted that Tyler was dining with Rhoda, who was dressed in a white skirt that seemed very short for late November, while Gottlieb, Branford, and Chainsaw were arguing at another table that Denise had just left.

Foster said, "Looks like we got some new information in. Seems like Blackwood Police have brought someone in for questioning. His name is Eddie Cragg, Caucasian, about 5'8", skinny and suspicious. Apparently he's a local drunk who walks around aimlessly in the middle of the night—sometimes drinking and throwing away beer cans in other people's yards or on university property, and sometimes collecting whatever he can to scrape up enough money for more beer."

"When did they pick him up?" Malkin asked.

"Not sure—sometime this morning out on West Willow Road," Morgan said. "He was pushing around a shopping cart full of ragged clothes and empty beer cans. The Blackwood Police Department is questioning him to see exactly what he knows."

"We're still learning," Malkin said. "We need to rush questioning—need to ask students and staff more questions, because the more they talk, the more we learn, and the more the guilty party tells us—but there is no reason to rush logic."

Malkin noticed Tyler eyeing Denise as he walked over to the drinks section and fumbled for a glass. She was flirting with Chainsaw, and Chainsaw was flirting back. She whispered something in his ear.

It was obvious what was going on. Denise was trying to get Tyler flustered so that he would feel jealous. No way that was going to happen, Tyler told himself. That bitch would die before she embarrassed him in front of the whole damn university.

George and Mindy came over to the officers' table. "Nice of you to try our gourmet cooking," said George. "Sometimes you just got to go with cereal, because everything else is marinated in lard and then basted in butter. Talk about disgusting."

Malkin agreed with George's assessment and smiled at Jackie as she fiddled with the buttons on her sweater. He assured her that he would do everything possible to track down Jenny's assailant and bring him to justice. A breeze of relief swept across Jackie's strained face. Meanwhile, as was his habit around 1 in the afternoon, Charlie came down to pick up some snacks—usually fruit or yogurt or nutrition bars—for himself and Abby to hold them over till their late lunches.

"Hey," Charlie said to Malkin, "a little birdie told me that you guys think that Eddie Cragg guy killed Jenny. I agree. You guys should arrest him fast. I've seen him walking around Edgar Hall—very suspicious character."

"Thanks for the scoop," Malkin said.

Suddenly there was a terrific scream from the buffet line, where Mindy, Chainsaw, and Branford were selecting items to eat.

It was Mindy. "Help!" she hollered. "Help me! Help me!"

Sheriff Foster and Malkin ran toward her, and Officer Morgan followed them.

Mindy stood there agape, holding her plate in both hands. She had helped herself to chicken fingers, when suddenly . . .

"Good God," Foster said. He grabbed her plate carefully and asked all the students to remain calm and seated. Morgan took Mindy out of the cafeteria; she needed help walking. Malkin examined the plate as Foster looked befuddled.

"I'll be damned," he said. "Look at that!"

Jenny's index finger had somehow found its way into the buffet. It was about three inches in length, thin but pale under the brown coating. Mindy had picked it up by accident. The officers and food-service personnel examined all the other food and cafeteria areas and found nothing, just the one finger that Mindy had discovered.

Upon hearing what had turned up on Mindy's plate, Rhoda threw up her meat right in front of Tyler. He helped her up and took her upstairs. He was concerned about Rhoda's psychological state, figuring she'd been through too much trauma and now might be the best time to schedule a session with the counselor.

Malkin helped Foster put the finger into a plastic bag given to him by one of the cafeteria staff. He couldn't believe the macabre nature of the violent criminal acts that had consumed the day, and it was only early afternoon.

"Gives new meaning to finger food," Malkin said to Foster. "This goes to your department. Send it out of town for forensics now, though they'll find nothing given it's been cooked well-done."

Officer Morgan had just returned from bringing Mindy up to Abby and Charlie for medical attention. "I think it must be one of the staff," he said. "Everything is happening in the basement."

Chip stood near the buffet line, and his darkened eyes stared a mile deep into the food pan. "It's an evil world, don't you think so, Jenny?" he said softly. "Looks like something just happened again."

While Foster and Tanner went upstairs to notify the front desk and their respective offices, Malkin and Morgan approached the cafeteria staff and a few other workers. They inquired about the finger. No one had seen it or had seen anyone act suspiciously that morning. Furthermore, they insisted that no one had entered the cafeteria overnight because it was locked—or at least, it was supposed to be. They indicated that besides all those now eating in the cafeteria, Chip and Chainsaw had grabbed brown-bag lunches to go, and Shaggy, Charlie, and Abby had come down early as they usually did.

"So they finally found the missing finger, eh?" Shaggy asked with a sneer. "I wonder why they would cut that one off. Not much meat there."

"Reminds me of Idi Amin," Malkin said. "Servants Stew—now that's a good name for a dish!"

Malkin wondered what Shaggy knew. He was talking too much. As for the rest of the cafeteria staff, he thought they were useless.

*   *   *

"I see the first report on the murder has hit the papers," Malkin said to Tanner, Foster, and Gull. "They got all the gory details, all right. So the media circus begins. Any thoughts, fellows?"

Tanner looked befuddled. "I've got no idea what to do next," he said.

Gull was more optimistic. "We need to look around a little more. Thing is, with this bum Cragg in for questioning, he could have done it, but could he have put Jenny's finger into the cafeteria? Very little chance."

"I've seen stranger things happen," Malkin said.

Morgan came up with what he thought was a brilliant plan: "Let's do this—meet with Jenny's parents tonight—they might know something. And then we'll search the whole premises again—in fact, the whole damn campus."

Malkin supposed officers in Blackwood faced more traffic violations and basic burglaries than first-degree murders, let alone those in residence halls on a respectable campus. He felt it was time for him to take control of all the hesitation and complacency. But first he had a question that had been burning in his mind.

"I was wondering," he said, "whether one of you could brief me on various unusual happenings in and around Blackwood the past couple years. Have there been any strange occurrences? Enlighten me."

After a minute, Sheriff Foster cleared his throat. "Well, let's think back. About a year ago or so, there was a doctor murdered—shot to death in his home. He lived outside Blackwood, about five miles out in the country. A lunatic who'd escaped a mental hospital in Richmond and had been the doctor's patient at one time is still unaccounted for.

"Then a few years ago—don't recall how many exactly, maybe five or so—there was the James River Killer. He murdered two young female employees about fifteen miles from here, in Richmond, but they were Blackwood workers. I think one of them may have worked at Blackwood College for some time. Law enforcement spent a lot of time on the case, but didn't get far.

"And if it's weird you want, here's a story that will really test you. A couple years ago some weird nut—we believe it to be the same James River Killer—was going around stealing women's shoes from shops. A few women were found dead next to the James River. Strange stuff, like knocking out a girl south of campus and shoving two left shoes in her ears—the ends of those high-heel shoes women wear, you know? Like decorating a Christmas tree. He left notes: 'Sorry I killed you, but I had to leave you before you'd recognize me.' Bizarre, I tell you."

Malkin rolled his eyes and understood that contrary to its image of peace and quiet, this area had had its fair share of criminal phenomena.

"We've got one hell of a task ahead of us," he said. "Everyone we've interviewed has told us very little."

He continued, "Except that Jenny had just broken up with her boyfriend, Chip. Also, she had just received a strange e-mail—doesn't really make sense. Then another girl living here receives a similar e-mail—Denise Lansing—with photos of Jenny's dead body. Then this afternoon, right when they reopen the cafeteria for lunch, we discover that someone must have put Jenny's finger in the buffet, and this must have happened sometime in late morning. I'm sure someone could have sneaked in there once they saw the buffet table set up, and it would be easy to do so unnoticed since the staff were busy preparing the dining area and food and rushing back into the kitchen and then into the dining area. Then we hear that an alcoholic vagabond has been picked up for questioning; it's well known that this Eddie Cragg used to walk around West Willow Road and North Street close to Edgar Hall and is not mentally balanced."

The other officers listened as Malkin continued. "This might be an inside job."

Morgan said, "We should make sure a security guard is on duty."

"More like ten," Malkin said. "I need to contact my family so they know I'll be staying on a few more days. Sure my wife will be thrilled."

"We appreciate your assisting us, Tom," Foster said. "Hope we find this maniac soon."

The officers decided again to divide duties. Gull would meet with students and staff from neighboring buildings to see if anyone had noticed anything strange the night before or that morning.

"And I'd like to check on Cragg and other possible outside suspects," Foster said. "I can make a few phone calls to local hospitals to see if any mental patients have been recently released—thanks to some liberal jackass lawyer, of course." He added, "Remember that John Hinckley is out on unsupervised weekend trips—his reward for trying to assassinate President Reagan but following that up with about twenty years of angelic behavior in the slammer. I think we call it justice, right?"

Tanner indicated that he felt it was his duty to meet with the victim's parents. Malkin and Morgan would meet with the students from Edgar Hall.

"Give someone a chance to talk, and they'll say something they shouldn't have. Let's meet up tomorrow morning for breakfast—anything but Edgar cafeteria food."

"That was your idea," Foster reminded him.

"And look what we came up with," Malkin smiled. "Nothing like a finger to ruin your meal."

As the others walked toward their vehicles, Morgan asked Malkin, "Can I really watch how you solve crimes?" He sounded like an excited child.

"Look, Morgan," Malkin said, "you've got a lot to learn. I've been in this business about fifteen years, and it's not pretty. This is the worst I've seen in a while—someone sick out there is trying to ruin everyone's Christmas, if we can still use that word on a college campus, and it's our job to get the killer before he strikes again. And I do mean *again!*"

Morgan accepted Malkin's assessment. After all, Malkin was the one who'd captured that al-Qaeda terrorist just a couple months ago.

Chapter Four

Zach barely ate any lunch, for had a guilty conscience. Returning to his room, he strummed his guitar without passion. He found it difficult to listen to the chords. His head ached.

Poor Jenny. This was clearly his fault. Zach decided to visit Chip and tell him everything. He hoped Chip wouldn't be home, for he feared his floormate's quick temper. Unfortunately, Chip answered the door.

"Oh God," Chip shouted. "Hi, Zach. Thought it might be a cop."

Zach felt uncomfortable, and Chip's words didn't make him feel any better about the situation. "We need to talk," Zach said.

"Have a seat," Chip told Zach, pointing to his desk chair. Chip sat down on his bed and grabbed a Coke.

"I don't know how you're going to take this, Chip," Zach started, "but I couldn't get much sleep last night. I was worried about what you might think."

Chip laughed. "What's up?"

Zach continued, "You see . . ." He fumbled to find the right words, which were always easier for Zach to discover when he was writing, not speaking.

"The past couple weeks . . . I mean before Thanksgiving break," Zach said, "Jenny and I spent some time together."

Chip sneered at Zach. "What the hell do you mean?"

"I mean . . ." Zach was wringing his hands and cracking his knuckles. "We were sort of seeing each other while you guys were dating. Nothing serious and she probably forgot all about me, it's just she told me she wanted to have some fun and focus on her classes at the same time."

Zach felt a load drop from his shoulders onto the floor. Chip looked flustered and banged his hand right into the wall.

"Are you insane? Have you completely lost your mind?" he asked. "Jenny never even mentioned you. This is all in your head. You're a psychotic mess. Go get yourself analyzed for some sort of psychosis."

Zach wished he had brought his Telecaster with him; he would have bashed Chip's head in without remorse. Zach knew that Jenny wanted him, not Chip. And Zach knew he would have had her if not for Chip's interference.

"She said she wasn't too happy being with you," Zach said. "So sometimes she would tell you she was going to the library or someplace, and really she and I would just take walks. One time she took me to a nearby wooded area, and late at night we would just read and talk, waiting for the raccoons to stop by and eat some of the leftovers we'd placed close to this garbage can that they would rummage in."

Chip couldn't believe his ears. "So you killed her?"

Zach felt his head spin in several different directions. He was experiencing vertigo and dizziness at the same time. He had been so wasted the night before that he had no idea what he might have done. All he remembered was staring at the walls and the ceiling of his room, hoping Jenny would stop by. Or Cindy might drop in, his imaginary high-school girlfriend.

Zach said, "I—I did, I mean . . . I didn't kill her."

"You hesitated!"

Zach felt a sudden bolt of rage erupt from within his chest, and it migrated into his brain. "I think *you* killed her," he yelled at Chip. "It's obvious. She dumped you and you killed her."

Chip got up and pounded his fist against the window, but it didn't break. He scowled at the little musician and couldn't believe his ears.

"You've lost your mind or something. She was too classy to go out with a misfit like you. I think you're just jealous that she was mine—and she was, she would have come running back to me within a few days if you hadn't killed her. Get the hell out of my room before I rearrange your skull."

Fury thrust into Chip, and he wielded punches on everything. He challenged Zach to a fight. Zach backed off.

"Look at the pussy back off a fight," Chip said. "I bet you killed her!"

Chip pushed Zach out the door, and Zach screamed back, "I'll prove to the cops you killed her." Chip flipped him off and slammed the door. He was so livid he had half a mind to follow Zach to his room and strangle him dead.

* * *

Just before dinner, Denise was busy printing out the e-mail from her younger sister in the computer lab in Edgar Hall when Tyler walked in. He looked surprised to see her there. She was sitting between Gottlieb and Chainsaw.

"I tried calling you, but . . ." he started.

"Don't bother," Denise said. The usually strong-of-mind woman seemed fearful for once, Tyler thought. He wondered if she had told the police about that e-mail from iKill.

"Denise," he said, "er . . . you haven't told the cops about that e-mail, have you?"

"No."

"I mean, you could, if you think it would help . . ."

"Why should I? I already know who sent it." She looked at him accusingly.

Tyler's face flushed red. He felt like he'd swallowed a live octopus and imagined eight tentacles squirming in his stomach and feeling their way through to his colon. "I—I didn't send them," he stuttered, and then quickly went on the offensive. "So why don't you tell me what's going on with him?" Tyler nodded in Chainsaw's direction. The latter was too busy reading information from a website to notice their dialogue.

"Oh, just a little fun. I imagine you're having lots of fun with Ms. Academics."

"I'm not going out with her," Tyler said. "I don't see why you're playing games."

"Do whatever the hell you want, Tyler. I'm taking off next semester—transferring to another university."

Tyler was incensed that Denise had not consulted him prior to making up her mind. "What do you mean transferring?" A brief fear signal ignited in his brain, but he took a detour to avoid tormenting himself over losing a beautiful woman.

"Like changing colleges," she said.

Tyler logged on to check his e-mail.

"You could have asked me first," he said.

"Yeah, but I didn't want to interrupt your rendezvous with Rhoda."

"There was no rendezvous, Denise. Don't do this."

Suddenly Gottlieb and Chainsaw logged out and excused themselves. "I'll catch you later, Denise," Chainsaw said. She started sending text messages.

Tyler stared at the floor. "Who do you think did it?"

"The police think it might have been someone from outside—a madman."

"Oh! Uh . . . I think so too."

Denise appeared dumbfounded. "See, that's what I don't get. How can you get straight "A" grades and yet be so damn stupid? I want to know."

Tyler noticed he had gotten a few messages from friends back home. He informed them about the murder that had taken place this morning in his residence hall. He wrote with all the excitement of an adolescent unconcerned with the finality of death.

"We're not all as sharp as you, Princess," he said.

"I told the cops that I got a strange e-mail too, but I waited a while."

Tyler pretended to be surprised. "Go ahead, make my day. I didn't send that damn e-mail to you, so you can shove it down your lack of cleavage for all I care."

Denise shot Tyler a look of incrimination.

"Maybe you should see Head Case Stacy," he said. "She's into voodoo and other scary stuff. She might know something."

"I can't stand that bitch," Denise said. "What could she know?"

Tyler laughed. "Probably a lot more than you do. And she might be mixed up in this somehow. Being into strange things is a good cover for committing brutal crimes."

Denise still suspected that Tyler had sent her the wicked iKill e-mail, and she wouldn't put it past him to murder Jenny just for fun. He had gone crazy a few times while they were dating. She told Tyler that she never wanted to see him again and that she thought he was dangerous.

Tyler told Denise to go to hell. "I cared about you," he said, "but now I just wish you were dead." The words rolled off his tongue like water cascading down a waterfall.

Denise told Tyler to stay away from her, to which he responded that Rhoda wouldn't be disappointed with that idea. Denise shook her head and marched down the hall to Stacy's room.

*   *   *

Denise banged on the door of the girl known as Head Case Stacy.

"Hi, Denise," Head Case said. She was dressed in a long wide black dress and wore black leather boots and a nose ring. "How's it going?"

Denise launched an offensive strike against this woman she considered a menace to society. "Why the hell did you send me that weird e-mail?"

"Send you what?"

"I got an e-mail from some sender known as iKill, and it had a picture attached showing Jenny's dead body. I told the police all about it, so don't pretend you don't know what I'm talking about. You're usually up to weird stuff. I'm gonna . . ." Denise wasn't sure if she was losing her mind or not. "I'm not saying you killed her, but maybe someone gave you that picture and then you sent me the e-mail with the photo attached. If you tell me the truth, I promise I won't go to the police." Denise knew full well that she would report any confession to authorities immediately, but Stacy didn't.

"Well, as a matter of fact, I was up late, but I didn't send that e-mail to you, and if you don't believe me, you can check my computer. The police already have."

Denise shot her a look of impatience. "Thought you didn't know about it."

"Well, I didn't say I wasn't into black magic, but I'm no e-mail witch."

"Then who sent it?"

"Jerry."

"Why him? I don't even think he's back from break yet. Are you insane?"

"Yeah, but he's a madman, a freak, who likes to play around with everyone's mind. He's scaring the hell out of you so that you'll back off and let him continue this wave of wickedness."

"How do you know all this?"

"I've got Nellie, and I've got Mr. Wizard. They give me the lowdown on all the characters here. At least, they give me a notion and let me take it from there. You've got to have the gift of ESP and clairvoyance, and I've got both. You may be in danger."

Denise couldn't believe she was wasting her time with this common mongrel and walked out the door. Stacy was capable of wicked mind games, she thought.

*   *   *

Branford aimed a six ball at the corner pocket and missed by half an inch. He held his pool cue like a hockey stick and whacked the long side of the pool table.

"You got quite a temper, kid," Chainsaw said. "Better watch it, or you'll end up in prison one day."

"Takes one to know one," Branford shot back. "Thank God I'm not a Labrador."

Branford, playing pool to distract his mind from numerous other obsessive thoughts plaguing him throughout the day, couldn't believe Chainsaw's comment. The latter repeated his statement.

"Sure you're not talking from experience?" Branford shot back.

Chainsaw made two consecutive shots, and Branford gave him a "beginner's luck" look. He missed the third shot, a rather easy one, and Chainsaw took a swig of rum.

"Keep hitting the juice and I'll have this game," Branford said. "Then again, keep hitting the juice and you'll need a liver transplant."

Chainsaw dismissed Branford's opinions with an air of superiority. "I'm stronger than an ox. I can take my liquor, man, and by the way, you ain't no one to talk about holding your liquor." Chainsaw rarely got in trouble with alcohol because he rarely went without it.

Branford, who disliked alcohol and most people, asked Chainsaw, "So were you drunk when you hacked her to death?" He stared at Chainsaw, who appeared to react to the question in disbelief.

"What the hell do you mean?"

"You know exactly what I mean," Branford said. "I know you weren't asleep last night. You told the cops you were sleeping, but I heard you walking down the hall."

Chainsaw stuttered and tried to regain his composure. "I was . . . I mean, I was sleepin' all night except, yeah, I think I went to the bathroom once. That's probably when you heard me."

"I thought I heard you talking to someone late last night. I was in my room writing up that stupid computer program, and I heard you up and about. It was the middle of the night, and that's when they say Jenny got killed."

Chainsaw studied the cue ball to distract his attention. Branford made the next bank shot into a side pocket and looked at his competitor.

"Hey man, don't worry," he said, "I won't tell anyone. Never mind that you killed my future wife. I'm sure your reasons were good. But just between you and me, how the hell did you do it so fast?" Branford issued a laugh that sounded like it came from the depths of hell.

"Man, you need to see a shrink," Chainsaw said, waiting for Branford to make his next shot.

"No, in contrast to *you*," he emphasized the last word, "I am quite sane. That is, I don't bludgeon my enemies. That's more along the lines of you and Chip. Was he in on this too?"

"No. I mean," Chainsaw struggled to find the right words, "it's like this, man. I was up because I couldn't get to sleep. It's been another bad semester—no women, no good grades, and everyone's getting on my case. So I just want everyone to shut the hell up and leave me alone. Got it?"

"But why Jenny?"

"I told you, you moron, I had nothing to do with that!"

"Then who did?"

"How the hell should I know?"

"I just figured you would, since I heard you staggering back into your room around the same time Jenny was killed. I can do differential equations, but putting one plus one together isn't all that tough either. You got drunk at the bars, or in your room, and came back and killed Jenny."

"No I didn't. Maybe Chip done her in."

"Why drag him into this? I think you did it."

Chainsaw got furious. He threw his pool cue at Branford, rolled up his sleeves, and challenged him to a fight.

"You want to piss me off? You want a piece of me? Let's go, you stupid little prick."

Branford knew he couldn't take Chainsaw, who could probably throw the billiards table into the wall, and tried to calm him down. But he also wanted to play with the guy's mind a little more. "You hit me, and I'll tell the cops what you were up to last night. They might find it interesting that you were so inebriated that you were probably the only person walking the halls of blessed Edgar when she was murdered."

Chainsaw stopped short of strangling Branford but held him in a half nelson for a few minutes before letting him go. Branford touched his neck, which was slightly sore from Chainsaw's grip, and prepared for the next shot.

"Game over," Chainsaw said.

"Ah come on, man, let's at least finish what we started, just like you did last night with Jenny." He added, "Got to dry the clothes after you wash them."

Chainsaw was enraged, and Branford ran out the door.

It's an evil world, Branford told himself. He returned to his room and prepared to resume work on another computer-science program assignment, but first he played a few Wii games. He took out his favorite game, *Assassin*, and turned on his TV, looking out his window with an assassin's eyes.

The rain was pouring down like in so many of the horror movies Branford had watched. He enjoyed the idea of killing and watching people suffer; the sadist in him appreciated dealing cruelty to those deserving. In the back of his mind, he was confident that Jenny had a violent death coming to her, and he was proud of not feeling sorry.

* * *

Denise rolled over in bed for the hundredth time in only half an hour. She couldn't sleep. It was only 6:00 p.m. She'd tried to nap, but her efforts were in vain. Her mind was racing, and she was trying to keep up with life.

Why should she receive that e-mail? And who was this iKill? Was it just a joke, or did Jenny's violent murder have anything to do with her receiving that wretched e-mail? What does it all mean? She thought of some people . . .

Denise suddenly felt an urge to be a private eye—nasty but exciting work.

Murder was a different story, though. There was nothing thrilling about going head-to-head with a psychotic killer. It made her stomach turn and her blood curdle.

The murderer had done a good job killing Jenny, that's for sure. Denise checked her train of thought. *Slow down*, she thought. *Slow down*. She was headed down a one-way road to mental implosion. The nausea and dizziness were resurfacing like a high-speed hurricane.

Was Tyler secretly trying to play mind games with her in order to scare her away? She doubted it. Was Tyler a psychotic killer? He was the quiet angry type who could fit the description . . .

There was that one time he had thrown his laptop through the window, breaking both. Tyler had screamed at Denise for what seemed like hours, and Charlie had to come upstairs to break things up or else call the police. Tyler told Charlie he had thrown the laptop at Denise's head in order to kill her so she would shut up. Unfortunately, he had missed. He looked out the window, cutting a few fingers on the jagged glass at the bottom of the frame, and yelled at people crossing the street below: "I hope you all get run over by cars tonight. Go ahead—play in traffic morons!"

Denise recalled that she had been stupefied by Tyler's outburst. But his tantrums were few and far between. Denise realized that a psychotic must have done Jenny in. Someone in this building had it in his mind to deliver a message.

Denise couldn't take the mental onslaught she'd unleashed on herself and decided to go for a walk. It was still light out, and she thought a brisk stroll down to the highway would do her good. Much better than staying here and torturing herself.

She put her coat on and wondered if she should she call Chainsaw. No, she decided. She wouldn't be able to tolerate his lack of ability to hold a decent conversation for more than three minutes. Most of the other students were sticking to their rooms or mingling with Charlie and Abby at the front desk or with the police, who were still looking for evidence. They're all focusing on us students, why don't they check Charlie and Shaggy out?

What she needed most, she figured, was some exercise and time to think clearly, in fresh air as opposed to this stifling, gas-heated residence-hall room of doom and gloom. But everyone had been told not to leave the building.

She played some of her favorite songs on her iPhone and logged into her e-mail. She opened her inbox and found she had five new messages. One from Mom and Dad, she guessed, and the rest of it junk mail.

She viewed the inbox and recognized one message from her parents. The rest of the messages looked like spam. Denise scanned them and then noticed one in the middle of the five new messages that came from a sender named "iKill."

That's weird, she thought. iKill . . . so he was sending her another e-mail? It could of course be a joke. And if it was a virus, well, that's what Norton was for.

She clicked on the e-mail. It took a while to open. She went to her closet while the file was still opening and put on a coat. The wireless connection was much slower than her mind. She looked out the window and saw that the rain had stopped but the weather looked cold and gray. The e-mail finally opened and she read:

Dear Denise,

> *Just thought you'd like to see what I've been up to. Got up early this morning to take some pictures. Think I captured a Kodak moment. Check out the attached pictures below. What a beautiful sunrise. Hope to see you real soon. Don't let me down, darling. Remember what happened to Jenny . . . you don't want to be next. Love, iKill.*

She looked at the first picture. Denise thought she'd stopped breathing. Her heart clung to her throat as she glanced at a purple body stuffed into some kind of machine. It looked like there was blood . . .

"Oh my," she said, struggling to rescue her emotions before they abandoned ship. "Oh God . . ." She scrolled down to the next picture— the same body taken from a different angle. It was Jenny, Denise realized. She started to cry. More pictures of Jenny in the dryer!

She gritted her teeth and felt her chest heave with a pile of panic, and her tongue grew heavy, filling her mouth.

It was Jenny, someone . . . Denise couldn't think. Her mind was a blank. After a few moments it hit her: Head Case was right. She was in danger.

Denise covered her mouth. She was sure she was going to throw up. Her mind raced and her breath grew tight. She slammed the keyboard into the desktop and got up. She looked around the room. She checked under the bed and under the pillow and in her closet. She scanned her desk; everything looked normal. It was getting dark outside.

Without thinking, she grabbed her keys and a hat and rushed out the door.

A few students were hanging out in the hallway. Denise saw no faces. Her teeth were clenched so tightly she thought others would tell her to stop grinding her teeth. She couldn't think of anything but Jenny's murdered body, all purple and disfigured, slumbering in the dryer. She heard a couple students say her name, but she kept walking fast toward the elevator.

"Open up, damn it!" she screamed. She felt like she might fly off the edge of the earth if she didn't get out of that building.

A few students came up in the elevator. She heard various voices— one she thought was Gottlieb. She recognized his voice, and the others were Chip's and Sheila's. Denise thought she also saw Branford run up the stairs and turn left toward his room.

She saw nothing. Nothing was worth seeing. The voices in her head cautioned her against going out, but she seldom listened to that inner critic.

Now she was running scared for the first time in her young life. Denise decided to sneak out of Edgar Hall for a brisk walk.

*   *   *

I followed Denise down Willow Road. She was walking much faster than usual. Wonder what was troubling her. Hope it wasn't my e-mail. Hope it wasn't the pictures of that angel Jenny. Denise the Doll. Such a pretty face.

She picked up the pace about half a mile west of Edgar Hall. A car drove by and honked. I hid behind some bushes so they couldn't see me. They yelled something at her, but she ignored them.

Smart girl. She remembered she had a date with me tonight. She stammered and shivered, bent down to tie her shoes. I'd seen her practical shoes before. She was so beautiful.

I walked faster. Denise jumped at every noise she heard, but she didn't notice I was trailing her.

Denise didn't react, but I'm sure her nerves were unraveling. I didn't want to make her nervous.

I caught up with Denise, and she turned around sharply. I smiled. What a coincidence . . .

"What are you doing here?" she asked, surprised.

I'm studying you.

Denise thought I was acting weird and demanded to know more. "Going for a walk? It's a little chilly for that, isn't it?" she asked.

"Well then, what are you doing out this evening, Divine Denise?"

"Had to get away," she said. "I . . . I got chased out of Edgar Hall, I suppose, by some kind of ghost or spirit."

Did the e-mail chase you away? Or was it the pictures? Did you get my e-mail, honey?

Denise froze. Her heart might as well have jumped out from behind her rib cage and fell beating on the pavement. She didn't know what to say or believe.

"You mean . . . you? I . . . I . . ."

She was speechless. Logic had caught up with emotion, and disillusion reigned supreme within the practical chambers of Denise's mind.

She felt a sharp twinge between her breasts and thought she was going to have a heart attack. It was fun watching self-suffocation. She looked around at the dirt road and moist pavement and dead trees and wondered if this was what hell looked like.

She felt trapped. She was trapped; there was no outlet.

I took out my chef's knife from inside the sleeve of my winter coat.

How you like this one, dear Denise? Stole it from the cafeteria and no one knows it's missing. You see, they don't keep inventory down there. Utensils come and go just like bacteria and leftovers. I bet we could have ourselves a murder every day for a week and no one would know what to do about it.

I kicked her down to the ground, and she cried out loud.

Go ahead and scream, Denise. No one can hear you way out here. I could have done this on campus and saved you the walk, but it was your decision to come out here.

The chef's knife shined dull and gray in the fading daylight of the death of November. Death was everywhere. And I couldn't wait to slit Denise's throat.

Denise tried to crawl, get up and run, and crawl again. She looked like she was moving in the direction of some tree. I jumped on top of her, and she tried to bounce me in a most violent, catatonic way.

"Get off me, you!"

That's not very nice, Denise. I'm just trying to show you a good time.

I plunged the knife once into her heart. Blood gushed upward and missed me but stained the ground and soaked her shirt. Denise wailed like an animal in pain, and her arms and legs flinched in seizures.

To make certain, I plunged the knife several times into her neck and chest. Blood rushed everywhere like manna from heaven. I finished my assignment.

I took a few pictures and called it a night. I could write a song and call it "The Love of Blood."

I wiped any prints off the knife and dumped it into a large-size garbage bin outside the residence hall.

Time for a little more excitement at Edgar Hall. No need to for finals week to be boring.

Chapter Five

Tom Malkin was barely into the second bite of his plain oatmeal in the hotel restaurant when Sheriff Foster broke the news.

"Two developments, Tom," he said. "You're gonna love this. First, we have another student missing. Name's Denise Lansing. No one has any idea where she might be. A couple of students saw her take the elevator down from her floor at around six p.m. or so."

"And she hasn't been seen since?"

"No. We're doing our best."

"Do better than that. So she never returned to her room?"

"Nope."

"Well, she might have just sneaked out and gone over to a friend's place. Or visited a boyfriend. Sure she wasn't at a friend's apartment or with Tyler?"

"Yep. It gets worse, Tom."

"Pray continue," Malkin said as he took another bite.

"This morning I asked Tanner to get someone to break Denise's door open. I mean, the girl wasn't answering her phone. And we tried calling all her friends, but no one had a clue."

He continued, "Her computer was still on, and I carefully tapped against the mouse to see what she'd been working on before she left."

"Online shopping?" Malkin guessed.

"Funny. There was an e-mail with an attachment of two photographs of Jenny Curtis's body in the dryer in the basement of Edgar Hall."

Malkin pushed his bowl aside. "Damn it all!" He pounded his fist on the table. "Similar to the one she received the morning Jenny's body was found—the one she told us about a little too late?"

"That's right—and there was some sort of ominous message too," he said, reaching for a piece of paper in his suit-jacket pocket. He read the e-mail message in such a way as to not attract much attention from customers sitting at nearby tables.

Malkin pounded the table again. "We're dealing with a special breed of madman," he said. "Yes, we'd better be careful."

"And one more thing," Foster said. "This Jerry Fowler guy showed up late last night around midnight. No one was working the front desk, but one of the guards we placed on duty to watch over things saw him use his key to get in. He showed ID—sure enough, it was him."

"We'll have to question him," Malkin said. "Doesn't look good for him at all."

"I'm a step ahead of you," Foster said. Malkin wasn't used to hearing that. "I called his folks up—they live in Alexandria. They claim that Fowler drove down here Sunday night and should have been around. He didn't leave late as we'd originally suspected."

"Excellent work, but it doesn't mean he didn't stop by a friend's place on the way. Maybe he's got a girlfriend in Fredericksburg or God knows where. We'll find that out when we question him."

Malkin paid his bill and left the restaurant to join Morgan and Gull at Edgar Hall. Many students were hanging out in the lobby, curious to find out if Denise's whereabouts had been discovered.

Sheila was busy flirting with Gottlieb close to the vending machines. Malkin overheard her say something about Denise's tendency to suddenly take off on shopping sprees. "I bet she took off to DC by train or just drove off to Petersburg to get some peace. A woman has to do that sometimes, just get away from men and clear her head."

Gottlieb just grunted. If a woman wanted to spend time with him, Gottlieb would agree with just about anything she wanted to say.

Close to the reception area, Charlie and Abby were talking to Officer Tanner. Charlie said that he had last seen Denise sitting alone after lunch. He said she was crying.

Big surprise, Malkin thought.

President Keyes made a short statement about Denise's disappearance and announced classes would be cancelled. Malkin asked Charlie to phone up to Rhoda and Tyler to check if they were in. Charlie called Tyler's room and handed the phone to Malkin.

"Tyler, it's Tom Malkin here," he said in a low voice. "You haven't seen Denise around this morning, have you?'

Tyler explained that he hadn't seen his ex-girlfriend, as he referred to her in a somewhat malicious tone, since the little spat in the computer lab around two in the afternoon. He added, "I don't think she exactly misses me, either."

"Too bad," Malkin said. "And have you seen Rhoda by chance?"

There was silence for a moment or two, followed by muffled sounds and soft whispers.

"No . . . uh . . . well, yeah—yes," Tyler said.

"May I speak to her?" Malkin asked with a smile on his face.

Malkin waited a moment and then heard Rhoda's voice. He asked if she had seen Denise lately.

"I saw her this afternoon sometime," Rhoda said. "Must have been like three or three thirty. Sheila and I were hanging out in her room, and Denise said she was exhausted and wanted to take a nap. She looked like she hadn't slept for a while. Poor girl."

Malkin explained that Denise was missing and hadn't been seen since early evening. Rhoda reacted with shock and broke the news to Tyler, who took the phone and spoke to Malkin.

"You sure?" he asked. "Maybe she's just at someone's house or something?"

Malkin said he was sure. He added that he would notify them if he heard any more news.

Tanner joined the other officers, and the five of them gathered in the lounge.

"Well, the plot thickens," Malkin said.

Gull spoke first: "I questioned everyone I ran into. No one saw or heard anything unusual. I also asked professors working in neighboring buildings, but no good leads. Nothing to go on from my angle."

Foster coughed and examined his notes. "First of all, concerning this fellow Cragg, he doesn't seem to know much. In fact, doesn't know much of anything. He's a general loser, but I don't think he's mixed up in the Curtis slaying. Says he just pushes his cart around campus to try and make ends meet. So if no one disapproves, I think we'll let him go."

No one suggested otherwise. "What's another bum on the street? Big cities are full of them—and they all ask for money while holding a cup of Starbucks coffee," Malkin said.

It was Tanner's turn. "I had the unpleasant job of telling Jenny's parents everything that happened. Her dad was in a state of shock but could control his emotions. I was impressed, actually; don't know if I'd be able to handle it that well. But her mom was a wreck. She kept vomiting and started spitting up blood—her gums were bleeding a river. We gave her some sedatives to calm her down."

He added, "Oh, and that fine lady from the counseling center—Teresa something—she was great. She handled it from there and took good care of them. They spent some time with Chip. Said that they knew Jenny had just broken up with him and wanted to make sure he was all right. The mother was very sympathetic, but I could see the look of scorn in the father's eyes. Don't think he trusted or liked Chip very much, so we might have to approach that case from a different angle. Before leaving town to make funeral arrangements, the parents met with Jackie and George as well. I guess Jackie had known Jenny since before they came to live in Edgar Hall—sort of a friend-of-a-friend Internet chat partner type thing. And George was still in a state of shock over Jenny's death."

"About what time did they finish their meeting?" Malkin asked.

"Around three thirty p.m. or so," Tanner said. "I remember because Mrs. Curtis said she didn't want her husband to drive back too late given the strain on his nerves and bad eyesight at night."

"Makes sense," Malkin said.

"Then we took a look outside, North Street, Willow Road, but nothing came up. I'll have my men do a more comprehensive search to be certain."

The cafeteria staff brought a tray of drinks and snacks. Malkin grabbed an apple and a cup of coffee.

"That brings us to this Fowler fellow," he said. "Let's bring him in and find out what he's been up to."

Tanner went downstairs and a few minutes later returned with a scraggly young man. Jerry's appearance was a contradiction, in that his shoulder-length brown hair was unkempt and his face looked haggard and weak, his eyes bloodshot and surrounded by black clouds, but his clothing was stylish. He looked like he had just walked out of some expensive store, wearing a clean formal white shirt with a designer suit jacket and what looked like new slacks and shoes.

Jerry was not in a good mood as he growled good morning to the others. "Why the hell wake me up in the middle of the damn day?" he asked.

"Don't you usually get up before two p.m.?" Malkin asked.

Jerry looked at him with disgust. "Not if I can help it."

Malkin self-censored another insulting comment.

Foster informed Jerry of the previous day's tragic events and asked about his whereabouts. Jerry shrugged his shoulders. "Wow! Jenny murdered! Imagine that!" He whistled as if surprised. Morgan thought he was putting on an act.

"Well, please tell us where you were yesterday," Morgan asked.

"Yesterday . . . let me think . . ." He was buying time. "I took an extra day off and stayed home to finish a paper." His eyes shifted from Foster to Malkin and back to Foster.

Foster explained that they had contacted his parents and gave details about that conversation.

Jerry got on the defensive. "I . . . that's right, uh—what I meant was, I stayed till Sunday, and I meant to come back on Saturday to finish this paper I—that's due this week and I uh . . . came back Sunday instead."

Malkin gave him a stern look. "Maybe you should tell us the truth, Mr. Fowler. Where were you yesterday?"

Jerry's speech stammered when he explained that he came back on Sunday but decided to stay with friends in another residence hall instead of coming back to Edgar Hall.

"I'm sure it will be no problem for you to tell us with whom you were staying last night," Malkin said.

Jerry said he had spent the night at Webster Hall in a friend's room. "His name is Nick Ludlow. He's in the same class as me, and we had a paper to finish. So I just went straight to his place and we worked on it there."

Malkin didn't believe Jerry's story and asked for Nick's phone number. Jerry couldn't remember it but said he might have it on his cell. He read the number to Malkin. Jerry's hand was shaking.

"We're just following up on every story," Morgan said. "When did you finish your paper?"

"What's that?"

Gull repeated Morgan's question, and after some thought Jerry said he had finished it sometime after midnight.

"And what was your paper about?" Malkin asked. "I used to be a student, and I like hearing all about term papers." Jerry did not notice the sarcasm.

Jerry wrung his hands and moved one of them nervously through his hair several times. "It . . . uh . . . is on residence-hall life."

"How appropriate," Malkin said. "And what is your major?"

Jerry looked unsettled. "It's, um, right now, uh, College Student Life," he said, looking out the window.

Malkin laughed. "College Student Life, eh? The majors they think up, I tell you. Seems like everything requires a textbook to learn. Next thing you know they'll have a major for beer-can collectors on the side of the road."

Malkin thought of Eddie Cragg—what a sad person, just like Jerry. Something wasn't right about the young man sitting in front of him, that's for sure.

Foster asked one more question: "And there's a student that is missing. Her name is Denise Lansing. I assume you know her, since she too lives in this building." He was careful to keep the verb in the present tense.

Fowler looked surprised, but Malkin again was uncertain as to whether he was genuinely shocked.

"Denise gone?" he asked. "When did this happen?"

"Sometime late afternoon or early evening," Malkin said.

"That's a shame," he murmured, staring at the floor. He rubbed his darkened eyes and scratched his shoulder. "I hope they find her," he added.

"I hope so too," Foster said.

Malkin stood up. "Jerry, are you sure you've told us everything you know?"

Jerry looked up at Malkin and felt intimidated. "Yes, I'm sure. Why do you ask?"

"Because I've been in this business long enough to know you're hiding something from us," he said.

"No—no, I've got nothing, I told you everything. But really, you gotta believe me. I have no idea where Jenny—er, I mean, Denise is. And I had no idea about Jenny till just now."

"You don't read the papers or the news online?"

"Sometimes, but like I said, I had that damn paper to work on all night."

"The news was all over campus, and you heard nothing?"

"I just finished my paper and slept. I don't like people very much."

Malkin pounded his fist against the wall and shouted, "This is a murder investigation, Mr. Fowler! This isn't a game. If you have any information about either Jenny or Denise, I suggest you tell us right away. If not, we have means by which to entice you to tell us the truth." When Malkin raised his voice, everyone sat up straight and dared not blink an eye.

Jerry swallowed hard.

"Do I make myself clear?" Malkin asked.

"I told you everything . . ." He paused.

Malkin looked cross. "Did you kill Jenny Curtis on Monday night?"

Jerry was stunned. "No—no way! You gotta be kiddin' me!"

"Ever heard of someone named 'iKill'?"

Jerry shook his head. "'iKill'? That's a strange name. Nope. Can't say I've ever heard that name before."

Malkin shook his head. He looked down at Jerry's pathetic, strained face.

"And since when have you been collecting women's shoes?"

Jerry sat up. "Hey! You had no right to go through my stuff."

"Actually, we did. And what are you going to do about it—pilfer a pair of high heels from Macy's just to prove you can get away with something? Like I said, this is a murder investigation, not a fashion show. Why the shoes?"

"I keep a pair for . . . er . . . I don't know . . . it's just a weakness on my part. I guess . . . I guess I just like them. So I keep them. They're from girlfriends, but none of them live here in Edgar Hall. You can check on that. It's not like I have any of Jenny's or Denise's shoes in my room—I promise that's true."

Malkin shook his head. "Ever heard of the James River Killer?"

Jerry hesitated before he answered with a quiet, "No."

Malkin shook his head again. He felt like slapping this kid silly.

"Why don't you believe me?" Jerry asked again.

"You tell me," Malkin said, and stormed out of the room.

∗   ∗   ∗

Malkin checked into Jerry's story and discovered there is no student named Nick Ludlow. Big surprise, he thought. He then went downstairs for some coffee and a chat with Charlie.

"Oh, hi, Tom," Charlie said. "Surprised to see you down here."

"You don't look too busy, got time to talk?" Malkin asked.

Abby was stunned. "We're just finishing inventory for the month, let me save this and then we can talk."

Malkin and Charlie walked to the end of the lobby and sat down. "There's one thing bothering me, Charlie. I can't seem to get anywhere with the students."

Charlie put one finger on both lips and looked upward. "Hmm, I'm sorry to hear that, but it doesn't surprise me."

"Why's that?"

Charlie said, "because everyone here has something to hide, but at the same time, they are very good at holding things in. Trust me."

"You're right, but without water boarding, how do I get those kids to talk? I'm asking you because you know them better than anyone else around here."

Charlie hesitated. "To be honest, these students are lucky. Many are on scholarships or fat student loans paid by people like me. You know, I never got the chance to go to college. That's how I ended up a front desk manager. But I had to work my way up, and I did." Charlie added, "I think Eddie Cragg is your man myself."

"Could be," Malkin said. He asked, "you ever heard of the James River Killer?"

Charlie's face turned red. "That was scary, yes I remember that very well. I don't think the police got their man on that one. That Cragg guy could have been the James River Killer too."

Malkin nodded in agreement. "Think there might be a connection?"

"Uh, yes, I think there could be, but he would have to really have it out for some people. He would have to be so full of rage that he could kill anyone for any reason. I don't even think there was any motive found in the James River Killer case, was there?"

"I've discovered there was some speculation, but nothing concrete. Tell me, Charlie, what is your view on mankind?"

"Oh, I try and be very positive. That's my role."

"Yes, but deep down, what do you think? Give it to me straight."

Charlie's eyes scanned the lobby. "I'm imagining all the students in this lobby now, and all I can feel is anger. Resentment. Someone's not telling you everything, Mr. Malkin, and that goes for Cragg as well."

"Any students you think might be mixed up in this business?"

Charlie waited a few seconds before answering. "I hate to say it, but I've had my eye on Jerry, Chip, and Zach. They are all lost and have no idea what's going on in their dirty little minds."

"Thanks for your time, Charlie," Malkin said. "Wouldn't it be funny if it turned out not to be one of the students?"

"You mean like Cragg? Yes, that would be very funny. Like a game of Clue or something."

Malkin's perspective on Charlie shifted a bit. Better keep an eye on that one, he thought. He might know too much, might know who iKill is, or be working with iKill, or even worse.

* * *

Zach returned to his room and turned on the television to give his mind something else to focus on besides death and suicide. His head spun in cycles of high and low as his body wasted from skinny to emaciated. Zach hadn't eaten in days and was hardly aware of the fact. His best friend during the past few years was darkness; now things looked like night. If only it would always be nighttime.

He turned his attention to music. He reached for a CD loaded with minor chords and covered his face with both hands. Even the music, slow and severe in dark tones, hurt his ears. Zach longed for a dose of eternity—that resting place where no wicked obsessions and gods of insanity picked away at his darkest fears.

Maybe that was hell, he thought. It certainly felt like death. And the topic of death brought him back to the current situation. Jenny was dead, and Zach had no idea what kind of blind rage his mania had steered him toward that fateful night. Now Denise . . .

She was probably dead by now, poor girl.

A fog descended into the room and infiltrated his head. He tried to see through the mist and felt an overwhelming desire to cry. Burning within his heart was an equally strong urge to scream until his windows shattered. He could jump through the fog and clear the window, dropping onto the cement pavement three floors down.

Not far enough to die, he reasoned. With his luck, he would catch a branch of that maple tree and dangle till a firefighter rescued him.

He shook his head. He had to remain positive. Teresa had told him to stay strong, but no matter how attractive she was, he knew she had no idea what harsh thoughts permeated his polluted skull. He could be a musician, a decent and well-respected songwriter, and his musical heroes never gave up. Or did they? Maybe he'd end up like Kurt Cobain.

Or Jenny and Denise . . .

He switched on the TV to clear his mind. The first station showed a man with an ax breaking down a door. He looked possessed. Zach wondered whether he could ever get so possessed. Possessed enough to kill? Why not?

He wondered where Jenny was now. Probably lying on some gurney in a hospital postmortem room. Zach wondered if Jenny had any regrets. His mind was racing so hard he thought he was developing a fever. His hands shook and were sweating as his face grew paler. What if he were called on to conduct the postmortem on Jenny's body? Zach considered whether some of those experts ate limbs or organs of dead bodies following their examinations. This was a relatively sane idea, given the other things that originated in Zach Gillett's brain.

Life is an opportunity for regret, Zach thought. Missed chords, bad chord progressions, out-of-tune broken guitar strings, selling next to zero CDs.

He was wearing what he called the death collar. He didn't even play his guitar, his best friend. Nothing was working. Nothing was worth working. He should just jump out the window and retire from life. He was lost in a death obsession.

No use doing this, he said to himself. The third floor was surprisingly quiet. Perhaps everyone was sleeping. No, he thought— everyone was trying to make sense out of Jenny and Denise.

No one knew what was going on. But someone in Edgar Hall had to know something . . .

Zach leaned back to ponder the idea. A flash of white fog crept in through the closed windows and enveloped his mind. He stirred his thoughts and swirled round the room. The room was circling him. He had no idea what was going on. The mist filled his eyes, and he screamed as tears ran down his face. A crushing anxiety suddenly lifted from his chest and shoulders. He felt instant relief.

Out of nowhere, Jenny emerged. He awoke from what had been an altogether intolerable nightmare. There were no police downstairs. There had been no dried-blood body abandoned in the dryer in the laundry room. And there had been no fried finger in the buffet line.

Jenny smiled at him. She gave him a long kiss on the lips. He held her in his arms and swore never to let go.

"I thought you'd died," he said, wiping tears from his cheeks.

"You work too hard," she told him. "Listen, there's a great play running at the Community Theatre Playhouse tonight. Take me there!"

Zach would never again refuse to take her anywhere again. In the past, he had asked her out in his imagination many times and then chickened out at the last minute. He figured why try, since she would probably refuse and instead go out with that idiot Chip.

But now, Jenny was here! He couldn't believe it. No need for him to commit suicide tonight. He had thrown himself completely out of whack.

"You bet," he said. "Let's do the play and then rent a movie—your choice—and watch it in your room with popcorn and root beer." Such was their style of partying, and Zach loved every minute of it. Though he had partied with the real partiers in high school, that sort of thing bored him now.

Jenny gave him a big hug and felt his forehead. "Are you okay?" she asked. "You do look a little pale." Jenny always had that nurturing, caring motherly quality about her that he found so appealing.

"Give me a break," he said. "Five minutes ago, I thought you had left me. Gone forever."

"Never!"

"Where did you go?" he asked, not sure why.

"I was going over last-minute wedding plans," she said.

"Wedding plans?" he asked, somewhat nervous.

"No need to wait. Our parents won't mind. God meant for us to be together."

Zach wasn't ready to marry Jenny so fast, but he figured, why not? He had almost lost her to a madman and wanted to be around her all the time so he could protect her.

"This time," he said, "I won't let you out of my sight. You'll be mine forever. This is our future. God gave us a miracle to work with . . . you will never leave me again, Jenny. I'll always take care of you, night and day. You shall never again leave me! Do I make myself clear?"

Zach was on the verge of one of his anxiety-ridden rages, but Jenny was the right prescription for him.

Jenny smiled and kissed him again. Now they were standing in a chapel, and she had on a long traditional white wedding dress with a veil. He put the veil down and liked the sharp white tuxedo he'd donned. Where had he bought it? Jenny probably got it for him. She was his caretaker.

They were married. Suddenly, Zach couldn't wait to pick Jenny up and carry her out of the chapel and into the limo.

Inside the limo, Jenny ordered the driver to go straight to the hospital. Zach wondered what was wrong.

"Anytime," she said, smiling.

"Anytime what?" He thought this might turn into something good, but every time he hoped as such he was disappointed.

"Could be anytime," she said. "I hope it's a boy. Then he can be a guitar hero just like his dad!"

Zach smiled. That thought had a pleasant ring to it. It sounded like the ring of a well-struck E chord in one of his favorite riffs. The limo driver asked Zach if he would be willing to sign Zach's latest CD; Zach didn't remember recording one and offered to do so without knowing how or why.

The limo pulled up next to the hospital, and nurses dressed in black took Jenny away in a wheelchair. They were all crying and had forlorn, sullen expressions on their faces.

"Meet us in Room 310. That's where you'll identify her."

Zach felt a 500-watt guitar shock the middle of the head. He was dizzy, and he tried to grab on to something to keep from falling down.

He fell down to the ground and had no idea which way was up. He came to after a minute and stared at human beings who blinked on and off like neon-lit stars in a melting Milky Way galaxy.

"Identify her?" he asked, his heart beating faster and his face growing pale. "Why should I have to identify her?"

"Because she died yesterday, and you killed her."

Zach retreated in terror. He screamed, "I didn't kill her! I didn't kill her! Somebody listen to me . . . I didn't kill her!"

He woke up drenched in panic.

*   *   *

For the first time in her life, Mindy Adams spent the day buried under her bedcovers. She didn't want to look at the world, and she didn't want the world to catch a glimpse of her. She felt guilty about Jenny's death, and now Denise's disappearance. She should have been there for her friend. She should have offered to do laundry with her. After all, Mindy knew that she was probably the last person Jenny had spoken with before she was . . .

She looked at the clock—7:08 p.m. She had slept the day away, but now sleep had forsaken her. She tossed and turned in her twin bed with the covers pulled up over her head. Mindy slammed her eyes shut but failed to doze off. Sure of herself and positive, Mindy seldom doubted herself or her ability to give life 110 percent, just like Jenny. She had always striven toward success. Jenny was to become a veterinarian and Mindy was to be a family physician. That's the way it was supposed to have been.

Not this time. Not in this lifetime.

7:12 p.m. . . . Goodnight, world, she thought.

The words "never escape" passed through Mindy's mind. Interesting words—they spoke of one trapped in a bottomless chasm in perpetual waiting for the fires of hell.

With those words echoing in her head, Mindy finally gave up on lying around in her room and walked down to the Lighthouse, a cozy little coffee shop on campus that served food and drinks till late at night. Students were now allowed to leave Death Hall but had to inform police of their every move. Many students brought homework to the Lighthouse and indulged in caffeine long enough to finish what they'd started. Tonight, however, Mindy just wanted a change of scenery and a hot chocolate.

Head Case Stacy sat at the table next to Mindy's and was talking with a female friend who Mindy didn't recognize. Mindy overheard whispers that were too loud to be inaudible. She overheard discussion of a séance and the mystery killer of Jenny Curtis. Mindy thought Stacy, or Head Case as most people called her, was crazy.

Séances? Ridiculous! Mindy thought.

The Lighthouse felt cold. Mindy put on a sweater, opened her psychology textbook, and shivered. The page she happened to open to was on abnormal psychology and theories about psychosis. As she read various descriptions of murderers through the years and their psychological bases for committing the acts, Jenny's face popped up from each page. Mindy froze and considered returning to her room.

Outside the south bay window that faced West Willow Road, she saw hundreds of students and what looked like media officials standing around.

Waiting for Denise to return? she wondered. She grew tired of the depressing atmosphere of the Lighthouse, a cheerful place to hang out during happier times. She paid for her hot chocolate and returned to the death zone to talk with Charlie and Abby.

Charlie was busy with inventory while Abby was working with a new computer program designed to maintain more efficient records of residence-hall data. She slammed the mouse down against the desk, and Charlie came to the rescue. Within a few minutes, Abby was smiling again and back to work.

"I usually don't get upset over little glitches like that," she told Mindy. "But I had no idea why it kept saying 'data input error.' I swear, I know technology makes our lives easier, but sometimes it's just a pain."

Mindy laughed. She recalled many a time she had to rewrite a paper because a mysterious virus had wiped out everything she had saved. "One thing's for sure, when something's on paper, it's there. Nothing can take it away—well, except for water. But with computers, you never know what you'll recover and what will disappear forever."

"Just like Jenny," Charlie said, his face looking at once melancholy and lost in some sort of distant memory.

"Yeah, and what about Denise?" Abby asked.

"What about her?"

"Apparently she got like one of those strange e-mails from this iKill character. It all seems a little creepy to me."

Charlie rubbed his hands and reminded Abby that the officials did not want too much information leaking out. He said, "I don't think they want everyone to know that this iKill person might have struck again. They want us to lay low and make sure no one says anything."

"It's a little late for me," Abby said. "I make sure a security guard or Charlie here walks with me to Webster Hall if it's after dark—like tonight. You will take care of me, won't you, dear?"

Charlie blushed. "Of course I'll make sure you're safe, as with any student."

They exchanged a few more pleasantries and gossip surrounding the two recent incidents before Mindy returned to her room. She felt exhausted and just wanted to sleep for a few days.

As she turned around to face the elevators—only the middle one was in service since the renovation had started—Mindy imagined them as giant teeth eating her.

When she walked out of the elevator on her floor, it was so quiet she could hear a finger drop. My God, she thought, where did that thought come from? Mindy walked into her room and locked her door. She sat next to her desk and felt colder. The warmth flowing through the vents failed to register any comfort in her bones. She glanced outside the window again.

Psychotic. Strange word. Who was so ruthlessly and irrationally unstable that he would stoop to hurting people?

Malcolm. That was Mindy's first guess. He had a violent temper. He had missed out on his chance to play football at UVA, just like Chainsaw had, and he could care less about his studies. Besides, he was hardly around and supposedly hung out in Webster Hall most of the time. But when he was around Edgar, he appeared listless and often paranoid, as if he was on pins and needles waiting for something to happen. He had the strength to take an ax to her and . . .

Stop. Enough. Mindy had decided that Malcolm was the murderer. She wanted to prove it, but finding evidence against him would be difficult. From what she had heard from others, he had quite the rap sheet. There were all sorts of rumors out about him.

Chainsaw was another possibility. He was also tough enough to do the job. And he was a hater. Mindy had no idea what Denise could see in him, other than someone stupid with whom she could get back at Tyler for liking Rhoda. Chainsaw had been an animal torturer when he was in middle school—a real winner.

Anyone capable of harming anything innocent is capable of killing students, Mindy thought. Perhaps Chainsaw was the man responsible.

There was one more guy who got on Mindy's nerves every time she laid eyes on him: Gottlieb Heiner. He was bad news. Nicknamed "Hitler Heiner," he had a temper that rivaled those of Malcolm and Chainsaw. Chip and George were always getting on Gottlieb for losing his temper in front of the guys or for throwing stuff out the window because of some small political or economic matter. Mindy was a pre-med student and didn't understand much of what politics entailed—not to mention what Malkin had talked about—but she understood enough to know that Gottlieb could kill if he didn't get his way, and kill again.

Stop. Her mind was doing overtime again. Jenny was gone. Mindy thought if Chip killed Jenny, then that would be the ultimate revenge.

Strange thoughts. Mindy shook her head. She was starting to get drowsy again. She felt her head spin in one direction, stop, and then spin in another direction. After a few minutes, she felt as if she had gotten off the ride and the room was starting to spin. She was tiring of all this.

Suddenly there was a knock at her door. She didn't want to open it. She had no idea who it could be. She didn't want to guess. If it was one of the girls on the floor, she would usually say, "Open up, Mindy, it's Rhoda," or something like that. No such warning now. It scared her.

The knock came again. She began to sweat and thought about hiding under her desk or under the bed. Better yet, she could lock herself in the closet; there was enough room in there to hide.

Mindy just wanted to hide away from life. The knocking was only a symptom.

Then she almost jumped as she heard a third, louder knock. It was followed by a voice: "Mindy, are you in there? If so, open up. It's George."

Mindy still didn't feel like opening the door but got up anyway. She threw on a sweatshirt and jeans and winced at her breathing. She felt like an elephant was sitting on her chest.

George's face looked grim. Jackie was standing next to him, and it looked like she had been crying. Her eyes were worse than red and puffy—they looked possessed. To her left was the intrepid Tom Malkin. His jaw was square, and he had a serious, dour expression on his face.

He said in an official manner, "I'm afraid we have some bad news to pass on to you, Mindy. Denise was found dead about an hour ago—in

an alleyway off West Willow Road. If you don't mind, Mindy, we'll need
to have a few words with you and the other students."

*   *   *

OPS head Frank Tanner assembled all the residents and staff of
Edgar Hall into the lounge on the fourth floor. President Keyes, Vice
President Flanagan, Tom Malkin, Officer Morgan, Sheriff Foster,
Officer Gull, and Teresa Martinez all stood beside him.

Sheriff Foster cleared his throat and spoke to the students and
staff. "I want to thank all of you for coming here on such short notice
Unfortunately, things have taken a turn for the worse. Blackwood City
Police, headed by officer Peter Morgan, and OPS, headed by Frank
Tanner, teamed up to look for Denise Lansing, who was declared
missing early yesterday evening. We found her stabbed several times in
an alleyway off West Willow Road about two hours ago and pronounced
dead on the scene. She was taken to Blackwood Hospital, where an
autopsy will be performed."

A chorus of incredulous exclamations could be heard from every
direction of the lounge. Malkin studied the students' verbal and facial
reactions. He noticed that Mindy, Jackie, and Rhoda were trying to
control their emotions but were on the brink of crying. Most of the
men stared in shock. He was surprised that no students—not even the
temperamental ones like Branford, Chainsaw, and Chip—showed any
sign of adolescent rebellion. Zach kept his head down and Sheila, sitting
next to him, watched as if she were at a movie premiere. Two of the staff
members had taken out handkerchiefs, and Charlie was sulking in his
chair, trying to ignore the update. Malkin noted that all the students
were present except for Malcolm and Jerry.

Sheriff Foster continued, "Indeed, this means there is a killer on the
loose. We've had two victims in two days. As law-enforcement officials,
we will continue to do everything in our power to bring to justice the
individual or individuals responsible for Jenny and Denise. We ask
that you take every precaution to ensure the safety of yourselves and
your friends. As such, I'd like to introduce the president of Blackwood
College, Dr. Arnold Keyes, who has a few words to say."

The students stared in awe. President Keyes, usually upbeat and
encouraging, was understandably subdued. "Good evening," he began.

"As Sheriff Foster just mentioned, we regret to inform you that Denise was found stabbed to death by an unknown assailant off West Willow Road just an hour ago. Once we have the medical evidence, which we're awaiting from the hospital, we'll have a more precise time of death.

"Regardless, I want each of you to know that OPS—led by Frank Tanner here and his staff of excellent officers—will do everything they can to assist the Blackwood City Police as well as the Virginia State Police. We will not stop looking for the murderer until he or she is caught. Having said this, I would like all of you to do two things.

"First, I want you to abide by an eight p.m. university-wide curfew. This means you'll have to return to your rooms by that time. Anyone out later without prior permission from OPS will be sent to police headquarters for questioning. Along these lines, I want everyone to be proactive. Try not to walk outside alone, if possible, and if not, ask for a police or OPS guard to escort you.

"Second, I want you to cooperate with police officials. I have agreed to allow all law-enforcement units to search the entire university. The two victims were residents of this building; therefore, the murders appear connected in some way.

"Finally, there will be an all-campus meeting concerning these killings tomorrow morning, and classes will be canceled tomorrow, as I announced upon hearing of Denise's disappearance. We'll have a memorial for Jenny and Denise in the Commons, followed by a message from Teresa Martinez of the Counseling Center, who will be on hand to offer grief counseling to those who wish to speak with a professional.

"It goes without saying that if any of you have any information whatsoever concerning one or both of these murders, it is imperative that you tell the authorities. Thank you."

President Keyes stepped aside to let Teresa speak next. "I just wanted to let everyone know that the crisis hotline part of the Counseling Center is open twenty-four hours, and we have additional experienced and professional staff members ready to assist anyone who feels overwhelmed. So if you need anyone to talk to—me or someone else—please stop by or call us at 947-4357, or 947-HELP."

Tom thanked President Keyes and Teresa for speaking. He indicated that everyone could leave and then motioned law enforcement toward him. "This bastard is beating us, and that's shameful. Two killings, two too many—so let's turn on our brains and find the beast."

Chapter Six

Malkin had some unfinished business in the lounge to attend to before returning to his hotel. There were two girls lingering in the room: Rhoda and Stacy.

"How are you holding up, Rhoda?" he asked.

"Terrible, Mr. Malkin," she said, still sniffing and taking out some used tissue from her jeans pocket. "Everything's going to hell."

"It's tough, but you'll be fine, Rhoda. Keep your head on straight, and don't let anyone stand in your way."

Rhoda appreciated the confidence he exuded but explained that she felt guilty about Denise's death. "You see, I think I'm responsible for her death," she said.

"What?"

"I mean, I didn't kill her, but . . . it's hard to explain. You know how it was when you were in college. We're always, like, dating a lot of people. Anyway, I started going out with Tyler, who had broken up with Denise. I didn't think she cared. I mean, she always acted all confident and poised. And Tyler and I got along fine, but I guess he told me that she took it pretty hard. So she started going out with . . ."

Malkin knew where this was leading, and he had the impression that Rhoda was trying to make herself appear important.

"We'll talk about this tomorrow, Rhoda," he said. "But remember what Teresa said. If you need someone to talk to, you can call the hotline or the Counseling Center. And I'm sure they would take good care of you."

"I'm too embarrassed to call them," she said.

Malkin took five minutes to convince Rhoda that she needed to talk to a counselor this evening. He called Teresa himself and set up an appointment for Rhoda at 10:00 p.m.

As soon as his attention turned to Stacy Nutter, however, the smile disappeared from his face. She was bouncing in her seat, anxious to speak to the detective. Malkin saw her double chin and thought Stacy looked like an excited Cabbage Patch doll. He sat down next to her.

Head Case had a lot on her mind. Malkin agonized through minutes of detached observations till Stacy, looking around to make certain they were the only two in the room, told Malkin, "I know who killed the girls. It was Jerry Fowler!"

"And how do you know that?"

Stacy sat up as if she were the hero of the evening. She imagined her story being broadcast on the radio and featured in the papers and online. "It's easy," she explained. "I approached the crimes from a sleuth's point of view, but I looked at it from the outside in, rather than the opposite way. Jerry was gone the morning Jenny was killed; he planned that to give himself an airtight alibi, which he knew the police would try to confirm. He just had his friends make up something.

"Then I thought that this crime was done by someone with a vicious temper. A lot of guys have bad tempers on this floor, but Jerry is the quiet, passive-aggressive type who holds his anger in. He probably had a thing for both girls, they rejected him, and he got back at them. And what fixes it for me is what the Wizard said to me," she said.

"Wizard? I should have known there was a wizard on campus."

"He's in my room. He's my energy in the form of a crystal ball. I give him all the information he needs—he asks questions, and we communicate through telepathy—and he gives me the answer."

"And?"

"And I spoke the facts of the case, and the Wizard started to get cloudy white inside. I'd never seen anything like it before. I had all the lights out and I stared into the crystal ball, and eventually I saw a picture. It was vague at first, but then it grew clearer. It was a face. It was Jerry's face."

Malkin couldn't believe he was listening to a sociology student with a minor in black magic explaining how she solved a murder case. They ought to send this Head Case Stacy out to the Middle East to track down al-Qaeda insiders, he thought.

"If you're right," he said, "I'll recommend you to Scotland Yard. But for now, there's still a killer at large. Don't tempt fate," he said. "And don't try to be a hero either. If anything happens, call me or the police immediately." Stacy promised to do that and walked to her room confident she could be a hero.

*   *   *

Mindy returned to her room obsessed with order and fear. Everything looked all right, but she still felt uneasy. She changed clothes, fixed herself some tea, and made sure the door was locked.

She tried the lock and door handle three times to make certain no one could get in. But why would anyone want to get in? Mindy knew she was thinking too much.

She checked her closet one more time; there was nobody inside. The floor was unusually quiet. She didn't like the quiet at all. Most of the time she disliked loud noises; now, Mindy would give anything to have some semblance of normalcy return to this haunted hall.

She had to calm her nerves, and she had to sleep. She opened her door and was relieved to find the hallway empty. The lights were dimmed, and she heard the din of various typical noises for a residence hall.

Mindy returned to her room, took off her socks, and slipped between the covers. She didn't like the dark but was too lazy to get up and turn on the light. The last-quarter moon cast a midnight-blue shadow upon the fright of night. All the tree branches and lights from outside formed strange shadows on the walls. Even though the windows were closed, she could hear every car that drove by and watched the lights from each car bounce off her walls.

The murderer—whoever this iKill was—could be in any of those cars. He could be driving up to Edgar Hall this minute. He could even already be in Edgar Hall, just a few doors down. An avalanche of anxiety brought tears to her eyes.

No way she was going to get any sleep if she kept this up. There was no point trying. She picked up a novel and started reading.

If thinking feels anything like this, Mindy reflected, then it would be better not to think at all.

She decided to go online and see if any of her friends were chatting. That would cheer her up; she could chat with friends out of town and forget all about iKill and the mess Edgar Hall was in right now.

After a few minutes, she signed in and checked her messenger pals. Much to her surprise, no one was online—except for Zach, who lived just a few doors down! She had logged on and knew that Zach could see her user name, but she wasn't sure she wanted to chat with him. She had chatted with him only once briefly back in early October, and she wasn't exactly a very good friend of his.

However, Mindy reconsidered, given that she knew she couldn't sleep and felt that chatting with a mere acquaintance was better than chatting with her inner ghost. She was about to initiate the chat session when Zach sent her a message. A dialogue began:

> **Zach**: I knew where to find you!
> **Mindy**: How are you?
> **Zach**: Fine. You know everyone is too scared to leave his room?
> **Mindy**: Yeah, it's crazy.
> **Zach**: I'm surprised you can relax.
> **Mindy**: I can't. And you?
> **Zach**: No. I've decided to kill myself.
> **Mindy**: Shut up.
> **Zach**: I'm tired of life.
> **Mindy**: You're not serious.
> **Zach**: I let everyone down.
> **Mindy**: You don't let me down.
> **Zach**: You don't have to play the protective older sister.
> **Mindy**: What?
> **Zach**: My family already hates me.
> **Mindy**: Not good enough of a reason.
> **Zach**: Plus I have a guilty conscience.
> **Mindy**: Why's that?
> **Zach**: I've done some bad things the last few days . . .
> **Mindy**: Like what?
> **Zach**: Can't say.
> **Mindy**: I won't tell anyone.

Zach:	Like hell you wouldn't! If I told you, you'd call the cops ASAP.
Mindy:	That bad?
Zach:	Yep. That's why I got this knife right here and I plan on—
Mindy:	Don't.
Zach:	I've made up my mind.
Mindy:	I'll come to your room now.
Zach:	What makes you think I'm in my room?
Mindy:	Where are you?
Zach:	Not telling . . .
Mindy:	Stop being such a child and tell me where you are.
Zach:	Could be right outside your door.
Mindy:	I don't think so.
Zach:	Go ahead and look.
Mindy:	No tricks.
Zach:	Suit yourself.

Suddenly, Mindy heard a door close. It came from the stairway. She was beginning to feel nauseated and was running out of patience with this little chat session. She logged off and reflected on her conversation with Zach. He was a lot weirder than she imagined. She had no idea he was so fearful and suicidal—or at least not to the extent indicated in his chat. Fearful, just like her. Just like her and everyone else in Edgar Hall, thanks to the mysterious iKill.

Mindy suddenly remembered how utterly paranoid she'd felt just before going online and chatting with Zach. She felt better now. "I'm not paranoid then," she reasoned. If the fear was based in rationality, and she knew she was being rational and that she was of sound mind, then Mindy was certain she was not paranoid. She breathed a deep sigh of relief and went to knock on Zach's door.

"I'm sorry I scared you," he told her, holding the door open so she could walk in. "I'm just lonely and depressed. I needed someone to pick me up."

Mindy looked Zach over from head to toe and thought he looked like death. His skin almost matched the color of her light green bathrobe, and she could have sworn he had not changed clothes in the last couple days. He still had on a blood-red sweatshirt with indecipherable black print on the front and faded jeans. Some morbid music was playing on the stereo. He sat on his bed across from Mindy, who was standing next to the door and keeping it slightly ajar, just in case.

"Again, Mindy," Zach pleaded in a self-deprecating tone, "I'm really sorry. I didn't mean to scare you."

Mindy was feeling more like a mother figure than an older sister. Somehow that feeling was comforting. Perhaps Zach wasn't a bad guy after all. Maybe he'd had a bad childhood and was raised by uncaring parents. That might explain his suicidal tendencies.

"You need to talk to Teresa, Zach," she said.

"I know."

"Promise me you will?"

"Yes."

"When?"

"Tomorrow. First thing. I promise." Zach held his head low and sulked like a kid being punished for coming home late.

Mindy smiled and gave him a big, maternal hug. For Zach, it felt soothing in a more sensual way. He smelled remnants of Mindy's perfume; their eyes met for a moment, and then hers fell to the floor.

"One more thing," she said. "Where's that knife?"

"Why?"

"Give it to me. I don't want you to keep it. I'll return it to the cafeteria tomorrow."

"Then they'll arrest me, I know it."

"No they won't. I won't tell them you had it."

"Swell—then they'll slap the cuffs on you."

"Then just return it to Malkin or Foster and tell them the truth."

"Then they'll lock me up and slam a straitjacket on me!" He raised his head, besieged by doom. "I'm done," he said. "I just know it."

Mindy was bewildered by his exaggerated claims. She knew he was doing it for attention, but at the same time she believed he was truly messed up.

"I gotta keep the knife," Zach said.

"Why?"

"I think I used it on Denise."

Mindy almost ran out the door when Zach forced her back into his room. He shut the door. Mindy thought twice. Sometimes Zach just wanted to get attention.

"Don't tell anyone, or you'll be next. Do you understand me, woman? Tell any of these cops anything you know, and you'll wish you'd never met me."

Mindy stood paralyzed against the door. She wanted to run away but was trapped. She thought she might be Victim Number Three and almost screamed for help. But Zach couldn't be thinking straight.

Suddenly Zach slumped. "I won't hurt you, Mindy. I could never hurt you." He got down on his hands and knees and begged forgiveness. "Don't even listen to me. I don't know why I said that. My family stopped listening to me years ago, and now I can see why—I'm a loser. Just go back to your room and leave me to my business here."

Mindy couldn't believe her ears. Here was this privileged, talented young man on the floor squandering everything. She told him to try to get some sleep as she closed the door and walked back to her own room to seek some rest herself.

She stared out the window into the midnight-blue sky. It looked more gray than blue, as there were clouds floating by. Outside looked like a dark, dense fog. It looked like it might storm; the wind was picking up, and she could hear it howl through the windows and into her nerves.

This was nuts. Jenny was dead. Denise was dead. One was killed in the morning, the other in the evening. Police officers were on the case. Malkin was here to help out. And no one knew a thing.

Maybe Zach really was iKill. Perhaps he was trying to warn Mindy out of kindness. That didn't make sense. But then who could iKill be? Gottlieb! Mindy's mind flashed back to memories of ideas and things he had said that made her believe he was the top suspect. But she had no hard evidence, only intuition.

It was no use thinking up the worst. This was real misery, lying awake around midnight and staring into nothing.

She decided to check her e-mail. She hadn't checked it for a while and thought her friends might be worried about her if they had heard about the murders.

She logged back on and saw that Zach had signed off. She opened her inbox and went to the mini-fridge to grab a Diet Pepsi. Suddenly, the phone rang. She jumped. Just calm down, she told herself. The phone rang again. It could be anybody, so why was she afraid? She picked up the receiver. There was no one on the line, just a busy signal. So much for scaring the hell out of herself.

Suddenly she recalled how George had warned her that Gottlieb enjoyed making prank phone calls. Mindy wondered if he liked writing prank e-mails too.

And then she looked at her inbox. There was only one new message. She looked at the sender's name. In bold type was a short word. She dropped her can of pop and felt her heart rate double.

It read "iKill."

Her hands began to shake on the keyboard. She dragged the mouse in anxious circles around the computer screen. This had to be some kind of joke. No way she was involved with all this. No one wanted her.

She imagined that was what Denise thought about the e-mail too. Mindy rubbed her hands and ran them through her hair. She breathed deep and debated whether or not to open the message.

She bit her fingers and opened it. There was a short note and two attachments. She felt her pulse quicken to a thick, driving beat. She could feel it down to the soles of her feet. Her chest ached. She read the message:

> *Hi Mindy. Just wanted to let you know that Denise is safe.*
> *I made sure. She was walking kind of strange and looked lost, so*
> *I put her in a place where she could find herself. See for yourself.*
> *I'm sorry to e-mail you; I'm not a bad person. Get some rest*
> *tonight. Now be a good girl and don't tell anyone about this*
> *friendly little note, or you might be next . . . Love, iKill.*

"Oh my God," Mindy cried. She wasn't sure how loud she had said that, but she could hear herself screaming inside. She imagined a paper cut on her tongue and a large man forcing an ax into her skull. She thought of a ghost with scissors cutting into her throat. She grabbed her neck; it was getting hot in her room, and she couldn't breathe.

"Not a bad person"? That sounded just like Zach.

She scrolled down to see the attachment. Then she stopped, figuring she didn't want to see whatever was there.

"See for yourself," iKill had written. Who would send this stuff?

She scrolled down a little further and saw the top part of a picture. She hesitated and didn't want to look. She closed her eyes and then opened them till they looked like narrow slits of gray, like an unforgiving sky. She looked at the picture. The top part was just grass.

But the lower part featured a bloody body mangled by a heavy instrument into the ground. It was Denise, Mindy was sure. That was her shoulder-length brown hair dyed dark red with her own blood. Disgusting. Her clothes were stained with blood. Denise's face was unrecognizable, but Mindy recognized the clothes and the hair.

Mindy shivered. She wrung her hands and kicked her desk. She was angry and afraid at the same time. Her arms were numb. Mindy felt her fingers tingle but scrolled down to look at the second picture. It was the same picture as the first but taken upside-down, from the opposite angle. What a warped person.

The idea that she might be next was enough to paralyze her. She sat frozen at her desk for a few minutes and suddenly quelled a horrendous scream coming from some place lit up in her brain. She covered her face with her hands and fell into bed crying.

No use considering sleep. She wasn't safe. Zach was right. No one was safe. Or maybe Zach had sent that e-mail. Anybody could have sent it. This whole building, the campus, the world, is warped. She bit her white knuckles.

Don't go there, Mindy ordered herself. She didn't want to consider how the murderer had killed Denise. Probably the same way he had killed Jenny, though these looked more like stab wounds. Zach thought Chip had done this, but why would Chip want to get rid of Denise? Did she know something about his killing Jenny? Mindy doubted it.

She thought about Tyler. Today at the meeting, he didn't seem all that emotional about losing his girlfriend. But he had broken up with her to go out with Rhoda. Or had he? She wasn't sure. Maybe no one was.

Of course, not much in this world made sense. People got killed every day for crazy reasons. Accidents. Suicides. Senseless murders.

Mindy's mind kept racing. For a few moments, she imagined how Chip, Tyler, Chainsaw, Malcolm, Jerry, Gottlieb, Branford, and Zach could have done Denise in. Mindy had to stop her mind before she gave herself a nervous breakdown imagining a hundred different ways to commit murder and get away with it.

Tyler definitely could have done it. Denise had been flirting with Chainsaw; Tyler had been flirting with Rhoda. Big deal. That's what college kids do. Sorority chicks are ten times worse. It's as if something is written into the script of life mandating stupid behavior during the college years.

Mindy remembered that there was a security guard downstairs. She considered informing him of the e-mail. But she was afraid to go downstairs alone. And she needed to think about this some more.

She walked back to her door and listened. It was dead quiet. Dead— why had she chosen that word?

Mindy smelled her T-shirt. It stank. She took it off and threw it in her clothes hamper.

Her mind kept walking down an imaginative pathway toward death in Blackwood. This was probably what Jenny did after she and Jackie talked about that picture she'd received. Mindy put on her robe. She had no clean clothes, and she was sure there was a murderer waiting for her in the laundry room.

That was impossible, she chided herself. He might be a lunatic with pictures of dead victims and a creepy e-mail name, but he can't possibly know when someone has to do laundry.

Mindy was fed up with trying to negotiate the cause and effect of the murders and the e-mails. She decided to play it safe and stay in her room.

But she couldn't stay there forever, she knew. She considered going down to the basement and looking around, but Zach was right—she shouldn't go anywhere alone. She had to be very cautious.

Zach still had that knife in his possession . . .

Mindy was losing her mind. She was imagining too many horrific scenarios and chose to put them to rest by taking a long, calming shower. That sounded like a good idea. She could relax and then maybe even catch a few hours of sleep. But something deep down spooked her.

Then she remembered why, and felt sad again. Memorial services for Jenny and Denise. Incredible. It seemed like she had just welcomed them back from Thanksgiving break.

Mindy tightened her bathrobe. It hung down below her knees, and she made sure her front was covered in case some nut was outside. She didn't want to have Sheila's reputation. She didn't want to show off in front of everyone like the tall, leggy blonde did almost every night.

"Nonsense," she mumbled to herself, "everyone is asleep." She knew that.

She grabbed her bathroom bag and keys and opened the door. It creaked. She looked around. The lights were off in the hallway but on in the bathroom—just as usual at this time of night. The only unusual thing was that it was so quiet. There were no more stereos, computer and video games, and televisions on.

Mindy closed her door and walked to the bathroom. She decided not to wear slippers and instead go barefoot so that no one would hear her. As she approached the door to the bathroom, located in the middle of the floor, it opened suddenly.

Mindy jumped back with what must have been a hesitant scream. She felt a sharp twinge in between her breasts and adrenalin rushed down into her legs. She dropped her bathroom bag containing shampoo, soap, and various lotions.

"Hope I didn't scare you," Sheila said. She had just finished taking a shower and had a skimpy white towel wrapped around her torso and another around her hair. The towel barely covered her and showed ample cleavage, and Mindy remembered that Sheila was the only girl on the floor who walked to the bathroom wearing only a towel. All the others wore T-shirts or robes.

Sheila clearly craved the attention of men—she showed as much skin as she could get away with, Mindy thought. She didn't want to be like that, not like Sheila. She didn't have Sheila's legs or long neck, but Mindy was good-looking enough to show off some skin. She just considered such behavior low-class.

Mindy found it difficult to speak. She collected her breath and said, "No problem." Sheila looked at Mindy for a few seconds; she thought Mindy looked pale.

"Are you sure you're okay?" Sheila asked. The fact that Sheila was a fast-talking extrovert who could filibuster for a living made Mindy feel nervous. "You look like you've just seen a ghost!" Sheila continued. "Don't worry. You're afraid of the killer, aren't you? Don't be—there is a very cute guard standing watch by the elevator downstairs. And he checks up here from time to time. I gave him my telephone number. He seemed interested but hasn't called yet. Who knows? Maybe there's a message on my answering machine." Sheila laughed. She took everything lightly, another trait that bothered Mindy. Sheila told Mindy to take it easy and headed back to her room.

Mindy looked around the empty bathroom and felt on edge. She walked past every shower and toilet stall to make certain she was alone. She looked in one of the mirrors and noticed her hair was untidy and her face looked exhausted. She felt frustrated. She thought a nice hot shower would do her good.

Mindy brushed her teeth and then flossed. She kept looking at the door, wondering if anyone else was going to scare the hell out of her like Sheila had just done. But she heard nothing and turned around to go to the showers. She walked up to her favorite shower—the third one from the door with the good water pressure. She took off her robe and hanged it along with her towel on the hook next to the shower curtain.

She turned the shower on, waited till the water temperature was exactly right, and got in. She felt better under the water and let the blast of hot water wash away her fears, beat out the terror that was tightening her neck muscles. She reached for her shampoo and, in the process, knocked her bottle of body wash over. As she picked it up, she thought she thought she heard a faint noise outside.

Mindy was stern with herself. She wouldn't let her imagination run away with her like she had earlier. She'd only drive herself crazy worrying about all those things.

Mindy shampooed her hair and rubbed a thick lather all over her nice, smooth skin. She was happy that Zach would see Teresa tomorrow. That was a soothing thought. Mindy thought it was funny that Zach thought Chip was the killer; she disagreed. She still thought it had to be someone who was mad from outside Edgar Hall. It was hard to imagine that someone on her floor was a—

Mindy froze. She heard a noise, but this time it was a louder noise like the sound of a door closing. She dropped her soap and stepped back against the wall of the shower stall. She listened carefully and thought she heard someone's voice. The sound of the water jet in the shower reminded her of a poisonous snake about to bury its fangs into her neck.

She wanted to say something to reassure herself it was just someone going to the bathroom in the middle of the night. That was normal. She had nothing to worry about. It was probably Sheila coming back in to get something, or maybe Rhoda. Perhaps Head Case had a late-night séance scheduled for the restroom.

She had to know who was in the bathroom. "Hello," she said. There was no response.

This reminded her of the time when, as a child, she got lost in the supermarket. She thought her mother had abandoned her forever as she ran crying into the sympathetic arms of a store employee. Mindy recalled that memory as if it happened yesterday. She didn't stop wailing for hours and pounded on her mother's face and chest till the latter promised to never let her out of her sight.

She felt like a child right now, a helpless child waiting in the wings for imminent doom. There was another sharp noise . . .

Mindy thought perhaps she had just imagined hearing a door. Or it could have been a door in the hallway. The door that led to the stairs wasn't far away, and that one was really loud when it banged shut. That must have been the one she heard. It was probably the security guard keeping watch.

But she wasn't sure, and Mindy had the kind of personality that had to be sure. She hesitated and eventually got up the nerve to say, "Sheila? Is that you?"

There was no reply. The water felt good on her skin, and she looked down at her bare feet. Her feet reminded her of how fast she could run if she had to.

"Rhoda?" she said. No answer. Mindy figured there was no one in the bathroom and that she was just paranoid. That seemed to be the word for the night. Zach had come across as paranoid, and now Mindy felt that way.

Had Zach gone to sleep? Or was he . . . Mindy divorced that thought from her mind and instead focused on completing her shower. Everything was moving in slow motion. Life was stuck ankle-deep in mud, and Mindy was trying to get out of the quicksand.

"Hello? Anybody there?" she asked again. Nothing. She started talking to herself just to fill the quiet. "Don't worry, just finish your shower and get in your room. At least you can lock your room; then you'll know you're safe. And lock your window too, and check under the bed and in the closet to make sure everything is—"

Mindy heard another noise; it sounded the same as before, but now she heard footsteps. At least, she thought they were footsteps. Or maybe she was just imagining all this, and it was the water in her ears that was driving her to madness. Suddenly she heard a whistling sound and relaxed. It was probably Shaggy or one of the guys staying up late. The whistling stopped, and she heard louder, firmer footsteps again.

And then, suddenly, the lights went out.

"Who's there?" she asked, her voice echoing through the hollow darkness.

There was no answer. She turned the shower down a little and listened carefully. Her heart rate shot to about a hundred and fifty beats per minute. She heard more footsteps and then more whistling. Charlie whistles, she thought. So does Shaggy. And Chip, George, and of course Zach the musician. Maybe this was all imagination.

"It's not funny," she said. "Turn the lights back on. Is that you, Sheila? Rhoda? Somebody say something please . . ."

A large knife cut through the shower curtain and barely missed her. Mindy screamed. She hit her head against the wall as she dodged another swipe that missed her chin by a centimeter. All she could see was a long black arm and a shiny blade. She couldn't see through the dark steam, but she thought the man was tall and had a dark mask on. Maybe it was a white mask. She thought she was going to pass out. She screamed as loud as she could scream, and then a third swipe caught her shoulder and bicep. Suddenly, her assailant ran away from her and out the door.

Blood dripped down Mindy's arm and onto the dark gray tiles of the dingy bathroom. She looked at her arm and knew she had been cut badly. She stood there vibrating in what by now was a mountain of dark steam enveloping her baptism in blood and water. She was hurt, but she was alive.

Mindy felt pain all over her body and began to cry. She heard sounds of quick movement outside the bathroom and several doors opening and closing.

She tried hard to breathe at all, never mind normal breathing. The shower was still running, and hot water pulsated all over her skin, mixing with the blood on the tiles.

Mindy was standing under very hot water but felt as if she was frozen as she realized she had just escaped a murder attempt—an attempt on her. Her back pressed up against the wall, she prepared herself for anything and prayed that nothing would happen.

She tried not to look at the torn flesh on her shoulder, but she looked anyway. Her mind's eye saw white tendons intermixed with blood and gore reaching into the joint. Mindy thought she was going to die—this is it.

She grabbed her robe with her left hand and somehow got it around her while running toward the door. For a moment, she imagined the killer standing in wait for her behind the door. She looked back at the shower stall and saw the torn curtain. She looked into the mirror.

She had to have courage; she had to leave now. Mindy ran out the door, turned left, and bolted down the stairs to the main lobby.

Chapter Seven

Harry Sampson looked as if he hadn't slept a wink. He was on his third cup of coffee, and breakfast had not even been served. He fumbled for his cigarettes before he realized he couldn't smoke in a public restaurant. Seated next to him were Malkin, Foster, and Tanner.

"Tell us everything you remember," Malkin said. He usually expected the worst and wasn't expecting to be surprised this morning.

Sampson explained the gory details of the night before. He'd been reading the *Sporting News* and keeping watch by the elevator on the first floor. He walked around the first floor and then took the stairs at the west end of the building down to the basement. Sampson saw nothing unusual and took the elevator up to the third floor.

"What time was this?" Foster asked.

Sampson tried to collect his thoughts and looked up at the off-white ceiling, as if the answer was carved next to one of the fluorescent lights. "I would have to say around one a.m., sir." He continued, "I walked around the third floor and everything seemed normal. I remember hearing some water running in the women's bathroom and thinking someone was taking a shower before going to sleep, something like that. But I didn't think anyone was in danger."

According to Sampson, he walked around the fourth and fifth floors of Edgar Hall—they were still under construction, but he had been ordered to keep an eye on all six floors. He spent about five minutes up there before taking the stairs back down to the main lobby.

Sampson said, "And then I got a Mountain Dew to keep me awake and was reading for about a minute or two when suddenly the Adams girl came screaming like hell down the stairs to my left—down by the east side of the building."

"That would be Mindy," Tanner said.

"No, the one from the TV family show," Malkin said. Tanner wasn't ready for sarcasm this early in the morning.

Sampson explained that Mindy was bleeding profusely in the right shoulder area and that the right side of her robe was soaked in blood. Mindy was very pale and in a state of shock, and he ordered an ambulance to take her to the hospital.

"Too bad they didn't take her to the Student Health Center," Malkin said. "She might have had to take a pregnancy test first before getting stitches."

Foster laughed. "You're in one hell of a mood this morning, Tom," he said. Malkin didn't respond but spelled the letters "iKill" with his knife on the faint yellow tablecloth. For a second, he imagined the linen soaking with blood like an inkblot permeating its surroundings with menacing saturation.

After that, Sampson explained that he had called Tanner, who in turn notified Foster and Malkin of the attack on Mindy and that she was sent to Lakeside Memorial Hospital for stitches. Morgan, the Blackwood city police officer, had come on the scene later, and OPS officers had searched for clues in the bathroom and taken blood samples and dusted the walls for fingerprints before searching Mindy's room.

Tanner nodded in agreement.

"That's when they found the e-mail from iKill," Foster said with a heavy sigh. Sampson repeated the contents of the e-mail, word for word, and handed a printed copy of the message and pictures to Malkin. Sampson was relieved to get those lurid pictures out of his possession.

Malkin examined them with cold dismay. He reread the message and glanced over the pictures of Denise clubbed to death in a ditch. She looked like a heaping mass of black, blue, and dark red. He'd seen much worse.

"So iKill strikes again. Mindy must have read this and panicked, and then decided to take a shower," Malkin said. "Denise reacted in a similar way, only she went for a walk."

"Mindy was a nervous wreck," Sampson said, "so the doctor recommended putting her on tranquilizers so she could relax and recuperate from the attack."

"Could she describe the attacker, this lunatic who goes by iKill?"

Sampson said, "Only that he looked dark—black mask and a long black arm or sleeve, and just the long steel-gray blade of a butcher's knife." He then filled in the background: "The way Mindy described it was like this—she couldn't sleep and tried reading, but that did no good. She chatted with Zach for a while and attempted again to sleep, but couldn't, and decided to take a shower. While doing so she thought she heard footsteps or breathing or doors opening and closing, and she thought it might be Sheila or Rhoda; in fact, she mentioned that Sheila was walking out of the bathroom when she entered and that they talked briefly."

He continued, "Said she was nervous but didn't tell Sheila why—it was of course because she had just read the e-mail from iKill. About five or ten minutes later, she heard noises again—couldn't really identify them but said they sounded like doors and footsteps, thought she might have heard voices. She called out to see if it was Sheila or Rhoda in the bathroom.

"Then suddenly the lights went out," he went on, "and she fell silent. She said she heard footsteps and braced herself against the wall of the shower and asked again if Rhoda or Sheila were in the bathroom. There was no response and then she was attacked—three big slashes through the shower curtain with that long-bladed butcher's knife. Probably stolen from the cafeteria. By the time she opened the shower curtain, he was out of there. She didn't hear anything else after that, and then she just put on her robe and ran downstairs, saying she felt like her arm was going to fall off. Can't say I blame her. That's when I saw her, and I called for the ambulance."

Malkin tapped his fingers on the table. "Bet no knife has been found."

"Not yet."

"Did you notice anything strange or see any suspicious characters?" Foster asked.

"Not at all," Sampson said. "That's just it. Everything was quiet and normal. Peaceful. Then suddenly Mindy's attacked and all hell breaks loose. All the students were buzzing about with questions and rumors, and it was mad. Fortunately the police came and got everyone back to bed. I stayed on the third floor with another OPS officer the rest of the night."

"And no one came in or left the building?"

"Not that I noticed, sir."

"How is Mindy doing now?" Malkin asked. He recalled last night's meeting and how he had warned them to be on guard. He thought Mindy was the sensible, cautious type who had just ran into bad luck—a psychotic killer.

"Much better," Tanner said. "Talked to her a few minutes this morning. Doctor says she can return home later today."

"Notify the parents yet?" Foster asked.

"Right before meeting with you here. Didn't see the point of calling them in the middle of the night. Maybe I should have, I don't know. They are on their way. As you can expect, they have pretty strong opinions about her staying here; they want to take her back up to Maryland this evening."

"And what does Mindy think about that?"

"She's against it, actually. Silly girl. Said she felt like that would be running away. She's got it in her head to catch this madman now. Can you believe it?"

Malkin thought for a moment. "Brave girl," he said. "Let's talk to the parents when they arrive. We could see if they would let her stay in an undisclosed location to finish the semester—under twenty-four-hour surveillance, of course, and with a personal bodyguard. That's the least this university could do for a woman who's got more courage than most."

Tanner, due to meet with Mindy and her parents at 10:00 a.m., said he would suggest Malkin's idea to them.

"Don't just suggest it," Malkin said, "order it!"

Their breakfast arrived. "I imagine this campus is going to blow up when this story breaks," Foster said. "First Jenny, then Denise, and now Mindy. But this iKill fellow didn't succeed the third time—she got away."

"That won't deter him," Malkin said. "This guy's clever and quick. He's a step ahead of the pack and demented. Killing people is no new profession, but taking pictures of them and then sending them along with short messages to his next intended victim—this is the psyche of a killer who's not only deranged, but I'd say he's got worse anger issues than Mike Tyson."

"Any ideas about the identity of iKill?" Sampson asked.

"The early-twenty-first-century killer," Malkin said. "I suppose before long, some bored, demented techie will create the ultimate computer virus that can kill a user with the push of a keyboard button or single click of a mouse. But for now, we'll have to settle for a traditional murderer who gets his kicks by sending e-mails of victims to prospective victims."

"Yes," Foster said. "This iKill is a computer whiz who knows his stuff. We need to focus on those students—*techies*, they call them—who possess excellent computer-science skills. At least that's one angle we can tackle."

"Tyler and Branford are the tech-inclined residents in Edgar," Malkin said. "But you don't need to know how to write JavaScript to send e-mails and include pictures as attachments. Any student could do that in minutes. Obviously someone is, and we're the fools without a clue."

"Why don't we just try to track down those e-mails?" Sampson asked. "Can't we find out from where the e-mails were sent?"

"Nice try," Malkin said. "We did that with the e-mail sent to Denise and just checked on this latest one sent to Mindy. One of Foster's tech experts looked into it. Best they could determine is the e-mails were sent from the large computer lab in Strong Hall, just next door. This iKill probably used three different computers but left no fingerprints. Anybody could have done that. It wouldn't take very long to walk to Strong—a five-minute walk—send the e-mail, and then walk back."

"We just ordered OPS to install video cameras in all computer labs on campus," Tanner added, "which they said they should have done by the end of the day."

Malkin doubted it; he had had enough experience dealing with bureaucracy in Washington.

Tanner said, "iKill . . . what a weird name."

"Then what about the pictures?" Sampson persisted. "I thought the police searched all the rooms last night. Did any of the Edgar Hall students have a digital camera?"

Malkin thought it strange that a young officer would be so out of touch with modern technology. "These days, Harry, everyone takes pictures with their cell and then deletes them after sending the e-mail. And most students have video record on their phones. I'm sure iKill just downloaded the pictures from his smart phone to the computer, sent them, and then wiped the computer and cell clean. So iKill wins again. In five minutes, everything is erased or destroyed. And the cell can't be tracked."

"But we'll be able to nail him if he tries again—the video cameras could catch him, right?"

Malkin's voice turned from informative to gloomy. "I don't think we have much time to waste. This iKill probably got his next victim picked out already. And it's our job to stop him. So how do you propose we do that, men?"

The four officers paid their bills as Foster received a call from Vernon Gull, who was staying with Mindy at the hospital. He said she was ready to be released and wanted to meet with Jackie and George.

"Go ahead and okay that," Malkin said. "Then she can work things out with her parents. But if they let her stay, again, I demand that Mindy live in an undisclosed location with a guard on watch 24-7. Is that clear?"

Tanner nodded. The officers walked out onto the cracked pavement of the parking lot. Before Malkin entered his car, he informed them that he intended to spend the day at Edgar Hall.

"Unless we watch firsthand exactly what the hell is going on in that damned place," he said, "we'll find ourselves calling another student's parents tomorrow."

Tanner shook his head. "Let's try and avoid another unpleasant death and another unpleasant phone call," he said.

"Then we've got no time to lose," Malkin said. "I'll call you later."

*   *   *

Following the memorial services and a quick lunch, Malkin returned to Edgar Hall to talk with students and staff. Fortunately for him, most of the students and all staff members with whom he wished to meet were present. Malkin situated himself in the new and comfortable fourth-floor lounge—the same one in which they had convened to announce the murder of Denise Lansing—and ordered Harry Sampson, who was on guard duty to send students and staff up one at a time to meet with him. They were otherwise not to leave the residence hall without permission.

Shaggy stopped by first. He had a sarcastically jovial personality and had worked in Edgar Hall and Harrison Hall—the newer residence hall across the cafeteria from Edgar Hall—for more than twenty years. He walked into the lounge with a spring in his step and whistling. He sat in a plush light-blue recliner opposite from Malkin and smiled.

"Never seen anything like this," he said, referring to the two murders and one attempted murder. He whistled in alarm, as if to place an exclamation point at the end of his short sentence.

"It's a damning business," Malkin said.

Shaggy laughed. "Well, all these murders—certainly wakes up a sleepy town."

"So it does," Malkin said. "Tell me about the students here. I want to talk with you before I meet them because I figured you've got a unique perspective on things here in Edgar."

Shaggy said, "Jenny had a great personality—studied all the time, that girl did. She was your typical daddy's girl who wouldn't do anything to upset anyone. That's why I was so shocked when I found out someone done her in. Like the killer must have got the wrong person. Scary thought, that one.

"Anyway, same with George—wouldn't hurt a soul. Totally into sports. He might drink a few beers with the other guys and bet on games, but pretty harmless stuff. He is a serious student and knows how to hit the books, you know. I'm not much on the romance scene, but you ask about what I seen, seems to me that George and Jackie are an item—seen it with my own eyes."

Malkin could care less about who was seeing whom unless it dealt directly with the murder.

"Malcolm is a cool brother, I think," Shaggy said. "He's not around half the time, and he's sneaky, if you know what I mean. Dumps out some weird stuff in the garbage sometimes—tubes, glassware, pills— think he's a chemistry major. Started out young; already got a wife and kid up in New York, and he goes up to visit often, but he also got a few women on the side here as well. This curfew you police imposed ain't his style. He don't like it, and he been whining about it to other students. Don't think he's into studying, but I could be off on that one. Got in on one of those minority scholarships, so what does he care? He doesn't like it when he doesn't get what he wants, let's put it that way."

Shaggy yearned for a cigarette but rejected the urge and continued. "Now Chainsaw, on the other hand, that boy can be downright cruel. Now there's a killer for you. He's been picking fights with guys half his size.

"And as for Denise, let me tell you, since you asked, now she was a smart one who knew how to get when she wanted it and didn't give a damn who stood in her way. So she and Tyler were pretty much the same—not sure they were a good fit, though. Tyler could have killed Denise; I'm talking rage, if you know what I mean, for what she did."

"How about Rhoda and Chip?"

"Like Chainsaw, Chip has a short fuse. He won't take no for an answer. Seems like if some madman didn't come off the street and put Jenny in the dryer, I would have guessed that Chip did. Now there's another killer for you. Could have been a twenty-four-hour state of insanity the shrinks keep talkin' about that he was in, and in that condition he decided to rip Jenny limb by limb. Chip is a possessive boy. He's got a mean streak, and man, was he pissed when Jenny dumped him. I could hear 'em screaming inside her room the day she . . ."

Shaggy stopped short of another explicit description of Jenny's body and moved on to Rhoda.

"As for Rhoda, the girl's got no self-confidence. No ego and just basically a follower. She is best friends with her neighbor, Sheila Underwood, who been trying to help Rhoda get into her sorority. Rhoda is just looking for Mr. Right to settle down. She's the typical marrying girl who avoids fuss and trouble.

"Her friend Sheila is more outgoing and has a ton of boyfriends. Probably count them on two hands. Pick a day and I might be able to tell you where she's staying, cuz she isn't in her room here in Edgar too much, you know. Sheila is no academic, but boy, she sure does like to party—the ultimate party girl, you know? Rhoda will end up a housewife with three kids and a husband who couldn't give a damn about her, while Sheila will go through two or three divorces and milk 'em for all they worth. There you go—you wanted my opinion. That's what I think."

Malkin said he liked a man who talked without spin. "Anyone else? Let's see here—how about Gottlieb, Branford, Jerry, and Zach? Anything about them you can share?"

Shaggy thought for a moment and laughed. "Zach is a good kid, not so big on life, and hates bein' a student, actually. His folks put a lot of pressure on him and all he wanna do is be in a band. But they want him to be an engineer."

"Much more admirable profession," Malkin said.

"He's a loner—most of the time he's staying in his room, drinking and smoking and watching TV and playing guitar. Don't study much. But check this out, Malkin: the best part is he obsesses about death."

"Best part?"

"Well, I mean, everybody got an obsession, right? He is obsessed with death. Seen it all the time when we go in to polish the floors once a month—like all his lyrics are about death and dying. I see and hear a lot, Malkin, and Zach is one hell of a morbid fellow, but he's all right—I think he'll pull through, or just kill himself trying."

Shaggy continued, "And Gottlieb—he's the German exchange student. He's a good kid, but he gets on people's nerves. I'm surprised it wasn't he who was murdered. He always gets into arguments with Chip or George about politics—you know, with the international terrorism and all that stuff. All them boys got a wicked temper, and all o' them could be killers."

That didn't surprise Malkin.

"Branford is another loner, but not as bad as Zach," Shaggy said. "Stays in his room a lot—but he's not playing guitar, he plays video games, computer games, does a little homework once in a while, and generally stays away from people. Tyler is another techie, good with computers, who stays away from people most of the time. I think they're antisocial. Branford and Tyler could be good murderers if they tried. They're both very bright and sort of bored. Maybe that's the type we're looking for here."

"We call that progress," Malkin said. "They don't need to know what the capital of Canada is, or Virginia for that matter. They just need a scholarship or financial aid with a cell phone and a new car from Daddy, and they're supposed to get a four-year education that way. In many ways, this isn't so much an education as a four-year exemption from responsibility. All professors want are good evaluations."

Shaggy laughed. He looked around and thought it was time for a cigarette break. All this talk had gotten him all worked up about the story of the century in Blackwood, Virginia.

Malkin asked, "So what about Jerry?"

"Much more into social life than school. Probably be on academic probation after this semester. He's not into school, and he spends most of his time up in Webster Hall. Strange kid, but smart—another techie, he could study more, but I know he likes to party, walks around with red eyes half the time—I don't mind, but I wouldn't want my son acting like that. And I heard he got some weird habits that I won't go into, some strange stuff that the other kids talk about. You know, porn and crap like that. Could be bad news all around."

"That's pretty much how I'd sized him up too," he said. "And how about Stacy Nutter? I guess the others refer to her as 'Head Case.' Interesting nicknames they've come up with for residents here: Head Case, Hitler, and Chainsaw. The latter fits the description and mood of this iKill the most."

Shaggy shook his head. "Impossible girl," he said of Stacy. "I mean, she's not even a chick. Nothing nice about her: weird and totally into black magic. Have you seen that girl's crystal ball and tarot cards and other crap in her room? It's scary stuff, man."

Malkin thanked Shaggy and said he had been most helpful. He asked Shaggy to call Charlie White up for a short talk.

*   *   *

A few minutes later, the lanky front-desk manager with a bureaucratic manner and friendly smile sat opposite Malkin.

"What can I do for you, Mr. Malkin?" he asked, pushing his glasses up his long nose.

Malkin studied Charlie closely. "Trying to solve this murder business, Charlie," Malkin said. "What can you tell me about Jenny, Denise, and Mindy?"

Charlie's eyes scanned the room. "Nice girls."

"Yes."

"They were very nice. All the boys took to them. They studied hard and would chat from time to time with Abby and me in the reception area."

"Anything you can recall that was unusual about them?"

"Not really, but you might ask Abby—she's the observant one and talks about all that girlish stuff. You know, Mr. Malkin, some of our boys have vicious tempers, but I don't think they're killers. Though Branford, Chainsaw, Chip, Tyler . . . could have . . ."

"And you could have," Malkin said.

"Why do you say that?"

"Because you also have a temper."

"Ha! That's ridiculous, I'm just a happy-go-lucky kind of guy."

Malkin smiled and Charlie wished him a good day.

Shaggy and Charlie . . . wonder if they're in on this together. Talk about smokescreens, Malkin thought, and then there is Mr. Cragg to deal with.

*   *   *

Harry Sampson informed Malkin that the rest of the students had gone out. As required by police, they had provided information on their whereabouts. Malkin opened his notebook. Jerry, Branford and Zach were downstairs playing pool while the others had left Edgar Hall. Tyler, Chip, Gottlieb, and Chainsaw were eating lunch at Madison's, another local student hangout, watching an afternoon NBA game.

Sheila and Rhoda were scheduled to attend the formal sorority announcements luncheon, while Malcolm was meeting with friends in Webster Hall but was supposed to return shortly. Stacy was still in her room, and Malkin was informed that Mindy, her parents, and George and Jackie were spending time together at Mindy's undisclosed location.

Sampson left Malkin to himself and the latter rested his elbow on one knee and his chin on his hand. He knew iKill had probably scheduled his next attack. Tom pondered the recent events and his mind took a trip down Murder Row. He was lost in meditation and considered every move and statement. He decided to go to the Recreation Hall.

"Good afternoon, gentleman," the detective said. "Just thought I'd watch you guys play. Go ahead—don't let me interrupt your game."

Zach was whistling an old rock tune while Branford was chalking his cue. Jerry stood in the corner with an indignant expression on his face. It was clear he didn't like the sight of Malkin in the room, in the building, or in Blackwood, for that matter.

Branford sank the last three balls to win the game. "These guys are no competition," he said to Malkin. "Care to join us? Everyone puts in a Jackson; winner walks away with eighty bucks."

"High stakes, I see," Malkin said. "Make it ten grand and I'm in."

"Give me a break," Jerry scowled. "That must be what you rake in per minute."

Malkin laughed. "Just like an undergraduate to overestimate the earning potential of someone like me. Go ahead and break, Fowler," he said.

Jerry aimed carefully but failed to sink a ball. He cursed and slammed his cue stick into the floor.

"Take it easy," Zach said, "or you'll have to buy the residence hall another one of those." To Malkin, he explained, "He's just like John McEnroe was a tennis racket."

"Go to hell and don't come back," Jerry said. "And while you're in hell, write a song about it. Just don't play it for me, though. I can't stand it when all the damn dogs howl like they're hearing the most cacophonic sounds on Earth."

Branford told the guys to calm down. He missed his ball, and Malkin sank two in a row.

"Old pro?" Zach asked.

"Not old, just a pro," Malkin said. He missed his third shot and looked at Jerry. "Missed that one—it was a bad miss, too. Just like with Mindy."

Jerry's hand began shaking as he took his turn. The cue was shaking left and right, and his shot wasn't even close. "Why the hell you asking me that question?" His nose was stuffed, and as tried to relieve some of the congestion, thin red blood trickled down from both nostrils.

"No question, just a statement," Malkin smiled. "You seem somewhat defensive."

Zach grabbed a soda out of the vending machine and noticed that Jerry was sweating. Jerry wiped his forehead with his sweater and said that it was unusually hot in the recreation hall.

"It's called heat," Branford said. "They turn it on in the winter so we can stay warm."

Malkin decided to cut to the chase. As Branford took his shot, Malkin asked, "Do any of you have any information that could lead us to discover the identity of iKill?"

Jerry turned around and walked awkwardly toward the vending machine. Branford put his hands in his pockets and waited for Zach to take his shot. Malkin noticed that Branford was the most calm, while Zach was trying to subdue some inherent nervousness.

"What makes you think we know anything about this damn business?" Jerry yelled. "We have no idea what's going on. Some nut walked in off the street and killed Denise and Jenny. Too damn bad. What the hell do you want us to do about it? Make up a killer just to put an end to it? Well, I've got no idea what's going on, so there. It's your job to find the killer, and our job to study."

"Is that what you were doing the day Jenny's body was found— studying?" Malkin asked.

Jerry hesitated. "Y-yes," he said. "I was writing a paper that was already overdue in Webster Hall with a few other students. Malcolm was there, you can ask him."

"I will," Malkin said.

"You're not doing a very good job," Jerry said. "Maybe you're all washed up. Maybe you can track down terrorists but can't find a village idiot."

Branford said, "Why so defensive, Jerry?"

Jerry screamed, "I'm not defensive. I just think everyone's scrutinizing me. What the hell for? There are plenty of people who could have done Jenny in. But it wasn't me. I have an alibi. So all of you can go to hell and stay there for all I care."

Zach thought about hell. "Must be a horrible way to go," he said. "Die and suddenly feel the burning fires of hell's front gates. Some way to go—eyeballs singed to sawdust."

"I'm not going to hell," Jerry said. "I've done nothing wrong!"

"I believe you," Branford said. "Now can you put your skirt back on so we can continue this pool game?"

Malkin gave Jerry a stern look, and the latter slammed his cue down and bolted out the door.

"I wonder what's biting him?" Zach said.

"You scared the hell out of him with all that hell talk, pun intended," Branford said.

"Well, the only thing one needs to do is die—just look at Jenny and Denise," Zach said.

"I'd rather not," Branford said.

Malkin leaned against the pool table and thought to himself, "That boy is hiding something. But what?"

Malkin checked his watch and realized he had enough time to catch the other guys at the Windmill, for a late lunch. He liked the atmosphere of the Windmill—black and white checkered floor with television sets propped in each corner, a small bar, and plenty of large round tables for students to eat, read, or just catch up with the news or games on TV. An old-fashioned red-and-white mill sat welcoming in the corner opposite the huge high-definition television. Malkin couldn't blame the students for wanting to get out of the morose halls of Edgar. He found them sitting at a round table covered with plenty of glass pitchers in the corner of the room.

"So this is the hangout spot these days," Malkin said as he approached the table. "Mind if I join you?"

Gottlieb pulled out a chair for the detective and said, "I think we all are happy to be out of the dormitory for a few hours, ya."

Chip looked around the table and coughed. He asked the waitress to remove the pitchers from the table as they all cleared their throats and looked around the restaurant.

"Don't worry," Malkin said. "I'm not here to bust you guys for underage drinking. A few beers after a couple bloody murders are understandable. Another cop might not be as generous, you got that?" He looked at the bar and thought the same of the ownership.

They all nodded.

Malkin ordered a Molson while the others ordered sodas.

"I came here to find out if you could tell me a little more about what's been going on this week," he said.

Chip shifted in his seat and looked up at the basketball game on TV, trying to ignore Malkin's call to discuss the week's events.

"It doesn't make sense," Tyler said with an awkward grin. Malkin thought he didn't look too bad for someone whose girlfriend had just been brutally murdered.

"Not at all," Chainsaw said. "If I find out who the hell this iKill guy is, I'd beat the livin' pulp outta him till he was nothin' but pus an' blood."

Malkin could imagine Chainsaw beating the hell out of animals and human beings if he had a mind to.

"That's not going to be easy," Malkin said.

"Oh, it will be very easy," according to Chainsaw. "I will pinch their jugular and put on a choke hold like that until his face turned purple and then squeeze the eyes out," he grunted as he used his hands and glass to demonstrate how he would carry this out.

"But who are you going to beat up if you don't know who iKill is? Or would you just take a wild guess and pounce on whatever your woman's intuition tells you?"

Chainsaw shut up and downed more beer.

"I meant finding the identity of iKill," Malkin said. "Any leads? Any thoughts? Any ideas you have would be greatly appreciated."

"I thought it was your job to find this iKill," Chip said with an angry tone, looking at Malkin as if he were incompetent.

"If only we could make arrests as soon as every crime were committed," Malkin said. "But it's not that easy, Sherlock, this loon is elusive."

"Obviously," Tyler said, slamming his glass on the table. He looked up at the score. The Celtics had pulled ahead of the Wizards.

"And what if you never find him?" Tyler asked. "What if iKill doesn't do anything more, just lays low in the background, laughing his ass off at having killed his share?"

Malkin said he was confident they would find iKill soon; however, he was intrigued by Tyler's mindset. What made him think iKill wouldn't act again?

Gottlieb looked down from the television set propped up in the northeast corner of the room and said to Chip, "I think you know something. Why you not tell us, because you are the iKill?"

Chip became livid and broke his glass. In his anger, he began shouting at Gottlieb and picking up pieces of glass with his right hand. Small beads of blood appeared on his fingertips, and he wiped them on his white polo shirt.

"Why the hell do you care, Hitler?" he shouted. "Did you want to bang her too? Why didn't you just get in line right behind Zach? How the hell should I know what was going on? Zach said some things, but he's such a wimp I can't imagine a smart girl like Jenny going out with . . ."

Chip calmed down long enough to throw a few of the larger pieces of glass off to the side. A waitress brought him a new soda and swept the broken glass off the table and floor and onto a pan. Chip's face was as red as the bloodstains on his shirt.

In a voice barely audible, Chip said, "Or maybe you just wanted to see if you could get away with cold-blooded murder. Maybe you sneaked down into the laundry room late at night and beat her up and threw her in the dryer. How do we know you didn't? What's your excuse? Were you watching another Nazi movie for nostalgia's sake in your room? Was my girl in your room before you took her downstairs and clubbed her to death?"

Chainsaw tried to calm Chip down, but it was no use. Gottlieb threw his glass at Chip, and it missed his head by an inch. Chip got up and lunged at Gottlieb. Tyler tried to hold Chip back but couldn't.

"We're past the Third Reich, go suck on Hitler's mama's tits for a while."

Malkin considered breaking up the fight as soon as Chip threw the first punch, but changed his mind, much as an NHL referee chooses to let players duke it out on the ice for a few minutes until they end up holding each other's jerseys without throwing a punch. He thought it best they got it out of their system now.

Malkin also observed the cool manner with which Chainsaw was watching the two go at it. Gottlieb had managed to whip two powerful punches from the left side that landed above Chip's right eye. Chainsaw was laughing inside, Malkin thought, and he definitely took pleasure in other people's pain and suffering. Not a good disposition, not a good man.

Chip and Gottlieb went at it a few more minutes before Malkin separated them. The owner of the restaurant came over to kick the kids out. Malkin explained he was a federal investigator looking into the recent iKill murders and that some tough questioning had led to tempers flaring.

"I see," the owner said. "Nasty business, this iKill mess. Any leads?"

Malkin said that leads were slim, but that they were slowly making progress with the investigation.

"I remember the James River Killer from a few years ago. Don't think they found him. Women's shoes, isn't that interesting?"

It was, Malkin thought, and he had a hunch that the James River Killer and iKill were one and the same—or else partners in crime. Malkin remembered what Gull had said about previous strange homicide cases in the Blackwood area and said, "That's not good." The owner walked away content that Malkin had everything under control.

Gottlieb was still perturbed at having been called "Hitler Heiner" and wanted another piece of Chip. "You attack me like that one more time and I kill you."

Chip laughed. "There you go, men. Did you hear that, Malkin? Hitler over here said the magic word—iKill. Did you hear that? Can I get a witness?"

Chip wasn't through with Gottlieb and got up to challenge him to a real fight. "No more of this," he said. "Get up, you stupid Nazi son of a bitch, and fight like a real man, not like some SS wimp who forgot that it was the Americans who beat the crap out of your country in World War I and World War II. And if necessary, we'll beat the crap out of you in World War III. We already know you're a bunch of al-Qaeda terrorist lovers!"

Gottlieb chose not to fight Chip. He was in the country on a student visa and any trouble he got into might result in an early flight back to Hamburg.

Suddenly, Chip jumped across the table and grabbed Gottlieb's head. He jerked it from side to side as Gottlieb tried to resist Chip's viselike grip on his scalp. Chip belted a series of punches with both fists all over Gottlieb's face, and there was blood dripping around both eyes.

"Take that, you asshole! You stupid German brick-for-brains! Won't you guys ever learn? You don't kill six million Jews for a laugh, and you don't come to this country to pretend to study and then kill American girls. Everyone knows you did it! I saw you follow Jenny down to the basement and beat her to death! You swine! And I know you followed Denise out to the alley off West Willow Road and did her in too. You stupid, sick prick! Must be that German blood! Must really be related to Hitler, because I can't think of another nationality on the face of the Earth that has been responsible for so many senseless deaths the past hundred years. Can you, you damn sinister sorry excuse for a student?"

Malkin thought to himself that they were lashing out and just inventing stories to blame one another.

Chip continued to pound away. Gottlieb was blocking most punches and landed a few of his own, but Malkin thought he wasn't fighting as hard as he could have.

"Or should we just call you iKill?"

Malkin pulled Chip off Gottlieb with one arm and told the boys to stop or he would have to press charges.

"Go home and forget this happened," he said.

Chip screamed, "Might as well press charges on the German joke—he's such a loser. He is iKill, I am sure."

Gottlieb wiped the blood from his nose. "If he's not iKill," he said to Malkin, looking at Chip, "then why does he lose his temper so like now?"

Chapter Eight

Rhoda envied the dresses of all the women pledging Gamma Phi Beta. She looked around the reception hall where this year's inductees would be announced and eyed her own dress. She never knew how to dress up because her mom never taught her. Rhoda imagined that if she had better fashion sense, she would have more friends and her pick of guys.

Rhoda felt somewhat isolated from the crowd. Everyone seemed to know everyone else. Girls were drinking punch, talking about various exploits with men from nearby fraternities, and laughing up a storm.

She saw Sheila talking with one of the Blackwood College alumni of Gamma Phi Beta and walked up to them. Sheila put her arm around Rhoda and introduced her to Mary Hamilton, a tall, platinum, sugar mama blonde who looked about fifty-five but tried to look more like thirty-five. Whatever she was doing, Rhoda thought, wasn't working.

"Good luck," Sheila told Rhoda and offered an encouraging but diplomatic social hug as Ms. Hamilton informed them that they would announce this year's inductees into the sorority in a few moments. All the girls giggled and sighed as they gathered in the living room.

Rhoda looked around and saw that there were fourteen girls trying out for the sorority. She remembered Sheila had said that twelve would be chosen to live in the house, and one would be chosen as an alternate who would belong to the sorority as a permanent member but would have to wait at least a year before living in the house. Rhoda was excited. This was her big chance to become someone. She felt her damp palms as she imagined her name being called first.

It wasn't. She felt disappointed but clapped for the girl who was picked. She repeated this eleven more times during the next few minutes as nearly every name but Rhoda's was called. Rhoda felt her heart sink into her intestines and had an impending sense of doom. She began to sweat as she noticed extremely happy faces with big smiles congratulating one another with big hugs and kisses on the cheeks. Some were even dancing with joy.

Rhoda didn't want to hear the last name. She already knew what was going to happen, and she wanted to disappear—just like that time on her sixth birthday when her older brother had thrown her into a mud pit and all his friends took turns throwing marshmallows at her when her mother wasn't watching. Humiliation and disappointment had been Rhoda's two best friends since elementary school. Why stop now? she thought. Might as well go with what she knew and see where it took her, even if it was to hell.

"Flora Smith," Ms. Hamilton called out.

Great, Rhoda thought. She'd worked her butt off for weeks trying to get into Gamma Phi Beta for spring semester and it turned out to be for nothing. She wished she could just fly away . . .

After they congratulated each other for a few moments, many of the girls offered brief, insincere condolences to Rhoda and then went their merry way. Rhoda was indignant. She did what she usually did when she didn't get her way: she shut up and repressed all her anger into a smoldering ball of molten lava ready to explode from within and cause all sorts of hell.

Sheila walked up to Rhoda and gave her a big consoling hug. "I'm really sorry, girl," she said. "I thought for sure they'd pick you. I voted for you. Hope you don't feel too bad. There's always next year. We'll get you in next year, Rhoda, I promise. This must be some kind of fluke or something." Sheila didn't seem all that disappointed, and rushed to join her girlfriends to celebrate the new inductees.

Rhoda smiled, even though she had white lightning and balls of fire playing in her heart. Sheila had voted for her, she thought. That was a terrible thing to know, for it in all likelihood meant that none of the other thirty-some girls in the sorority thought enough of her to vote for her.

Rhoda slipped through the crowd like an eel navigating the undertow. She found her coat, put on her shoes, and walked out the door. From an environment of boisterous cheer and proud affectation, she emerged into an atmosphere of cool, calm serenity. She was relieved to be outside.

She walked back to Edgar Hall, just half a mile east on West Willow Street. A few minutes later, Rhoda turned to her left and took a long, hard look at a piece of land taped off by police.

She shuddered. That must have been where Denise was killed. She imagined what the dead body must have looked like and felt like throwing up. At least she was alive, she thought, though she wasn't sure why.

How come iKill went after Jenny, Denise, and then Mindy? Why did he spare her? It just made Rhoda feel like more of a loser. She wasn't even worthy of being someone's exciting corpse. She felt like she'd failed at just about everything and wished there were an easy way out of all this stuff—out of this dull life she lived in.

Rhoda felt like crying. She wouldn't mind if iKill came after her tonight. It might be one thing she could be good at, she thought: being a victim.

*   *   *

Rhoda did not return directly to Edgar Hall. Rather, she walked east on Willow Street a few miles toward I-95. If she had a car, she thought, she could get on the Interstate and head west and . . . well, she wasn't very good with directions. At least she could escape to Shenandoah and jump off a cliff, turning herself into dessert for vultures.

Why is she thinking like this? Rhoda thought. After tonight's torture she wondered if she were suffering from some kind of delusional behavior. Maybe she suffered from temporary psychotic delusions, during which all the rage in her creates body bags of blood.

Don't go there, she thought. She was Rhoda Remlinger, and she recited aloud a few positive affirmations. To hell with them, she thought, nothing is positive about my life. Does she really need a boyfriend now? Is she so desperate to get into the god-forsaken sorority? Probably, but she wasn't sure. Had she really wanted to go to college? Or was she doing everything to make other people happy?

Rhoda wasn't sure, what the hell, maybe she is iKill and a delusional killer.

She was not iKill. That she knew. But who was? And why was she suddenly thinking of iKill? She tried to avoid the topic, but the more she pushed iKill out of her mind, the more he stared in her imagination.

Rhoda thought about all the rich girls at Gamma Phi Beta with their rich cars and their expensive makeup and designer fashions. She thought they could all go to hell because she wouldn't have anything more . . .

Her thoughts were interrupted by a tall man with a wooden face who suddenly walked out from behind a high wooden fence next to the sidewalk.

"Excuse me, little girl," he said. Rhoda jumped, and her heart began to race as if a hundred Dobermans were chasing her.

"I . . . I'm sorry," she said, out of breath. "You scared the heck out of me."

"Don't mean to be any trouble," he said, "but I'm collecting money for the police department."

Collecting money for the police department? This sounds weird, she thought. Although the man was wearing shabby clothing—an old sweatshirt with stripes and a name she could not make out—she doubted that he belonged to the police force. Rhoda wasn't even the cynical type, and she could see that.

"Sorry," she said, "but I don't have any money."

"That's what they all say, toots," he said in a low, rusty voice. He was wearing black and reeked of cigarette smoke. Rhoda noticed that behind him was a shopping cart with a few dirty belongings—most likely trash—and some empty beer cans.

"I can't help you. I have to go."

"You're not going anywhere till you help me out," he said. "Can't you spare some change for old Cragg?"

Cragg—why did his name sound familiar? She remembered he was the street beggar and aluminum-can collector who spent his welfare money on alcohol and cigarettes. But what did he really want?

"Thought you were working for the police," she said. Rhoda had been afraid at first, but now the man seemed harmless.

"Well, I was, but the cops let me go about fifteen years ago," he said. "Been looking for work ever since. And now I'm looking for iKill."

"iKill?" she asked. "How do you know about him?"

"All over the papers, dearie," he said. "He's living over down there in Edgar Hall. Been there killin' off woman after woman. Likes the good-looking ones. You might be next, honey." He had a warped, strange smile that minced logic and defied comfort.

"I'm not good-looking," Rhoda said.

"Don't know if I would say that," he said. "I bet you could make the music play all night long, if you know what I mean."

Rhoda realized she was dealing with a man who lacked a little upstairs. She turned and walked away. The man suddenly grabbed her arm and prevented her from moving.

"Don't forget the shopping cart man," he yelled at her. "You might think of me one day. Might just have to start doin' rounds down by Edgar again real soon."

Rhoda had had enough of crazy people. She was tired and wanted to get some rest. It felt like three months had passed since she had returned from Thanksgiving break.

She couldn't cope with people, she thought, because she was now more certain than ever that she had no place in this world.

*   *   *

Chainsaw didn't feel like going up to his room following his return from lunch and instead bought a Gatorade, grabbed a copy of *Guns and Knives* that someone must have left, and sat down. The back of his mind was clubbing his conscience with assignments, hourly tests, and final exams—all of which Chainsaw could do without. He took a big swig of his favorite drink, some of which spilled on his thick plaid shirt.

What was he doing there? "Nothing" was the answer that came to mind. He had learned nothing during his first semester at Blackwood College, and now he was in a heap of trouble. He struggled with his memory—goaded by a traumatized conscience plagued with bleak secrets not meant to see daylight—and fought the inevitable. Eventually, Chainsaw knew, he would have to tell the police everything. They were bound to find out anyway.

He looked around the lobby with slight paranoia but found he had the place to himself. He looked down at the magazine and turned to an article. He tried to read but couldn't get past a single sentence.

"This is worse than reading a history textbook," he sighed. He closed the magazine, rolled it up, and then slammed it against the edge of the chair. Damn if he was gonna burn in hell for what he'd done. They had it coming—all of them. Ain't no one gonna tell him he'd done wrong.

Still, his conscience beat louder rhythms of solemn regret. He couldn't take it any longer. He saw Branford walking out of the elevator and checking his mailbox. From twenty feet away, Chainsaw called him over.

"This isn't exactly your kind of hangout," Branford said. "What are you doing here?"

Chainsaw made a large fist and slammed it down on the arm of the chair. "I got problems. Have a seat."

Branford got a Coke from the vending machines before joining his floormate. "What's on your mind?"

"Not my mind, my shoulders . . . the whole damn world is on my shoulders, and there is nothing I can do about it."

Branford waited for the coffee to cool before taking a sip. He rubbed his hands over the cup to keep them warm on this cool November day.

"Got trouble?" he asked.

"Spades."

"Yeah, me too."

"I know. That's why I wanted to talk to you."

Chainsaw was about to tell Branford what was going on, but then Malkin and Charlie walked into Edgar Hall and sat in the lobby. They were within eyesight, but Chainsaw knew they were too far away—about thirty feet—to overhear his conversation with Branford.

"I need your help," Chainsaw said.

"Same here."

"Those girls—all these cops . . . the evidence . . . it's gotta end. Everyone's talking, and they know I got the nickname Chainsaw because I used to kill dogs and cats alive with a chainsaw."

"I know. It's driving me crazy. It's only a matter of time before they find out I raped a few girls back in high school and got away with it!"

"We gotta say nothing and cover ourselves—agreed?"

"Absolutely," Branford said.

"And you're gonna keep it that way," Chainsaw said. It was more of a command than a suggestion, but that didn't matter to Branford.

He preferred his face in one piece. Besides, he had a pretty good idea of what Chainsaw could do given an ax or a butcher knife.

Chainsaw finished his drink. "They're over there, going over notes. They think they know everything. Pretty soon all hell is gonna break loose, then they'll come knockin' on my door. They might not find me, Branford. I'm thinkin' 'bout cuttin' out while I got a chance—maybe hitch a ride to California or fly out to Canada."

"They'll catch up with you," Branford said. "Not with my help, but you know you won't get far."

Chainsaw shook his empty Gatorade container and bounced it on his leg. "Don't say a word—but I'm a killer."

Branford said, "You know they suspect you. Just because they know you tortured and killed animals back in your proud youth. So they'll keep an eye out for you—one of those anger management things."

"That's why I'm thinkin' of gettin' outta here." He lowered his voice. "Or maybe just wait things out. I don't know . . . what are you gonna do?"

Branford turned around to eye the law-enforcement officials and said in a low voice, "Not sure if they know everything, sometimes these cops are just too stupid to figure things out. If everyone stays cool, then we got nothing to worry about. They got nothing on us. I mean, they haven't asked us about rape or animal killing so far, right?"

Chainsaw liked Branford's attitude. The latter added, "And I trust you won't say anything about what you know."

"Promise—and you back me up too."

Chainsaw considered prison. He pictured himself being led in handcuffs into some prison cell that doubled as a torture chamber, and he'd seen many of those in movies. "Yep," he said, still banging his bottle against the rim of the table. Chainsaw's face turned red. He said nothing but grabbed Branford's Coke can and swirled the red aluminum in the palm of his hand.

"Let's get out of here."

Branford returned to his room while Chainsaw went for a walk outside. While the weather was cold and windy, the anger boiling within him fueled a reeling mind bent on annihilating anyone who crossed his path.

*   *   *

Sheila had enjoyed a great afternoon at her home away from home—the Gamma Phi Beta sorority house. It was there that she had learned how to really flirt with guys, lead them on, make them want her, and then leave them high and dry.

She got into her new white Toyota Sequoia and started the engine. Though it was only a short walk to Edgar Hall, she preferred to drive at night, even though tonight she was anything but sober. She had had at least four good drinks in the past hour and was on Cloud Nine, fueled by alcohol and pride.

But Sheila felt bad for Rhoda. As she fastened her seatbelt, her mind raced between Rhoda, boys, homework (forget it!), and the upcoming Christmas break.

She pulled out of the driveway and stopped at the intersection. Only six more blocks to go, she thought. She took a deep breath and popped in a breath mint just in case the worst happened and she got pulled over by the police. She couldn't afford another DUI. She had gotten one back in August when she first rushed Gamma Phi Beta, and it almost cost her a membership. Instead, she was allowed to be a formal member but was not allowed to live in the house for one semester as a result of her DUI conviction.

It was another stormy night, and she turned on the radio. One of her favorite songs, "Miss You" by the Rolling Stones, was playing. Sheila sang along: *"Oooh, baby why you wait so long? Oooh, baby why you wait so long? Won't you come home, come home?"*

Sheila thought back to high school whenever she heard this song. It was from the late seventies but they always played it at all the dances because it was such a cool tune. She missed her high-school boyfriends. She couldn't remember all their names, but somehow things were easier back then.

She reminisced about prom, homecoming, cheerleading, and all those boyfriends she had used as the biggest flirt at Medford High. She thought back to high-school parties—tame stuff compared with college—and wondered how all her old friends were doing.

Since arriving at Blackwood College, Sheila realized, she had not really kept in touch with her old pals. When she got back to Edgar Hall,

127

she would get online and try to chat with one or two. It had been too long.

"Miss you." Indeed, Sheila missed her old friends, her old school, her old boyfriends, her old house, her parents, and even her old teachers—in spite of not having tried very hard to be a good student. High school was the best time of a young girl's life, she thought. She was having fun now, she knew, but somewhere down the line life would start to get difficult. That was one line Sheila would wait to cross.

She sang along to the chorus again: *"Oooh, baby why you wait so long? Oooh, baby why you wait so long? Won't you come home, come home?"*

Sheila was two turns away from the Edgar Hall parking garage. The clock in her Sequoia—a gift from Dad for her eighteenth birthday—read 7:30 p.m.

Excellent timing, she thought. Just in time for that stupid curfew.

She turned left and hooked another quick left to pull into the garage. She found a spot on the second floor and parked the car.

Sheila breathed a sigh of relief. She hated driving while intoxicated, and she felt her muscles cramp up knowing that a second conviction would mean fifteen years of asking other people for rides.

Sheila's mind fast-forwarded to next semester. She thought of Rhoda and how she just didn't fit in with the rest.

"I was walkin' Central Park, singin' after dark, people think I'm craaaaaazy."

She knew that Rhoda would never get in. Some people never win.

"I just been foolin' with myself, it's just you and no one else, Lord I miss you chiiiiiiild."

Sheila leaned forward and turned off the ignition. She felt a strange sensation overwhelm her, and a knot formed in her throat. She was tired. It had been a long day, and now she'd have to deal with Rhoda and . . .

Suddenly she heard whistling right behind her. It was a familiar tune.

Of course, she thought, it was "Miss You," the song she'd just been listening to. But there was no whistling in that song that Sheila could remember. Was the radio still on? She was certain she'd turned it off but checked it again.

Maybe she was going crazy. She was hearing things. She had never actually listened to a song on the radio and then heard it later whistling in her ears. It was like a soft, whispery whistle echoing within the hollow chambers surrounding her painfully attuned eardrums. She'd had too much to drink, and now Uncle Alcohol was beating her senseless. That's what drinking will do to you, she told herself. Make you think strange things that aren't really happening.

She unbuckled her seatbelt and was about to get out of the car when she looked through the rearview mirror. She saw two eyes behind a black mask.

A low, creepy voice murmured, "Baby why you wait so long?" The voice followed the question with a demonic laugh. As the face behind the mask smiled and continued to whistle to "Miss You," a long arm raised a butcher's knife in Sheila's direction. She screamed into the dark of the parking garage as a November wind howled outside, accompaniment for another easy tragedy. Hers was a scream unheard.

*　　*　　*

"Oooh, Sheila why you wait so long?"
Shut up—stop screaming and you might live to see your friend Rhoda.
Just kidding—you won't get off that easy.
I thought you might leave your little social gathering with her.
I could get two for the price of one.
But you stuck around to help clean up. Nice girl.
And Rhoda went her sweet way.
Got any plans for tonight?
I was thinking of introducing you to myself.
My name is iKill.
Sheila shivered. "You're not iKill," she said. "You're—"
Now now now, won't you come home? Come home? Ah, come now Sheila baby, we got a good thing going tonight.
Don't mess it up just because you gotta get your way again.
If you do, you won't ever go home. Understand?
Sheila couldn't hold back the tears. She was trembling from head to foot and the steering wheel was covered in sweat.

Let me tell you a story. I want you to hear it all. All you have to do is shut up and not say a word. Listen to what I got to say, and I might not slice you up into a gooey pepperoni pizza.

Remember Jenny? Jenny was sweet. Thank God for Little Girls. I sent her this picture of a dead cat that I'd seen lying in the middle of the street

129

somewhere west of campus. *Thought she might like it since I know she's an animal lover, and since I was a Jenny lover, I thought we were a perfect fit. But I heard she didn't appreciate the picture I took for her. She should have—it wasn't easy taking that picture.*

And then later that night I knew she wouldn't be able to sleep, so I followed her and found her down in the laundry room by herself. She was wearing that cute pink robe that I had seen so many times and I thought she looked like a queen, but I couldn't bear the sight of her doing laundry all alone.

So you know what I did? I took this big ax I'd bought at Walmart and butchered her as if I was getting her meat ready for market the next morning.

Then I tossed the laundry in the dryer. It's no use leaving a job half done. But I forgot the fabric softener—and so did Jenny. So I ran the dryer on delicates just to be considerate.

Yes, Jenny was one of a kind. I miss her. Even today, I still think of her and all the chances we missed out on.

And how about Denise—she was next? Remember her? She got all upset over some boy stuff. It was just a joke, really. She was a smart girl, but she let her emotions run away with the moment that time.

I knew she'd be on the run. I followed her down Willow Street with the knife I'd taken—borrowed—from the cafeteria. That was easy enough. She was scared, but death comes to the cute ones in peculiar ways. I was having my fun. I hacked her up good and left her for dead in the alley. It was a pity I couldn't take a part of Denise to share with the others just as I'd taken Jenny's finger and put it in the cafeteria food.

Mindy liked that. And speaking of Mindy, how's the old girl doing? She got away from me. I knew I was in trouble when I risked going into the bathroom alone in the middle of the night. Mindy couldn't sleep and needed a pick-me-up. I slashed away three times and then made a break for it. Didn't have far to go, so no one knew what was going on. Mindy survived that one, but she should be careful because there are a lot of crazy people out there.

But I'm not crazy, Sheila. I know all these girls want me. I've become sort of an international star. Have you seen all the headlines? They've got my name—iKill—all over the place. And the police are clueless; they have no idea what is going on. Neither did you. You didn't pay attention to me.

Sure, you'd talk with me whenever it benefited you, but there were times when you were mean.

That's right, pretty girl, just plain mean. And you hurt my feelings. This is payback time.

I hope you understand I have no choice.

Up until that moment, Sheila had remained quiet except for spurts of crying and subdued screams. Her soft ocean-blue eyes trembled, and her hands were so cold they could barely feel the steering wheel.

She said, "I don't understand. I don't understand. Why you? Why Jenny? Why Denise? Why Mindy? Why me? Can't you just spare me and . . ."

Don't give me the lowdown on morality, Sheila. I've got a job to do, so do as I say.

Sheila obeyed and, much more sober now, regretting having driven such a short distance to the sorority house in the first place. She had a bad feeling about this situation and tried to come up with a way out. She tried to speak, but her tongue felt like a brick, impeding her ability to utter a syllable.

She wasn't a quick thinker, she knew, but she had managed to get herself out of some pretty bad jams in the past.

But this was the worst. She was afraid she was going to die—die at the hands of iKill. Sheila's mouth was dry, caked with fear, while her cold clammy hands clenched the wheel and her slacks.

Now she knew who iKill was. It all made sense. She wondered how long he was going to let her live.

I stabbed her in the neck. Her head hit the steering wheel. I took some more whacks at her back.

Sunny Sheila didn't even have the decency to face me. Her neck was broken in a few places and her back was frothing with blood. I figure she lost about two or three pints of blood, but I'm no expert.

Besides, why bother with details? I took a couple pictures to e-mail a friend . . .

This was so easy. Why do they make it so easy? I could have done this blindfolded and upside down. Maybe I'll try that next time.

I walked into Edgar Hall just before curfew; there was nobody around the entrance by the laundry room. You'd think they'd have learned by now.

That might be giving them too much credit.

*   *   *

Harry Sampson and Charlie were chatting by Edgar Hall's main entrance. Malkin was sitting in the lobby, talking on the phone, as Chip came up the stairs.

"How are you doing, Chip?" Charlie asked.

"All right, thinking about transferring to another university next year."

"Might not be a bad idea," Malkin said. "By the way, what were you doing downstairs? I saw you were coming up."

Chip couldn't handle it anymore. "I went to grab a bite to eat in the cafeteria and then thought about Jenny and her finger and had to have another look . . . I don't know why . . . I loved her so much, it hurts so much."

Malkin zoned in on Chip: "Best you go up to your room and get some rest. And don't even think of causing any trouble."

"I won't, sir."

Malkin reminded Harry to stay on the third floor through the night and bade Charlie a good night. "And both of you, be careful. I'll get some coffee at the Lighthouse and then head back to the hotel. Sweet dreams, of course."

*   *   *

Rhoda ran into Tom Malkin, who was drinking mocha at the Lighthouse, as she was leaving for Edgar Hall just before 8:00 p.m., barely making curfew.

"Let me walk back with you," said Malkin, who'd changed his mind about going back to the hotel. "I want to check things out on my own, see what happens at night."

Rhoda shivered but didn't say anything. Malkin noticed she looked forlorn and tired.

"What's the matter?" he asked. She ordered a cappuccino to go and walked with Malkin.

Rhoda explained the events of that afternoon. She said she felt like a loser and that she was certain she would never succeed in life.

He tried to set her straight. "You could try to be the pilot of your life. It's your plane. Fly it where you like."

Rhoda wasn't in the mood for a motivational talk, Malkin thought. She looked like a tormented girl. He suggested she get some rest and then contact Teresa in the morning.

"But I think that might be too late," she said.

"Why's that?"

"I don't know . . ."

"You can call her now if you want, or I could call her for you."

"Maybe it doesn't matter."

"They're there to help. Suit yourself. But I am not a counselor, so I wouldn't be able to help you out much. Call Teresa and tell her to come at once. I know she will. She's God's gift to compassion."

Rhoda thought for a minute, took the number from Malkin, and thanked him. He said he would be around Edgar Hall for a while that evening, so Rhoda should feel free to call his cell phone at any time. Rhoda thanked him again and gave him a prolonged hug.

"Just don't tell my wife about that one," Malkin said with a smile. He missed his family and hoped this serial killer iKill would be arrested soon.

Rhoda laughed even though she didn't fully understand the joke. She threw her coffee cup, half empty, into the trashcan next to the front desk and said hi to Charlie and Abby, who were pulling a double shift. Charlie asked Rhoda if she wanted to join them for pizza.

"Just ordered an extra large. Harry sometimes comes down and has a piece with us," Abby said.

Both Abby and Charlie knew the students well and could tell that Rhoda was feeling down. She told them everything about the day's events at Gamma Phi Beta, and Charlie sympathized with her situation. He said she could focus on more important things and that not getting into a sorority wasn't the end of the world.

Rhoda laughed. She hadn't laughed since early that morning when she imagined what she would say when accepting induction into the sorority. That was a faded memory; it was a dream that would never happen, like so many of her dreams. She thought it was sad that most of her dreams were painted in dark gray.

"Don't let this missed opportunity get you down," Charlie said. "Think on the positive side—you have a lot to offer, so just go for your dreams. You might not always get there, but you have to go for it."

He added, "And besides, who really cares if you didn't get into some stupid sorority? That won't affect your GPA or your ability to study."

"But *I* care. And it *will* affect my GPA and ability to study, because now I feel like a loser."

Abby smiled and put her skinny right arm around Rhoda's shoulders. Rhoda needed that. She felt better.

"Guess I'll join you for pizza. I'm kind of hungry."

Charlie said she should not pay for the pizza; it was Abby's treat. Abby laughed. "I don't think that's the way it works."

The threesome talked about anything but iKill, and before they knew it, the pizza was delivered. "Next time it's your turn, Abby," Charlie said.

Rhoda ate at half the pace of Charlie and Abby. She felt like everything was in slow motion. She was hungry yet had no appetite.

"I'm going up to my room and locking the door, and I'll do my best to forget about today. And the last few years, for that matter," Rhoda said.

Upon walking out of the elevator onto the third floor, she suddenly felt like crying. Not only crying, but wailing so loud everyone would have to take notice.

Rhoda felt lonely and afraid. She entered her room, knowing iKill had to be around somewhere—if only she knew whom and where, she would feel better. But of course, that's what everyone was thinking. She suddenly heard footsteps outside her door and felt a horrid chill rush down her spine. Who could that be? The whistling sounded familiar, but she couldn't place it. She hesitated to open the door, figuring it could be iKill.

So what? The worst that could happen would be that he would kill her. That wouldn't be so bad, she thought.

Rhoda opened the door and found Shaggy pushing his cart down the hallway. He stopped whistling long enough to wish Rhoda a good evening.

"Nice evenin' outside," he said, exposing several rotten teeth. "Not too cool. Could even take yourself for a little walk if you aren't afraid of getting cut up by that mean ol' iKill."

Shaggy, almost a sincere sadist, was too creepy for Rhoda. She decided she would stay in her room and lock the door.

Was all this just a big joke on her? Rhoda's high-school peers had enjoyed playing merciless pranks on her. Rhoda was always the gullible one, ever willing to play the fool for the enjoyment of others.

Rhoda needed to see a face she could trust. She walked up to George's room. He was watching a hockey game on TV. "Have you seen Tyler?" she asked.

"Not in a while," George said. "Want to watch the game with me?" Rhoda thanked George for the invite but declined; she wanted to see Tyler, or maybe just stay alone in her room.

Rhoda hated the idea of walking down a flight of stairs. God knows who or what was waiting for her, perhaps iKill in the corner . . . She tried Tyler's cell-phone number, but there was no answer. She didn't leave a message because it wasn't urgent. Besides, she was sure he wouldn't return her call anyway. He had other women on his mind.

The world was black, she thought as she returned to her room, locked the door, and looked out into the cloudy night sky. The branches of the large oak tree outside her room were banging against the window. Black on black. Rhoda hated when that happened. On nights like these, she rarely slept well.

But who cared about sleep tonight? Perhaps she didn't even deserve to sleep. She had missed out on joining a sorority. Rhoda even felt bad about the fact that she was alive.

Like Zach said, maybe the dead are better off. Dead—that must be the worst word in the English language, she thought.

Or was it the best?

Rhoda had no idea and fell onto her bed exhausted and too tired to sleep. For now, she let the world spin round her head and imagined she was eating a pixie stick like she had when she was a little girl.

"Rhoda, how would you like another ride on the merry-go-round?" She could hear her mother's voice in the background, distant yet clear enough to sound as though she were there with her. Rhoda remembered various favorite children's songs she used to sing with her mom and friends and cried a few tears in remembrance of the innocence and joy of a happy childhood.

*   *   *

Around eight-thirty, Harry Sampson—who had just finished a late steak dinner with Frank Tanner and Vernon Gull—returned to Edgar Hall to keep guard for yet another night. He hoped tonight would prove less eventful than the night before. No more blood donors were needed, he thought.

"Just had a good steak," he told Charlie. "Otherwise I'd grab a few bites. That pizza looks great."

Malkin went over details with Sampson, Following their short strategy session Malkin roamed the corridors of Edgar Hall and checked various rooms. He had in his hand a list of suspicious items found following the search conducted by Foster and his men. The list contained the following items in the corresponding rooms:

- **George Young**: baseball bat, screwdriver, hammer, camera
- **Stacy Nutter**: crystal ball, tarot cards, Ouija board, voodoo dolls, camera
- **Jerry Fowler**: several women's shoes, pornographic magazines and DVDs, metal wire, plants, camera, camcorder, bottle with lithium
- **Branford Smith**: hundred DVD/computer games, camera, camcorder
- **Malcolm Huntington**: benzene and other chemicals, camera, blood on pillow (DNA sample taken)

Malkin thought for a moment and then knocked on Malcolm's door. There was no answer. He entered with the key given to him by Frank Tanner and observed the bloodstains on the pillow. Surely Malcolm wouldn't kill someone in his own room and then drag the body down to the basement or off a half mile west on Willow Road. Something wasn't right.

Malkin also checked the bottle of benzene. Why would Malcolm need a bottle of benzene? Sure, majors in chemistry, he may have taken it from lab by accident, but Malkin doubted that scenario. Still, could Malcolm be iKill? Did he have the personality or the imagination? Malkin doubted the second scenario much more than the first.

He moved on to Jerry Fowler's room. This kid was crazy, Malkin thought, and he recalled that both Mindy and Head Case had suspected Jerry was iKill. It made sense, Malkin thought, simply because Jerry had not arrived at Edgar Hall till the day after Jenny's body was discovered. That left a lot of time unaccounted for.

In addition, each time Malkin spoke with Jerry, whether on the fourth floor or just recently in the recreation hall, he was sure something was missing. That is, Malkin believed they would be much closer to finding out the real identity of iKill if Jerry would just say what he knew or what was on his mind. But thus far, the boy had remained tight-lipped, and Malkin had a feeling it would be difficult to get any kind of information out of him.

Malkin entered Jerry's room and found the women's shoes stuffed in his closet behind his own shoes and piles of various other things. His mind flashed back to the conversation with Foster concerning the mysterious James River Killer. He also saw a stack of pornographic magazines.

"Pornography—now there's an example for America to be proud of," Malkin said, his sarcasm no longer in check. He figured Jerry had about twenty issues altogether on top of his closet just next to the laundry detergent. In the bottom right-hand desk drawer was a large bottle of lithium, prescribed. Malkin's eyes darted back to the detergent, and he wondered . . .

Malkin considered for a moment and then agreed that it was probable that Jerry took lithium to combat manic-depressive disorder. If true, would it be sufficient to throw him off mentally and make him a murderer?

Malkin found what he was looking for in Jerry's room and more, including hooks in the ceiling for hanging plants. He decided that Jerry remained a prime suspect because he was strong, big, and absent the night Jenny was killed.

About a half hour later, Malkin joined Harry Sampson downstairs and commented on the conversations from earlier in the day. Sampson said that two students were still unaccounted for that evening: Sheila Underwood and Malcolm Huntington. Otherwise, everyone had returned to Edgar Hall in time to make curfew and was around doing something somewhere.

Malkin was worried about Malcolm Huntington. He called over to Webster Hall and was told that Malcolm had left approximately forty minutes earlier. It was about eight-forty now, so Malcolm had left around eight. That made sense to Malkin, since it fit Malcolm's personality to leave for some destination right at the time he was supposed to have arrived there. But it shouldn't have taken him more than twenty minutes to walk over to Edgar Hall. Unless . . .

Malkin was surprised his mind went in that direction. "Unless, of course," he said to himself, "he stopped by Strong Hall to, say, send a few e-mails for the hell of it . . ."

Fifteen minutes later, Malcolm walked through the main entrance of Edgar Hall carrying his book bag. He walked past the front desk, said hi to Charlie and Abby, and checked his mailbox. As he turned to enter the elevator, Malkin asked him to step aside for a moment.

"What are you talking about, man?" Malcolm asked.

"Routine check, Mr. Huntington," Malkin said. "Where have you been today?"

Malcolm hesitated to answer. "I been at Webster Hall all day—working on a group project. It's due at the end of the week, and I don't wanna wait till like the last minute, you know what I'm saying?"

"I understand," Malkin said. "But now I want you to understand something. There is a murder investigation going on here, and it's not just the kind of murder investigation that you watch on Scooby Doo or your favorite sitcom or whatever half-witted television program is out there to poison malleable minds.

"So I would expect to have your full cooperation, as I asked earlier," Malkin said. "And I need to know what you know concerning this murder . . . this *set* of serial murders over the last few days."

"I got no idea, man," Malcolm insisted. "Most of my friends live in Webster. I got my friends and some other folk who live up there, and they always be helping me with my homework or studying for a test. I don't really hang out with many students from this dorm except for Jerry Fowler. Cool cat."

Malkin thought Jerry was about as cool as a slush fund accumulated from immoral donations amassed from various Buddhist monasteries around the country. He decided to challenge Malcolm and go with his hunch.

"I'll need to check the contents of your bag," Malkin said.

"I don't think so," Malcolm said.

"Open your bag. If you hadn't been fifty minutes late, there would be no need to check your book bag. But since you've exceeded your allotted curfew time, you need to show us you don't have an ax in there."

Malcolm laughed for a second, but it was a pained laugh. He was adamant about not opening his book bag.

"This is my private property," he said, "and I don't have to show it to anyone except airport security if I'm flying. You got a problem with that?"

Malkin took out his .22 Smith & Wesson and held it securely in his hand. "Show it to me, or you'll be answering a lot more questions than might be necessary. We don't want to unduly disturb you."

Malcolm resisted and pleaded for a few minutes to be able to first use the bathroom. Malkin suggested he obey police orders or face a twenty-four-hour detention in police headquarters.

Malcolm finally succumbed and opened his bag. He threw it over to the two police officers. He sat down on the egg-white sofa in the lounge with a somber expression on his face. He saw his life flash before his somewhat bloodshot eyes.

Malkin said, "Been studying all day have you?" He sorted through the bag's contents and was pleased with what he saw. It confirmed his earlier suspicions.

Malcolm tried to evade the inevitable one more time. "Yeah, with my friends back in Webster Hall. I told you, man, working on that group project. Man, can't you just leave me alone?"

"Very interesting," Malkin said. "Let's see here, you must have been thirsty today. Ammonia, sodium cyanide, ether, and benzene—all made a nutritious breakfast. Who needs steroids when you got this crap in your arsenal?"

Malcolm said nothing and merely shrugged his shoulders.

"Do you want to say anything or wait for a lawyer?" Malkin asked, raising his voice.

"I'm a chemistry major," Malcolm said. "I got chemicals with me all the time. So what's it to you? You can ask around, even my man Jerry knows what the lowdown is. I got a job to do and I do it right."

Malkin stuck out his chest and raised his voice. "Malcolm, I've dealt with international terrorism and intelligence issues, and I know my fair share about what's going on with the younger generation today."

The young student sat looking up at Malkin with an expression of arrogance and denial.

"And I know you've got enough chemicals in your possession to begin making and/or dealing methamphetamine. Now I suggest you tell us everything you've been up to this week before you hear the clang of the slammer."

Malcolm slammed both fists into his thighs and covered his face in his hands. Malkin asked Sampson to call the authorities and confiscate the contents of Malcolm's book bag.

*   *   *

Rhoda woke up from what felt like a trance. Her face was wet; she realized she had cried in her sleep. No wonder she felt miserable, she thought.

Her brain burst into a whirlwind of catastrophe. She wasn't sure what to think, let alone what to believe. There had been so many awful things happening over the last two days, two months, two years, and two decades that she wished she could just fall back asleep.

Forever.

She rolled over onto her right side and stared at her room. She hated her room, and since the middle of the semester she had hated Edgar Hall, but particularly since the beginning of the week.

Rhoda looked at the clock—it was 9:30 p.m. She wondered whether Sheila was back yet. She worked up enough energy to walk next door to Sheila's room and knock on the door.

There was no answer. Life never provides any answers, Rhoda thought. She walked back into her room and locked the door. She fell back into bed and began crying. She realized that little of what she had done in life was of any consequence. She couldn't even find any Kleenex in her room.

Everyone else was home. She considered getting some Kleenex from another student but rationalized that crying alone without tissues was more desirable than having to deal with floor mates she didn't care for.

But Rhoda was still interested in Tyler. He had come into her life as her first real boyfriend right at the time she was already neglecting her studies because of her involvement with Gamma Phi Beta. Tyler helped her with homework and studying for tests and quizzes, but Rhoda still bombed most of them. She was certain Tyler had gotten tired of her the same way he had grown bored of Denise, except that he had dated Denise for a couple of months while Rhoda had had him for just a fortnight.

Still, at least he was someone who cared, even if only for a few hours. Rhoda hadn't had many close friends she could depend on. She had a vague understanding of trust, but it encircled her like a distant, unreachable planet.

She felt a looming depression overcome her. She looked around the room and reviewed the status of her life. It was as blank as the walls.

The answer was clear: she had no life. She felt like doing something drastic. She thought about throwing all her treasured possessions out the window and then maybe herself.

Rhoda thought she knew how to go about things, but she now realized she had no clue. Still had no clue.

She felt the room spinning around her. When was the last time she ate? She had had a few bites of pizza. Was that it?

Rhoda got up and went to her desk. She took out a sheet of paper and wrote down the date and time. She scribbled a few lines of regret and failure.

Rhoda had learned a valuable lesson today: some people make it and some don't. Some people are destined to be great while others are destined to be losers, and most people are somewhere in between.

Rhoda was a loser. She had failed, and she could foresee no hope of achieving success in the near future.

This semester was a wash. Her life was over. There was no point in going on, she thought. If she tried to do something right and failed, everybody would laugh at her. It had happened time and time again. She was used to the same old song. She was accustomed to the same old result.

Rhoda realized her formula in life was easy to figure out: thought + effort = failure.

She wiped tears from her eyes, as she knew she would never see Jenny or Denise again. They were up in heaven. Or maybe she was wrong about that too—perhaps all those Sunday schools she attended were a big lie. You can't trust anybody, she was sure. Or was she? She didn't know. That feeling of not knowing was what hurt the most.

Rhoda tried to stop this onslaught of life analysis. She recalled Jenny's ubiquitous smile. Jenny always had a kind word for everyone. Even when she broke up with Chip, Rhoda guessed, Jenny couldn't have been cruel about it. She didn't have a cruel bone in her body. Jenny would have gone out with Zach had she not been . . . Rhoda didn't want to go there.

She looked out the window again and estimated the jump out the window would be about thirty feet. She could go for it and . . . She stopped herself. This tailspin of delusion and death wish was swirling in her fevered brain at breakneck speed. She had to slow herself down and rethink everything.

She was tired of failure. She was tired of trying. Most of all, Rhoda was tired of being tired. She despised being the nondescript woman walking down the street. She wanted to make something of herself.

And that is exactly what she set out to do that evening. While everyone would worry about iKill and his next victim, if there would be any more, Rhoda was going to win her last battle. She would pop the champagne cork in a big way tonight. And though she wouldn't be there to see it, she had a good feeling about her decision. It was about time.

Rhoda went to her desk and wrote a couple more lines. She thought about her parents, her brother and sister, her high school, her friends, her sorority, and her classes. Most of all, she thought about her dreams and visualized them twisting slowly down into the depths of a thunderous tornado.

Rhoda was desperate for self-protection now. She was sure Teresa could help her, and she would have loved to have Malkin help her.

There was only one way to get their attention, only one way to get the attention of the whole floor, all of Edgar Hall, the entire campus, and the city. And most important of all, there was only one way to get the attention of her family and friends, who she categorized as so-called, part-time, call-me-when-you-need-me-otherwise-pretend-I-don't-exist friends.

She had to do it. Rhoda reached for her pocketknife and took a deep breath.

She looked out the window. The wind drummed a steady beat against Edgar Hall, ghost-white traces of oxygenated fear with a beat from hell.

She imagined heaven as a place where worry and fatigue did not exist. Rhoda figured that in heaven, she would not need to please anyone. She would be happy there. The fact of the matter was that she was going to die tonight, and no one would know that the cause of her death was her inability to please.

She opened the Swiss Army knife her brother had given her. It was short—only about four inches long—but sharp, very sharp. She took the knife in her right hand and took another deep breath. She looked out the window again.

She hoped that a knight in shining armor would show up at her window and rescue her from herself. Or maybe some kind soul would come knocking and listen to her trials and tribulations, and then save her from what she was about to do in the nick of time. Rhoda waited a few minutes for someone to come, but no one did.

"Figures," she said to herself. "Whenever you need someone, they're no place to be found. People don't really care about other people."

But again, she knew that in the lobby downstairs sat two good people who did care. Rhoda hated Malkin and Teresa for not coming up to her room and checking on her; they should have done that if they were doing their duty. That damn Malkin suggested calling Teresa, as if she would answer her phone.

Rhoda would have to get their attention as well as everyone else's, and she knew exactly how to arrange that. She raised her right hand and lowered the blade of the pocketknife onto her left wrist, one inch below the base of her palm. She held the blade on the surface of her skin and once again began to weep.

She couldn't believe what she was doing. But somehow, it felt right. She didn't know if she had the courage to carry it out. Most of her life, she had lacked the courage to do anything right. This one, Rhoda was determined to get right.

She looked down at her note: five short sentences explaining her actions. She guessed that after everyone found her, they would laugh. She wondered again about death. As long as they didn't laugh . . .

Rhoda thought she would loathe having to watch others giggle at her own demise. But upon reflection, she could care less. She had made up her mind to go through with this and let history call it her first successful endeavor. She would earn at least one "A" grade this semester—in re-creation.

She wished Tyler were around; *he* could have been her first successful endeavor. Rhoda just wanted one good year of dating, marriage, and then becoming some sort of professional. That's what Rhoda had wanted. But it wasn't to be.

She wished Gamma Phi Beta could have been another successful endeavor, but instead that turned out to be a first-rate blunder. Rhoda should have known better. She should have known better than to trust Sheila.

And then she thought she should have known better than to trust anyone in the world. She began to believe the idea that no one was trustworthy. Perhaps learning this painful lesson was her first success, and the result of this lesson would be her second.

Two successes on the same day! What a day, she thought.

Rhoda lifted the knife off her wrist and set it down. She began to cry again. It was hard for her to think straight. She thought a short note was not enough; Rhoda considered writing an e-mail to everyone in her inbox address book.

She turned on her laptop and opened her e-mail. She checked her account and was surprised to see she had one new message.

A new message? For her? People were always e-mailing her, but most of the e-mails were boring, except for the ones from her friends still in high school. Maybe the e-mail was from her old friend Becky. Maybe, just maybe, this e-mail would be the one that saved her.

She clicked on "Inbox" and waited for the screen to load. It seemed to take forever. Rhoda glanced down at the pocketknife and back up at the computer. While it loaded, she checked to see if anyone was online. No one was online at the moment, and she . . .

Rhoda froze. It couldn't be. She pushed her chair back and slammed her right hand against her mouth to keep from screaming. She covered her mouth with her left hand as her right hand smothered its counterpart. She had received an e-mail from iKill, with an attachment.

She couldn't work up enough courage to open the e-mail. She almost deleted it without looking, but then she figured that she had spent her whole life avoiding courage and now was the right time to be courageous. Her hands were shaking; the cursor rested on the delete function for a minute before she clicked on the e-mail and read it slowly:

Hi Rhoda,

How are you doing? Thought you could use a little pick-me-up this evening.

Here's a little nightcap, on me.

Sheila's blonde hair contrasts nicely with the blood, and as you can see she bled a while. She didn't quite make it back from the house. You know which house I mean. It was getting late, and I was getting bored. Mindy had gotten away, so I had to settle for Sheila.

By the way, where is Mindy?

If you see her, send her my best. And tell her I didn't mean to scare her in the shower. I only meant to kill her, to cut her up and watch her bleed.

Rhoda, take care. Judge for yourself—I included a few pictures for your viewing pleasure. I call them "Sheila's Sequoia."

And you're not so bad yourself. You have that housewife kind of beauty. I've fantasized about you in the kitchen behind the vacuum cleaner. Don't go far or you could be next.

Love, iKill

Rhoda gasped and reread the last few lines. She was "not so bad" and had "that housewife kind of beauty." A hurricane of anguish and disillusion plowed through her heart and spilled into her arteries. She felt sick and wanted to throw up. For days, she had wondered about iKill, and now he had e-mailed her. All of life's coincidences seemed to result in eternal humiliation.

She looked at the pictures of Sheila her blonde hair and disfigured face, barely recognizable. Her neck and back had been stabbed several times. iKill strikes again.

What a sick thought. What a sick individual. Rhoda closed the attachments and didn't save them. Sheila was dead; it was hard to imagine. Now iKill had murdered three girls—Jenny, Denise, and Sheila. He must be some kind of sex pervert, Rhoda thought.

She felt a huge wave of guilt rise within her. The damn sorority could care less about her, but she was alive. Sheila had been accepted back in August and was now no more. It seemed odd.

Nothing made sense. Rhoda's brain burned with question after question. She got up to make sure her door was locked. Anxiety made her entire body vibrate like a 747 about to take off on a one-way flight to hell.

She checked her closet and under her bed. There was nothing. She felt weird; suddenly, her survival instinct had returned, thanks to a demented e-mail from iKill.

She began crying without tears, only desperation. She decided it was time to tell the world, this sick, sick world:

Hi,

> *I just wanted to thank the people who tried to help me in my eighteen years of life. I know I have caused a lot of pain and suffering to people who love me, or say they love me, and for that I am deeply sorry. I don't understand life and I have no idea about tomorrow, only that I won't be a part of it. That way all of you know I won't be around to ruin it for you. I hope I get it right in the next life, if there is one. I am sorry for everything.*

Love,
Rhoda

Rhoda hesitated a few minutes before finally clicking on "Send." It was gone. That was that.

Rhoda thought of Malkin and Teresa. Should she call them? Could she save face at this late stage, or was it too late? Do most people who do this go through this kind of maddening debate over life and death?

Rhoda picked up the pocketknife and placed it back on her wrist, perpendicular to the veins sticking out. She could feel her chest heaving. Suddenly rapid and violent pictures of her own death, Jenny's dead body in the dryer, Denise's dead body in the ditch, and this recent photo of Sheila lying dead flashed before her eyes a thousand times. It was too much. Rhoda pressed down with a trembling hand on the knife, and it cut a thin red line into her wrist.

Rhoda thought she would scream at the sight of her own blood, but she didn't. She laughed. She finally realized what she had known for most of her eighteen years on earth: she didn't care about herself. What a relief!

She pressed down harder and cut deeper into her wrist. More blood spurted out onto her forearm and desk. Rhoda suddenly thought back to happier times when she was a child with long blonde hair, running free in the meadows, playing with friends on the merry-go-round and hopscotch, playing jacks, smiling. She had smiled all the time as a child.

Rhoda could still hear her mom's words: "Hey Rhoda! Daddy's home and dinner's ready! It's time to come in. Tell your friends you'll play with them later, after you've finished your dinner."

Now it was all over. Everyone had done so much to secure her happiness—all except for her. She began to sob harder, and she cut into her flesh with rapid-fire strokes. Blood first trickled and then began to stream down her hand and onto the note she had left for people to find.

"If they care," she said. Rhoda felt a sense of relief when the blood translated into physical pain. She could not understand why the physical pain she had inflicted upon herself helped remove so much of the mental strain. Rhoda felt the burden on her shoulders suddenly disappear.

Her arm was soaked with blood, and she didn't care. She sliced her wrist a dozen more times and looked deep into the wound. She thought she saw tendons and other things she had only heard mentioned in magazines and on television.

Rhoda felt the urge to share her moment with everyone. She ran to her door and opened it. She looked left and right, and no one was around. Suddenly she heard a soft swishing sound at her feet and saw thousands of slimy pink snakes. They actually looked more like giant worms, Rhoda thought. She walked down the hall and ran her left hand against the wall just as she had done when she was a child walking through the school, singing love songs.

She smeared blood all over the walls. Rhoda had no grip on herself anymore. She thought she was going to pass out. How did all this happen?

She'd opened the door and drifted into a deadly dream. Everything fades away, she thought as she took a last breath. She was free.

*   *   *

Malkin and Teresa were pacing in the emergency-room waiting area. He checked his watch. It was nearing midnight; they had been waiting about an hour when a doctor approached them.

"She's going to make it," the short and obese Dr. Wiley said. "But it was closer than we thought. We almost lost her; she had lost a tremendous amount of blood and managed to cut through several vital veins and tendons in her wrist. We'll need to keep her here for a couple more days to monitor the progress of her wrist. If it heals like we hope it will, then she can go home. If not, we'll have to do surgery on the wrist."

Teresa breathed a sigh of relief. She put her hand on Malkin's arm and thanked the doctor.

"Of course," Dr. Wiley continued, rubbing his graying goatee, "she'll need to go through counseling for the suicide attempt. Whether she does that here or at the university is up to her. But we'll have to set that up relatively soon. In fact, I won't release her till I know she's scheduled for long-term psychiatric care. We're talking serious psychological trauma here—some sort of maladjusted depressive disorder."

Malkin said he understood and would call Rhoda's parents on their cell phone. They had already been notified and were on their way from nearby Oakville. What a way for them to spend their night, he thought. Teresa asked if they could see Rhoda, but the doctor said she was sleeping and it would be better for her to rest before seeing her parents.

They left the hospital and bought a couple of large coffees to go at a twenty-four-hour convenience store. Malkin's cell phone rang as soon as he walked out the door.

"Malkin here," he answered. "Who's that?" He didn't recognize the voice on the other end.

The voice was slow and stern. "Mr. Malkin, it's me, Charlie. I'm here at the front desk with Harry Sampson."

"Right," Malkin said, "didn't know who you were. What's up?"

Charlie explained that as soon as Teresa and Malkin had left with Rhoda in Teresa's car, he and Abby had followed the trail of blood left by Rhoda up the east stairs.

Malkin said, "Yes, and?"

Teresa blew on her coffee and listened as they waited to pull out of the parking lot. She opened up a sugar packet and spilled half of it on her blouse. Malkin looked over and wanted to help her dust her blouse off but thought better of it—wouldn't be professional, but temptation was pounding on the door.

Charlie spoke very slowly. "And we got upstairs to the third floor and there was blood, you know, all around . . ."

Malkin was getting impatient. "And?"

"And we kept following the blood all over the floor and walls—you know, the walls on the third floor have this sort of red stripe of blood because of Rhoda's suicide attempt . . ."

"Yeah and?" Malkin said. "Get to the point, for God's sake!"

Charlie's voice was shaking. "Uh, Mr. Malkin, so a few of the students went into Rhoda's room, because she had left her door open, and they saw her computer was on. This is the story that George told as he heard it from Chainsaw, Branford, and Chip—those were the guys up and about in that area upstairs. Stacy got up to talk to us afterward, but she didn't go into Rhoda's room."

"And what was so interesting that you have to call me to tell me about Rhoda's room?" Malkin asked.

"They checked out her room because they thought she had gotten attacked, because of all the blood. But it was suicide, right? But get this: on Rhoda's computer there was this e-mail from iKill. And there were these two pictures. It's terrible."

"What pictures?"

"They said there was an e-mail message from this iKill person. And you know what? Those pictures do look like Sheila. It's hard to tell because it only shows her back all banged up. But I think it is Sheila—the same blonde hair is there. Remember, she was the only student not to show up tonight after Malcolm got here. This is very disturbing, Mr. Malkin. I . . . I don't know what to do." Charlie knew what to do, but now he had to contact the authorities first.

"Hang on, Charlie," he said. "Go up to Rhoda's room. Stand guard there and don't let anyone in, whatever you do. Make sure nobody leaves the third floor. And don't touch anything. We'll be right there."

"Okay," Charlie said. "It's a damned funny business. I can't figure it out."

Malkin closed his cell phone and threw it against the dashboard. "Damn it all!" he shouted.

Teresa knew the news wasn't good. She said nothing but had a grave look on her face. She started driving back to Hell Hall.

"Charlie called to say that some of the students saw Rhoda's door was open and walked in to check things out and her computer was on. Apparently, Rhoda had just received an e-mail from iKill with pictures of another dead body."

Teresa was strong enough to ask, "Oh my God . . . I don't think I want to know, but I have no choice, right? Who is it this time?"

"Sheila Underwood."

Teresa quelled her emotions and turned into the circle drive in front of Edgar Hall.

"Thing is," Malkin said, "I don't think anyone knows where she was killed."

Teresa was alarmed. "I don't think we're going to get any sleep tonight."

Malkin nodded and put on his coat. "Or for several nights, if we don't get our damned act together and solve this thing before mass graves à la Saddam Hussein and Milosevic turn up, right here in Blackwood."

Chapter Nine

Blackwood area police conducted a brief search on campus from midnight till 2:00 a.m. for the body of Sheila Underwood, after having viewed pictures on Rhoda's PC of what appeared to be Sheila's dead body lying next to what seemed to be a piece of glass. The search was unsuccessful and postponed till sunrise.

"Get the damn video from the computer lab now," Malkin said.

Gull called Malkin a few minutes later. "Uh, you won't believe this, but the surveillance cameras haven't been installed yet."

"That's the last thing I expected," Malkin said drily. We'll get on that first thing in the morning."

Teresa left Edgar Hall at 1:00 a.m., after which Malkin found himself in the same dreaded fourth-floor lounge adjacent to the recreation hall with Foster, Gull, and Tanner. Abby, still burning the midnight oil downstairs, brought up a pot of potent coffee and snacks for the men.

Malkin examined Rhoda's suicide note, decorated with drops of blood, and wondered what Blackwood College—or human nature—was coming to.

"What's next, a revolution?" Malkin asked, pacing back and forth along the far west side of the room on which two windows overlooked West Willow Road and the parking garage. He swallowed his coffee fast and threw the paper cup into a corner wastebasket. "Next thing you know, we'll have Flower Power and the sixties all over again, God forbid."

"Maybe this is it," Foster said.

Malkin grunted. "Unless we put a stop to these maniacal killings, we the law-enforcement branch of government deserve to be put behind bars—for incompetence if for no other reason."

Tanner said, "I have no clue what is going on. It's just ugly."

Malkin sat down in a plush brown reading chair, turned on the large lamp above him, and read from his notebook:

"Jenny Curtis—Victim Number One—hacked to death in a laundry-room dryer in the basement of Edgar Hall in the middle of the night. Her right index finger was cut off and placed on the buffet line in the cafeteria. No apparent motive. Weapon—an ax and probably a knife. No suspects. Received an e-mail of a dead cat lying in the middle of some road by an unknown person. Recently broken up with Chip Patrick, also a resident of Edgar Hall, and presumed to have begun dating another resident of Edgar Hall, a musician named Zach Gillett. Admired by many males in this building and altogether considered a sweet, gentle, innocent, caring girl—the last person you'd suspect anyone would want to harm. Wish I could say this was the first time I'd heard it happen.

"Denise Lansing—Victim Number Two—stabbed to death on West Willow Road about a mile west of Edgar Hall early evening of the same day. No apparent motive, weapon—a large knife—not found. Probably lying in any of three hundred adjacent fields surrounding campus; I'm sure we won't come across it. No suspects. Received e-mails shortly before she was murdered, the last of which contained an attachment with pictures of Jenny Curtis's dead body in the dryer downstairs. Recently broken up with Tyler Mitchell, another resident of Edgar Hall, who had begun going out with Rhoda this week. Smart, self-possessed girl who was considering transferring to a university in Massachusetts and who had expressed some interest in that kid posing as a student, Hank Kilger, a.k.a. Chainsaw.

"Mindy Adams—was to be Victim Number Three, but narrowly escaped an attack in the bathroom on the third floor the next night. Received four midlevel cuts to her right shoulder and arm while she was in the shower by an assailant she described as dark and tall and having long, dark arms. He ran away in part because Harry Sampson was doing his rounds in the basement and third floor as he had been instructed. Like Jenny, Mindy is considered a studious girl with a positive disposition and gets along with everyone. Received an e-mail from iKill containing pictures of Denise's corpse found in the alley off West Willow Road and a brief message. Guess that's the way iKill likes to communicate. No suspects, no apparent motive.

"Rhoda Remlinger—attempted suicide following her not getting into a sorority and over guilt for having dated Tyler while he was still going out with Denise. Rhoda is currently recuperating in the hospital, but her wrist is in bad shape and she lost a lot of blood. She didn't get into a sorority she had rushed and had been generally very depressed for several reasons, hence her decision to attempt to take her own life. Her parents should be here by now, and Officer Morgan is waiting to meet with them at the hospital. Received an e-mail from iKill with pictures of Sheila Underwood's dead body, can't tell where it was taken—still not found, but we'll resume the search in the morning—and a brief message. A very friendly but somewhat naïve and not academically inclined student who had been good friends with Sheila Underwood and most of the residents in Edgar Hall.

"Sheila Underwood—Victim Number Three—body not yet discovered but presumed to be dead after viewing the e-mail just referred to sent to Rhoda Remlinger and left on her computer screen. No video available from the computer lab, from where we assume iKill sent the e-mail. Active member of Gamma Phi Beta and not the academic type, Sheila was going to college more for social than academic interaction. So far as we know, she had not received any threatening e-mails from this iKill.

"So there we have it: three victims, all women living in Edgar Hall, and all brutally murdered; and one near-victim, also a female. We're not dealing with a sensitive criminal here. He takes every precaution to disfigure the face and torso. In one case, he actually dismembered a finger to put it in a food dish. I wonder if the Food Network has featured anything like that before."

Malkin continued, "Of course we're dealing with a homicidal maniac—a serial killer bent on wreaking havoc on women on this campus. I surmise this killer lives in Edgar Hall because of all the connections to the murders. The real question is, which one is iKill? We know it must be someone who is adept with computers."

Foster said, "This is the digital age, for God's sake. All the young kids are good with computers. They have iPads and laptops and MP3s and cells with digital cameras. Any of them could have sent e-mail messages. We now know that all of them were sent from Strong Hall, all on different computers. No fingerprints from Edgar Hall residents found.

"What makes this case maddening is that we can't simply track down the computer and user. This iKill logs on with his fake identity and downloads the pictures, sends the e-mail to what I suppose he considers his next victim, and then trashes everything in seconds."

Tanner agreed and hoped Malkin wouldn't fall into one of his ballistic moods.

Foster said, "Of all the students living in Edgar Hall, only Branford and Tyler are computer-science majors. Does that make them more likely suspects?"

"Branford, yes," Malkin said, "but not Tyler. I don't think he did it. We have iBooks, iPads, iChat, iPhoto, iMovie, iDVD, iTunes, and Blackwood's own special brand of traumatic technology: iKill. Maybe our serial killer is a Macintosh user, who knows?"

"Could be. Who owns a Mac?"

"I think we're dealing with someone who is not computer proficient but wants us to believe iKill is a computer genius. There is nothing genius, however, about the pictures and emails. I still think that if we don't go with our first theory, that some madman got in through a side entrance and killed Jenny in the laundry room, another possibility is that Chip killed Jenny and then got carried away with one and so either tried to get away with others—I'm not so sure he'd be that reckless—or else had to silence some girls who might have known more than he wanted them to, especially Jenny, who had dumped him before break. That could have happened—seen it a hundred times in urban areas, but not so much in smaller places like here."

"But if we're going by temper alone," Tanner said, "then a handful of suspects appear—Chip, Chainsaw, Jerry, and Gottlieb. And in Chip's case, more of a latent temper."

"I'm not so sure we're going by temper alone, men," Malkin said. "Would a temperamental murderer bother to spend time taking pictures and e-mailing potential victims? Could be, but we have to cover all the angles and think outside the box. We're dealing with a clever killer who wants us to praise him for his ability to outwit—hence his intelligence—to mystify, to frighten, and to inflict suffering in a most violent way."

*   *   *

Following a short break, during which some officers took power naps in their chairs while others scoped out Edgar Hall for clues, Tom Malkin slammed his fist into the south wall of the fourth-floor lounge of Edgar Hall and felt better afterward. He imagined finding the true identity of iKill and rearranging his face into a puddle of brains.

Malkin took a seat and gave stern looks to each of his colleagues. "We've been chasing this idiot iKill for a week now, and day after day he eludes us. This bastard has terrorized a small campus and a town of 15,000. Meanwhile, we've been walking around like a bunch of reality-TV dumb asses wondering how he's doing it and what he's got planned next."

Gull raised his hand as if to ask a question.

"This is no elementary school," Malkin said. "If you have something to say, Gull, just spit it out. But for God's sake, make sure it's intelligent."

Gull was smiling. "I think we've got our man. It's Malcolm. He was gone around the same time Sheila was killed; he returned to this building after curfew, and he had to know he was violating curfew; he was a drug addict, possibly a methamphetamine dealer, and was probably involved one way or another with at least one of those victims; and he is physically powerful enough to do it. Plus, remember that Mindy claimed to see a dark-colored arm. Doesn't have to mean someone who's black, but it's another point to look at."

"Go on," Tanner said.

"Well, it fits our psychological profile. Malcolm Huntington comes from a background of poverty. We did some background checks on him and it turns out he hasn't been paying child support for two years, he's had multiple affairs with other women all over the place, and his trips up there every two weeks or so were not to see his family, as we had thought and as he had mentioned to us, but to obtain heroin and chemicals like those found in his book bag from contacts taking the train down to Blackwood and Clark City—stuff to make methamphetamine with."

"Does that tie in with his connections to Webster Hall?" Gull asked. "He'd been known to spend a lot of time there."

"Exactly," Malkin said. "According to my notes and questioning, it seems like old Malcolm was quite the salesman. We should have known

155

there was something fishy about a poor kid from a bad neighborhood who has no scholarship, but drives a BMW around. He had customers in this residence hall plus four others, and it seems like his major base of operations was in Webster. That's why he was there most of the time, including tonight."

"What did Malcolm offer in terms of information regarding this business of his?" Foster asked.

"Seems like he was willing to save face," Gull said. "As soon as he found out he might get off with a lighter sentence if he cooperated with law-enforcement officials, he began talking. And check out what he told us: He's been in the heroin and methamphetamine business for about three years now. He did about three months of jail time for possession of heroin and then was let off for good behavior. Ain't that sweet—he turns into an angel almost overnight, and they kick him out to make room for the next damned deviant.

"In addition, Malcolm had clients right here in Blackwood. Seems like his routine was as such: go to the train station around nine p.m., pick up the stuff from a dealer who would not get off the train but continue on to Clark City and dump a book bag full of dope there as well. It is altogether a pretty slick drug ring, and police aren't exactly hot on the trail of students moonlighting as dealers handing off simple bags filled with drugs to innocent-looking people, especially in lesser-known areas like these."

Foster stopped writing and said, "Thanks, Gull, that's very helpful. I wonder what he hasn't told us yet."

"There's more," Gull said. "Malcolm apparently had clients in Edgar Hall. He mentioned specifically Jerry and Zach—and there are dozens of others he'll gladly expose, knowing we'll be more lenient with his sentencing. We're fortunate that he's talking and incriminating so many people for his own good. A snitch, but he might cut his jail time in half for being one."

Malkin straightened his tie and looked at Gull. "Still, just because he's into heroin and methamphetamine—Foster, get your men to search all of campus and Blackwood and the surrounding areas to find a BMW with a half-assed methamphetamine lab—doesn't mean he actually is iKill."

He added, "Malcolm could be the ringleader, or maybe it's someone else here in Edgar."

"True," Gull said. "But the facts point in that direction. I think he's our man; it's a sure thing."

Malkin said, "Let's examine the facts of last night, because a whole lot of hell broke loose between seven p.m. and midnight. It was one of those days we prepare for but hope will never happen, just like 9/11.

"Malcolm Huntington claims to have gone to Webster Hall sometime in mid-afternoon. He plans how he will pick up the dope at the train station and to whom he will distribute it. He heads to the train station shortly before 8:30 p.m. and returns to Edgar Hall around 8:50 p.m. No doubt he was hoping he would make it back without causing a commotion; instead, he found himself dealing with Charlie and me by the front door and reluctantly submitted his book bag to me for inspection. At that point, he tried to make feeble excuses, but he pretty much realized the game was up."

Foster nodded and Tanner added, "Teresa did point out that his manner went from tight-lipped and uncooperative to talkative and cooperative once he found out he might get off more easily. Wise choice."

Malkin threw Tanner a tell-me-something-I-don't-already-know look and continued. "We now turn to Sheila Underwood, the social queen of Edgar Hall. Her body has not yet been discovered, but based on an e-mail message still showing on her neighbor Rhoda's computer—to which we'll get in a moment—it appears she was slain sometime last night, right around curfew time. Sheila's movements last night were quite simple. She helped set up for the party at the Gamma Phi Beta sorority house in the afternoon, returned to Edgar Hall to change for the induction ceremony, and then drove back to the house around six or seven. The ceremony lasted till about six that night, and her sorority sisters present claim that Sheila left the house after helping cleaning—around seven thirty p.m. or so. Unfortunately," Malkin said, "she was never seen at Edgar Hall, and I know Charlie never saw her return, or so he says."

He added, "Then there's Rhoda's tragic episode. She had rushed the same sorority as Sheila's—somewhat as her protégé—thinking she would get in and didn't. The girls at the house said she was the only pledge out of a field of fourteen who didn't get membership. Rhoda must have taken it hard. Pity they didn't have consola . . . well, I probably shouldn't say that right now. Anyway, she left the ceremony around six thirty p.m.

and returned here around seven thirty p.m. Then I ran into her twenty minutes later at the Lighthouse coffee shop and walked her back here.

"Charlie and I suggested she talk to Teresa," Malkin said, "and Rhoda said she would consider it. Charlie left for his dinner break. Rhoda went upstairs to her room and wasn't seen by anyone. Most of the students here were not around till right before curfew ended, except for Malcolm and Sheila, of course. George Young claims Rhoda talked with him for a few minutes and was an emotional wreck. She wanted to talk to Tyler but Tyler was out, probably with some other girl. I don't think he cared one bit about Denise or Rhoda.

"It gets worse from there," Malkin continued. "Teresa, Charlie, and I were sitting in the lobby later—a little after nine p.m., just going over the case for about half an hour, when suddenly Rhoda came running— more like falling—down the stairs, bleeding to death. She had cut up her wrist—this was around nine thirty p.m. And there was a snowstorm of blood everywhere. It looked like a red X-ray of everything you wanted to know that was in your wrist but was afraid to ask. Teresa and I took her to the hospital in Teresa's car, and we left Charlie and Abby to watch things here. Abby stayed in the basement, Charlie took the third floor, and Harry monitored things at the front entrance of Edgar Hall.

"The doctors said that Rhoda would recover fine but may require surgery depending on the extent of her injury and how she recovers in the next couple days. Apparently some tendons and veins had been slashed. It was a nasty sight. Imagine all the blood and pus around the infected wound. I guess the knife she used wasn't all that clean; she said it was a present from her older brother. I'm sure he's on top of the world right now. Anyway, word is that she felt guilty about her fling with Tyler—which she thinks might have led to Denise's murder—and not getting into the sorority. She suffers from an inferiority complex, and I imagine suicide was one way of getting everyone's attention."

Foster smiled as he remembered Malkin had a bachelor's degree in law enforcement with a double major in psychology. He hadn't lost much of his knowledge over the years.

Gull asked, "What did you find out about the e-mail you found earlier?"

Malkin said, "I was about to get to that. It seems as if Rhoda went crazy and lost control of herself right when she received an e-mail message—a brief one, but to the morbid point—from iKill. Charlie was kind enough to call me, after Teresa and I met with Rhoda's doctor, to let me know about the message so that no one could tamper with it, in case someone there was responsible.

"The worst part, again, is that this insane nut iKill attached two pictures of Sheila's corpse. You can only see her back hunched over and a lot of blood."

"Can we find out who sent the damn e-mail?" Gull asked.

"No," Malkin said. "The best we can do is say that it was sent from one of the computers in any God-forsaken lab, and the user logged in simply as first name 'i' and last name 'Kill.' This must be a very deranged individual. Furthermore, I should mention that Sheila's SUV—"

Malkin paused a moment to kick a chair. "Gull, has anyone checked her vehicle?"

"No, just buildings and the surrounding areas."

"High-speed it to the parking garage immediately, Gull. We might find a clue or some evidence."

Ten minutes later, Gull phoned Malkin. "You were looking for a clue or some sort of evidence? We got it—Sheila Underwood herself. Stabbed in the back and neck in the driver's seat."

"I'll be damned . . ." Malkin provided Gull's report to the others.

"Should have looked there first, we knew she'd driven, damn it," Tanner said.

Malkin growled, "Jenny. Denise. Mindy, almost done in, and now Sheila. This is deplorable. What bothers me," he continued, "is that one always has to pay attention to the psychology of the killer. In this case, I can see Malcolm as an adulterer, a drug addict and a drug dealer, a bad father, and a bad student—an overall lazy, poor role model—but I don't think he's got that killer instinct."

Foster asked, "If you don't think Malcolm did it, then who do you think is this iKill character?"

Malkin said, "Great question, but we need to find more information before we can determine that. There are, as I see it, still several suspects in this case, but I think the field is narrowing. Best thing we can do now is use our minds, or try to get into the mind of our goddamn killer."

He continued, "Before Jenny died, she broke up with Chip; before Denise died, she broke up with Tyler, who was starting to see—albeit temporarily—Rhoda. Mindy had no boyfriend and Sheila was a flirt, with no doubt some sort of pick-of-the-month dating philosophy on this campus. Rhoda attempts suicide. And with each death we have the twenty-first-century killer—he bludgeons, takes pictures, and then e-mails them as attachments with cryptic messages to future victims."

Tanner, taking notes while barely awake, said, "We're looking for the digital killer."

"For now, let's make sure we beef up security in such a way that students can walk without fear on campus day or night and prepare for finals," said Malkin. He added, "This case has already made national headlines. The media is reporting every detail and now we have become the laughingstock of an entire nation."

The men decided to head home and continue the investigation the next day.

Malkin turned to tell the officers, "If we could find Saddam, and thank God we did—'former Iraqi dictator' has a nice ring to it, doesn't it?—then we can find this deviant iKill."

Chapter Ten

The next morning, Malkin joined Foster for another cup of coffee in the lobby. "Before leaving last night, I checked with Head Case Stacy. She had a lot to say—mostly rubbish—but she is convinced that Jerry Fowler is iKill."

"Is the proof in the crystal ball?" Foster asked.

Suddenly Jerry entered Edgar Hall and dashed to the elevator. He was in a shaking panic. "Wonder what's up with that guy? Another head case," said Malkin.

Jerry jumped into the elevator and rushed to his room. He closed and locked the door and dashed to the window to shut the blinds. He removed his coat and dark sunglasses. Jerry's eyes ached almost as much as his head. He fell onto his unmade bed and pounded it in desperation.

"Where the hell is Huntington?" he screamed silently. "Where the hell is that stupid black asshole?

His thoughts bounced off the walls and hit him square in the jaw. He needed a sugar fix, anything to quiet the tension melting the cells in his cerebellum. Jerry knocked over books and pens but found no snacks. He opened his closet and threw out clothes and magazines before staring at the women's shoes he'd been collecting since he was in high school.

"When will my damsel come rescue me? I don't need no damn wife, I need a nurse," he said to himself.

Jerry put everything back into the closet and locked it. He sat down in his desk chair and watched the room spin round and round. He covered his face with both hands and yearned for darkness. He prayed for God to take the sun away for a few more weeks—hell, a few more months or years would be even better. He uncovered his face to bite his

161

fingers till one of them bled. He felt like vomiting and looked around for his trash can; he couldn't find it. Probably sold it for more.

"Why did I do it?" he asked himself a few times. He felt terrible for Jenny, Denise, and Sheila. He imagined them in his room at this moment.

"I would have loved you if you'd just given me a little more time," Jenny said, purring like a tender white kitten in the corner of his bed.

Denise descended from a corner of the ceiling like a black widow, and Jerry thought he heard her hiss. "Come near me, darling . . . now now, don't be scared. Mommy's waiting for you in the nursery . . ."

He shook his head to clear the cobwebs; he couldn't believe the signals he was receiving. And then Sheila emerged from behind the shade of his desk lamp as a squirmy white mouse.

"Catch me if you can," she said with a flirtatious smirk. Jerry couldn't let her go and chased her across the room. He caught her in his right hand just before she could sneak under the door.

He smiled as Sheila quivered in his hand. "What do you want me to do?" she asked. "I'll do anything for you, Jerry."

He felt an uncontrollable fury erupt from within his fevered head and squeezed Sheila into a white pulp.

"Just like toothpaste," he said. "Don't mind if I try . . ." He licked her up and began chewing on his own hand till it began bleeding.

Jerry rubbed his eyes and realized he had better get out of the room before police came to ask him questions. He was in no mood to answer questions about anything, especially the girls. He fought his conscience till it backed into a corner of his mind and slammed his head against the door.

He looked around for the soft white kitten, the black widow, and the tiny mouse, but they were nowhere to be found. Then he looked at himself and wiped his bleeding hand on his T-shirt.

"I'm a goner," he said. "It might be too late if I don't make a break for it now." He reached for the phone and dialed Malcolm's number, but there was no answer. He slammed the phone down and thought about checking with Zach. Jerry got up and then realized he'd lost his keys.

He couldn't find his keys. Then his memory mingled with his imagination as he saw axes and knives pounding into flesh and bones cracked from their necks down. "Can't walk with a broken ankle," he said, smiling. Then Jerry began crying again, and this time he understood there was no way out but one . . .

*   *   *

Malkin ran into Morgan, back from the hospital, as the latter was walking out of Gottlieb's room.

"Find out anything interesting from Hitler?"

Morgan looked down at his little notebook. "Not much," he said, "though he seems unusually concerned about this missing Sheila Underwood girl. The fact is he wasn't particularly close to her. Maybe he's trying to play the sympathetic role, but again that doesn't seem his thing. The other thing is that he was unusually quiet. You know how that has a threshold beyond which it becomes somewhat suspicious? Well, I would say that Gottlieb was suspiciously silent and therefore uncooperative when I asked about the three murders. I bet he's got something to hide, but we can't pin anything down."

Malkin nodded. "It's consistent with what we know, nothing new there." He added, "But that kid has to be careful. He messes up once, and I'm ordering CIS to send him back to Germany and never let him back into the country again."

On that note, Morgan and Malkin split up to continue questioning. Malkin knocked on Fowler's door, but there was no answer.

"Jerry? If you're in there, open the door. It's important. Malkin speaking."

Still no answer. Malkin tried opening the door, but it was locked. He pounded on the door. "Open the door, Jerry, or I'll have to break in."

There was no sound. He decided to chat with Zach and found him lying in bed hiding from the light of the world.

"Didn't your parents teach you to get up when the sun rises?" Malkin asked.

"Who cares?" Zach fired back. "How wonderful. If I don't die today, I can always look forward to another sunrise tomorrow. Gee, think I might go for a walk, smell the flowers, and discover God while I'm at it."

"It might not hurt as much as you think," Malkin said. "Millions of people do that every day and are happy. But I didn't wake you up to give you a sermon." Malkin sat in Zach's chair and said, "I understand you might be in some trouble."

"That moron Malcolm snitched on me," he said. "I've got to report to the police this afternoon about these drug connections. It's all his thing; I was just a dabbler, but I guess the pigs want the dabblers as well."

Zach just stared at the wall. He shifted his attention from the wall with pictures of rock stars to the ceiling covered with stars and planets that glowed in the dark. Malkin thought that Head Case must have been born on one of those stars or planets.

"What's it matter anyway?" Zach said. "My life is over. I've got nothing left to live for."

Malkin asked, "Why heroin? Or were you into making methamphetamine as well? Malcolm mentioned heroin in connection with you, I believe."

"So what if I took both? It's not like anyone cares."

"So that's the way it is," Malkin said. "I see." His skepticism toward faith in human nature was increasing by the minute thanks to his visit to Blackwood College. His lack of faith in human nature was already sky high before arriving here.

Zach laughed. "I like my guitar. I can tune it to play any way I want. But I couldn't tune Jenny. She tuned me out. I wrote some pretty crazy songs, you know. You'll probably think I'm crazy, but when she didn't respond to my desires I wanted to kill her."

Malkin said, "So you are iKill."

Zach didn't respond to the statement and looked around his room.

"I like staring at my stereo. It's not the greatest—no separate amp and tuner and receiver like some of the other guys have—but it gets the job done. I like how even when the power is off, the lights flicker from left to right on standby. Those bright red lights blink on and off on the buttons you can press to choose what kind of bass and treble sound you want, depending on the kind of music you're listening to.

"See? Look at it. It blinks left to right, about half a second on each button, and it flashes on Pop, Rock, Techno, and Classical. You know something? It goes across twelve times and then stops after the first two, then goes across twelve times again, hitting all the different music styles. Isn't that amazing?"

"One of a kind," Malkin said. "Amazing how much you like to count."

Zach grunted.

164

"So which was it, methamphetamine or heroin?"

"Little bit of both," Zach replied, his mind still focused in an otherworldly way on his stereo. "I like to get high, then go down, then go back up again."

"And that's why you have the lithium?"

"Guess so," he said like he hadn't a care in the world. "I can name all the objects in this room in clockwise, counterclockwise, alphabetical, color, and size order. And yesterday I spelled all the longest words I know in the English language a dozen times the right way, then backward. I can also—"

"You might get yourself checked out by a doctor."

"I'm not addicted," Zach said, beginning to resent all these questions about his personal life. He sat up, rubbed his eyes, and opened them to find dozens of black snails and snakes at his feet. One snake bit Zach and told him he would be dead within twenty-four hours.

"That's good." Malkin said.

"If I were, I would have looked into buying a tomb for myself a while ago." Zach ignored the snakes but could feel the bite above his right ankle.

"Tomb?"

"It's one of those things they bury you in."

"Oh, I see." Malkin felt an impulse to get up and smack Zach into some sense.

"Something cheap. I wouldn't want my parents to worry about me." A brown snake slithered across his lap and bit hard into his stomach. Zach felt his body deflate and thought he was going to pass out.

"Better to start now than later."

"What do you mean by that?" Zach fiddled with his guitar case and threw it down onto the floor to smother the snakes. Malkin thought he was just letting off steam.

Malkin walked over to the corner of the room to examine a poster of a young female rock star wearing next to nothing with a caption, "God is Dead." He said, "You don't want your parents to worry about you, so you take drugs, play guitar, and neglect your studies. I'm not here to preach, as I said before, but it seems to me like you either want them to worry about you, or you just don't give a damn about your life."

"Maybe both," Zach said.

"So why did you kill her?"

"What?"

"I said, 'Why did you kill her?'"

Zach remained tight-lipped and saw a skinny black ghost with wispy white hair emerge from his closet. It seemed amiable, but Zach was certain it was an assassin.

"You said you felt like killing Jenny because she didn't follow up on your signals," Malkin said.

"That was then, this is now," Zach said. "I don't hold grudges anymore. Chip could have had her back if she hadn't been killed. I don't think that I killed her. Maybe he did." He added, "Though if I'm going to do jail time for this stupid heroin bust, then I suppose it wouldn't really matter if I said I murdered Jenny or not."

"Give or take fifty years, or as I prefer, a little electricity," Malkin said. "It's up to you. If you want to waste your life, I for one think it would be a shame."

"If you want to see something that is a shame, just look at some of the lyrics I've written and listen to some of the songs I've put down as demos. They're worse than a truckload of hogs being hauled off to the slaughterhouse."

"At least you know what you're worth," Malkin said.

"Maybe."

Malkin waited for more self-pity, but Zach offered no further comment. "Then where were you last night?" the detective asked.

"In my room," Zach said. "I was listening to music in my headphones and didn't hear anything that was going on. Later Branford told me what was happening, and I couldn't believe that Sheila got attacked. Someone said she still hasn't been found—is that true?"

"She's been found, all right."

"Dead or alive?"

"Dead."

Zach stared back at his stereo and watched his life drift away with the soft sounds of acoustic guitar coming out of the speakers.

He closed his eyes and was on the verge of breaking down. That black ghost was aiming a rifle at him. Maybe it was Head Case. For a moment, Zach realized Stacy might have been killed and brought back to life as a witch to torment him, and this was her now coming to kill him first. He almost made a break for it and then looked up at Malkin.

"Maybe those girls were lucky," he said.

"What do you mean?"

"Now they don't have to worry about going crazy or dealing with anything or anyone."

"That's preposterous."

"Sure, for someone who's as successful as you, anything depressing sounds crazy. But maybe they are the lucky ones. They don't have to worry about tomorrow—homework, jobs, bills, parents, marriage, children, all those negative things."

Malkin just laughed. Zach looked hypnotized for a few minutes and then broke out of his spell. He said, "You know, Mr. Malkin, I've spent many long days walking around graveyards at night. I call it my Tombstone Tryst. But I meet only dead people, of course. They have more interesting things to say than the living."

Zach noticed the skinny black ghost disappear through his door going to God-knows-where and breathed a sigh of relief. He was still alive, wasn't he? He wasn't sure of anything. Why had he mentioned his Tombstone Trysts? No one knew about that till now—no one.

"So you can communicate with the dead?" Malkin asked. "Maybe you and Head Case should talk about writing a book on the subject." He figured with the ratings that drab daytime television received, the book would be a bestseller.

"I don't know about really communicating," he said. "But I feel more at home in a graveyard than I do here in Edgar Hall."

"This place has been a graveyard of sorts lately," Malkin said.

"Feels like it," Zach said. "But sometimes I wonder if Rhoda had the right idea. She cut up her wrist nice and red and juicy just so that she could get past that frontier—the frontier between life and death. See, it's not much of a barrier, and it might not even be something unusual or unknown to us. Instead, death might be a welcome change—like a shift in perspective—that works in our favor. Have you ever thought a lot about death and suicide?"

"Death, all the time. I've killed people, Zach," Malkin said in a serious tone. "Killed criminals on the scene, killed terrorists on the scene, in the US and in other countries. It's a harsh world out there."

"Think I killed those girls?"

"I suppose it's within the realm of reality."

"Or maybe it was you."

Malkin laughed. "Keep up the creativity."

"I've read lots of books in which the serial killer is really the detective," Zach said.

Malkin looked at Zach's television and noted several horror DVDs piled next to the player. "So are you frightened knowing I have a 9 mm right here with me?"

Zach thought that was tame compared to the snails and snakes. "Nope. Maybe it was Chainsaw."

"Why do you think it was?"

"No, just suppose. Because he's the strongest one on the floor, and he used to torture cats and dogs." Zach's eyes grew large and blue but still suffered from some cloudy haze thanks to the last bit of heroin pumping through his veins.

"Could be."

"Jenny used to shudder—can't say I blame her—when Chainsaw would brag about setting cats' tails on fire or hanging little puppies by the neck till they wriggled their little bodies to death. He's a sick person."

Malkin thought Zach was speaking the truth. He respected that Zach hadn't even tried to lie about his drug use—though he might be in denial about the extent to which it was a part of his life—but he didn't sweep it aside altogether either.

"Just like iKill."

"Just like iKill."

*   *   *

Malkin joined the other officers in the lounge and briefed them on his conversation with Zach and the possibility of Jerry going missing.

"We're talking murder here, Vernon—no, bigger than simple first-degree murder. We're talking about a small community that's being terrorized by some serial killer who goes by iKill and who is still at large. As such, I don't think that we're looking for someone with a poor scholastic record or irregular attendance."

Gull agreed. "Ah, hell if I know who this iKill person is. You still think it's someone from inside the building? You don't think it's some madman stranger or alcoholic who came in because he was on the wagon and lost his temper?"

"Anything is possible," Malkin said. "I just know that we're dealing with someone who's very clever and not unwilling to murder again. He's gotten away with three in just a few days' time. Maybe Charlie is right, after all, and it's that Cragg fellow."

Gull said he would meet with Tanner to discuss their next move. Malkin suggested they meet briefly that afternoon to go over notes and strategy for the next day.

"Unless we capture iKill within the next two days, we're not only going to see a minor revolt in downtown Blackwood, but also a sharp reduction in enrollment at Blackwood College."

"Don't think President Keyes wants that," Gull said.

"Then again, if they take a whole week to have a surveillance cameras installed just because of some damn ticket order, maybe they deserve this." Malkin was still fuming over this simple yet incomprehensible bureaucratic blunder.

"Maybe," Gull said. He grabbed his pen and police cap and walked downstairs to meet with Tanner.

Malkin next went to Chip's room and found him busy working on his computer. He closed several files as soon as Malkin walked in.

"So how are you doing?" Malkin asked, taking a seat on Chip's desk chair.

"As good as expected, considering everything."

"I know."

"Heard anything about Sheila?"

"Yep—dead as Jenny and Denise."

"I just don't know what the hell is going on in this world anymore—or in Blackwood, I guess."

"It is pure evil," Malkin said.

There was a sudden knock on the door. It was George. He came in and asked if he was interrupting anything.

"Not at all," Malkin said.

George had stopped by to borrow a blank CD from Chip.

"We're talking about iKill," Chip said. "Any thoughts on the matter?"

Chip sat down on a chair in the middle of the room between his two guests and breathed deeply. He was glad to have George in the room so Malkin couldn't focus solely on him.

"I have no idea," George said. "All I know is Jackie has been a walking nightmare ever since Jenny was found dead. She can't bear being on campus and is planning on leaving early."

"Sorry to hear that," Chip said. "I know they were very tight."

Malkin thought at that moment that Chip didn't feel all that sorry for Jackie. There was some duplicity in that kid, he noted.

Malkin asked, "If I were to ask you to give me one or two names of the people you suspect most in this case, whom would you identify as iKill?"

George thought for a moment and answered, "I'm not sure. Are you certain it was one of us?"

"He wants names," Chip shouted. "We all know who killed all three girls; it was the same loser who tried to kill Mindy too. It was Heiner."

"And why do you think that?" Malkin asked, aware of Chip's enmity for the foreign student.

"Here he comes waltzing into Blackwood College acting all innocent and naïve, but I bet he's got connections. This drug thing that Malcolm is mixed up in, I'm sure Gottlieb's into that as well. His hands are dirty. It all probably started in Germany. He wanted to go for just about all the girls in this residence hall, but none of them wanted to spend any time with him," he laughed. "So I figure he killed them out of revenge, that's all. I think the case is clear. He had the motive, the ability to kill, and the opportunity. He was around when all three girls were killed."

"But many people believe you had more motive to kill Jenny," Malkin said. "After all, she broke up with you, not with anyone else, and there are rumors she was being courted by Zach."

"That little pansy? Jenny was all right just a couple weeks before Thanksgiving break. But we hardly spoke during break, and I could tell things were deteriorating. Then she brought up this thing with Zach— it was nothing, she just told me that he was wondering if we were still going out, and if not that he'd like to take her out to a concert or something. But Jenny declined. And by that time we were pretty much done with. I don't think Jenny would have gone for some musician like Zach. She liked real men like me."

Chip laughed then and admitted, "She might have, or she might not have. She didn't exactly let me go on an easy note. When we broke up, she was clear: 'This is the way it's going to be.' There was no hesitation on her part. Her mistake. Who knows? If Jenny had not broken up with me, she might be alive today." Chip had a mean, twisted, and satisfied expression on his face.

"I wonder why you say that," Malkin said.

"Because, in a way, I think she had it coming."

"Had what coming?"

"Something bad—for treating me like trash."

"As bad as murder? That's pretty bad, Chip," George said.

"She wouldn't be the only one," Chip said.

Malkin sat up getting ready to leave and said, "That's true enough." He added, "If either of you finds out any information leading you to suspect something, or if you already know something but want to tell me later, I would highly encourage you to do so. We don't really need a fourth victim, do we?"

Chip and George exchanged curt glances and said nothing.

*   *   *

Tom Malkin, increasingly frustrated by his inability to crack the iKill case and still waiting for that breakthrough realization, met briefly with Foster, Gull, and Morgan in the fourth-floor lounge and compared notes.

"I keep coming back to Malcolm," Foster said.

"Come to think of it," Malkin said, "there was blood on his pillow."

The three officers looked at Malkin with bewildered expressions.

"Blood on a pillow?" Morgan asked.

"There was about a square inch of dried-up blood on the pillow of Malcolm Huntington. It wasn't there the first time we checked rooms, computers, and cell phones, but he'd probably just washed it. The pillowcase was different. Anyway, he'd managed to hide most of his stash in Webster Hall with friends or in various lockers around campus, but he had benzene on his desk and blood on his pillow. Frequent methamphetamine users will often get nosebleeds if they snort the crap enough, and I guess that's what Malcolm did."

Foster asked, "Do you think Malcolm Huntington is iKill?"

"No," Malkin replied.

Tanner said, "He doesn't seem the type who would e-mail people of his exploits."

"That's exactly right," Malkin said. "Remember, men, we're looking for a savvy, experienced, cunning criminal who wants acknowledgment for his actions."

"That could be any of the students," Foster said.

"Not any of them," Malkin smiled, "because I think we can eliminate more than half. I've narrowed it down to a handful—I'd say three suspects."

"Seems like most of the students I asked have a hunch that either Chainsaw, Jerry, or Chip is iKill," Morgan said.

"If it's not Malcolm Huntington," Tanner added.

"We have physical evidence," Malkin said, "and we have times and places. But we don't have motive. No one stands to gain financially— unless it was Malcolm, and he thought the girls knew what he was up to, but I highly doubt that. I don't see this as a crime of passion either."

Gull agreed. "I don't think this was done for greed."

"Pull your lazy minds toward the psychological angle," Malkin said. "Some cases aren't so complex, but I have a feeling this one is. Hence our pathetic amount of evidence thus far." He asked the others, "Did anyone talk to Jerry Fowler? I think we have notes on everyone, but I didn't see him. I knocked on his door a couple times, but he didn't answer."

The other officers looked at each other. They all shook their heads.

Malkin said, "Not good. He's mixed up with the Malcolm Huntington drug ring, and I'm sure Fowler has information that can help us. I know he's been hiding something from me ever since this whole drama started."

"All right, I'll look into that," Morgan volunteered. "I spoke with him last night after Malcolm indicated Jerry had been a recipient of regular shipments from DC—through Malcolm the distributor—and he tried to deny everything. He got pissed off at me, and I swear he had half a mind to punch me out."

"It would have been great if he'd tried," Tanner laughed. "I think I've had it with all these spoiled brats. They don't know how much they've been given, and yet they're so willing to throw it all away. Amazing."

"That explains the lithium in his room, not to mention Zach too," Malkin said. "I bet they mixed that in with the methamphetamine. Smart kids." Malkin added, "And Tanner—I think you've got something there. Can we talk about that later? I think I'll go with Morgan and see what our friend Jerry Fowler has to say."

"And if he won't talk?" Tanner asked.

"Well then, we'll just have to pull out some old police-officer intimidation tricks and see just how brave our little suspect is."

Foster said, "Nothing too extreme, Malkin. We don't have the authority to use intimidation techniques like you had when you were with the CIA."

"Let's hope it doesn't come to that."

"Of course, we're assuming he's hanging around here. He might have taken off this morning and tried to split town before the cops rounded him up for questioning on the drugs allegations." Malkin turned to Morgan. "At what time was Fowler to report to the police?"

"At two p.m.—same time as Zach."

"Well, let's find out."

Malkin got up to leave and added another thought: "Always remember that, as far as I'm concerned, there are three basic motives for murder: profit, fear, and revenge. Sometimes those overlap, but in this case it appears we are not dealing with a killer bent on gaining some significant income."

"So what are you trying to say?" Morgan asked. "That we're not dealing with a case of high-stakes blackmail?"

"That's my educated guess," Malkin agreed. He continued, "I think our motive is revenge. Revenge stands out as the primary motive, and fear may be secondary. But we need to focus on the revenge factor. This iKill character is committing brutal murders, and it must be for some sort of revenge. Why so deliberate and violent? I am not sure, but we'll find out. Maybe Jerry Fowler knows something we don't."

"Let's hope so," Morgan said.

*   *   *

Malkin and Peter Morgan took the stairs down a level to look into the whereabouts of Jerry Fowler.

"Shoes," Malkin said. "Why did Jerry Fowler keep women's shoes in his closet? We have to find out what the boy is up to. Something about him is disturbing."

Morgan recalled, "He's the only one we couldn't track down for questioning this morning."

"Let's hope he's hanging out in his room," Malkin said. "So far, no news from iKill. Maybe the server isn't cooperating for serial killers doing business online."

Malkin recollected the first time he had set foot in this residence hall back in 1980. *Right at the end of the Carter years,* he thought, *and the whole country was ready for the Carter years to end, just like everyone is ready for this iKill mystery to end.*

Morgan walked up to Room 307 and knocked. There was no answer.

Malkin pounded on the door several times and shouted Fowler's name. "Police! Open the door immediately!"

But there was no sound heard inside the room. Malkin put his ear to the door and knocked one more time, this time more quietly.

"Strange," he said. "I knocked earlier this morning, and there was no answer. Maybe Jerry made a quick stop and went out again, or maybe he's just sleeping off some fun drugs."

Malkin knocked a third time: five dull thuds. There was still no response. "Go downstairs, Morgan, and have Charlie come up with the master key. I think we should go in; it could be filled with drugs, unless Fowler has decided to make a break for it knowing that Malcolm has incriminated him in this methamphetamine ring."

Morgan was not unhappy about being sent downstairs again. One more chance to see Abby's navel.

He wanted Abby. And cracking this iKill case might mean a big promotion—more money might impress Abby.

Morgan asked Charlie to help them unlock Fowler's door and managed to flirt with the blonde bombshell at the same time. As Charlie searched for the master key, Morgan said, "You know, Abby, there's a great new barbeque restaurant down on the east side of town. I hear they have great chicken sandwiches with potato wedges. What do you say?"

Abby couldn't accept right away, of course, though she appreciated Morgan's boldness and thought it was a good idea.

"That depends," she said, smiling like an excited teenager on her first date. "There haven't been any murders around in that area lately, have there?"

Morgan laughed. "No sightings of iKill in that neighborhood, unfortunately. Why? Do you like crime?"

Abby knew she had him in the palm of her hand. "I have always been fascinated by murder mysteries," she said. "But of course, I've never been involved in one till now. And it does kind of give me the creeps."

"It gives you experience so that you can develop skills as to how to manage certain situations," Morgan said. He'd never felt prouder.

Abby realized Morgan was approaching bragging territory. She decided to claim her own fame to boasting: "I'm just glad I was able to shed some light on this business," she said. "After all, I was the one who first told you that it was a friend of Malcolm's who had come by here during break to see him. But he wasn't around, of course."

"Very bright of you," Morgan said. "You know, you'd make a great private detective. Have you talked about homicide cases much with Malkin or Foster? They are the real experts."

Abby enjoyed the flattery. "Between taking care of things here, working another job, and taking twelve graduate hours of credit, I don't really have much time for anything.

"Anything except barbeque chicken for lunch," Morgan interrupted her. "You have to eat. And with your figure—hope I don't get in trouble for this, but understand that a man has got to say what a man has got to say, just reporting the facts as nature delivers them—let me just say that you have absolutely nothing to worry about. I think you could down three of those sandwiches, and it wouldn't even add a milligram to your weight."

"Just one sandwich will do," Abby said.

Charlie returned with a batch of keys after what seemed more than an hour. "One of these should do the trick, but I'm not sure which," he said. "Hold the fort for a few while we get that door opened," he told Abby.

They went upstairs to open the door. Outside Jerry's door, Malkin was chatting with Branford, who said he had seen Fowler in the bathroom last night but hadn't seen him this morning.

"Probably made a clean break for it," Branford said. "It wouldn't surprise me. That kid is a pervert and a loser. I'm not surprised at all that he was mixed up with Malcolm and this whole drug thing. I prefer alcohol myself. Zach, on the other hand, he's a cool cat, and I was shocked to hear he was in on this whole sordid mess as well. I wonder what the hell got into him."

"Probably problems at home—or the fact that he's already eighteen years old and still doesn't have a top-twenty song in the charts. I think he's secretly competing with One Direction. No offense to Zach."

Malkin said he thought music these days was a waste of time. Right now, he was less concerned with pop music than with getting into Jerry's room.

Charlie tried several keys and apologized. "Sorry, Mr. Malkin, I usually let Shaggy do this kind of stuff, but one of these keys must work. I think . . ."

He fumbled with the keys and tried at least a half dozen before one finally turned in the lock. The door opened, and a foul stench hit the men like an avalanche of body odor from some Third World sweatshop.

But the smell was nothing compared to the sight. Morgan gasped and Charlie jumped back against the opened door as Malkin looked straight ahead in disbelief.

"Nobody touch anything," he ordered.

Branford whistled and turned away in horror. "Now that will wake you up in a hurry," he said.

Malkin couldn't believe his eyes. Jerry Fowler was hanging from some thick metal wiring entangled around his neck and suspended from a plant hook nailed into the ceiling. A chair was toppled on the floor with the back facing the bed. His eyes were gray, dead, and open, staring down onto his desk from a snapped purple neck. The thin metal wiring had cut several narrow slits into Jerry's neck, hence the trail of dried blood from the left side of his neck over his sweater and down to his jeans. It seemed as if Jerry had decided to hang himself in his usual clothing style: a black suit jacket with a blue shirt and expensive jeans. His arms dangled on either side of his body, the hands semi-clenched and blue.

Behind the hanging figure was a computer with the screen saver on. Morgan asked Malkin's permission to click the mouse to see what Fowler had been working on right before he decided to hang himself.

"This is strange," Morgan said. "Looks like a suicide note—twenty-first-century style." Everyone leaned forward as several other students lingered outside the room, wondering what was going on.

Charlie said, "Mr. Malkin, please allow me to stand watch outside. I won't let anyone in, and if anyone asks any questions, my lips are sealed. I don't want a major scene. God knows we've had enough with the media circus the last few days."

Malkin agreed. "Good idea, Charlie. But please come back in if trouble arrives.

Malkin rejoined Morgan and Branford and read the note, written in a large font in a Microsoft Word document:

> *I couldn't help it. I had to kill them.*
> *I had to watch Jenny tumble-dry downstairs.*
> *I had to watch Denise squirm to death in the ditch down the road.*
> *I had to watch Mindy's naked body in the shower. She has great breasts.*
> *And her eyes! You should have seen the shock in her eyes!*
> *But she got away—the smart ones always do.*
> *I had to butcher Sunshine Sheila in her own SUV.*
> *Have you found her yet? Take your time.*
> *I couldn't give the police the satisfaction of solving this crime.*
> *So I solved it for them. I did everything for them.*
> *I confess to killing all of them.*
> *I am iKill. The one and only.*
> *At least I'll go down in history. People will remember me forever.*
> *They'll remember the e-mails.*
> *They'll remember the way I hanged myself in my residence-hall room.*
> *They'll remember how Edgar Hall became a haunted house.*
> *And for Jenny.*
> *For Denise.*
> *For Mindy.*
> *For Sheila.*
> *I loved all of you. Good-bye.*
> *Love, iKill*

Malkin clicked on the mouse with a handkerchief to check what else was on Fowler's hard drive. He found a folder labeled "Photographs" and opened it.

There were about twenty JPEG files saved in that folder, each one labeled with initials and a date. Malkin read out loud:

"JC-11/29 . . . DL-11/29 . . . MA-11/30 . . . SU-12/1 . . . God, this guy was beyond sick. I don't think there is anything that could have helped him. He was the embodiment of evil."

Malkin wheeled around to look at the disgusting figure hanging from the ceiling and said, "Hope the bastard rots in hell for an eternity."

The others left the room hanging their heads in disbelief. They turned back to make sure Jerry Fowler's head hadn't moved.

Charlie asked Malkin what he should do.

"Lock the door and get forensics here, and call the hospital to have the body removed. And I'll contact President Keyes and Joe Flanagan and make sure they schedule press conferences to inform the media of all the details before they swarm around this building like flies on garbage" Charlie locked the door behind him and returned downstairs.

Branford went back to his room and was mobbed by other residents on the way. They asked him a million questions about what had happened in Jerry's room. He was happy to have witnessed something most people never see in a lifetime. Branford actually bragged about having seen a dead man hanging in a residence-hall room.

"Always knew he was a weirdo and a pervert," he said, "but I had no idea he was iKill. Makes sense, though. Remember, he wasn't here the night he killed Jenny. Must have stayed at a friend's apartment or even gotten a hotel room. Sick fellow. I'm glad he's dead."

Morgan pumped his fist in joy and shouted "Yeah!" He turned to Malkin, who was dialing Tanner's number, and said, "Well, I guess that's that."

Chapter Eleven

"It will be nice to be able to walk on campus and feel safe again," Jackie Lowell said. "I'd made a habit of turning around feeling sort of paranoid every time I heard some strange sound."

George put his arm around Jackie and said, "From now on, you have nothing to worry about. I'll take care of everything. Leave it all to me."

Rhoda agreed and was happy to be back . . . sort of. "I think I have a new outlook now. I'm happy that I've been given a second chance, and I think I'll make the best of it. I never thought I'd say this, but I look forward to having the opportunity to prepare for finals."

Tyler, sitting next to her, smiled. "You'll do just great. Let me know how I can serve you, my dear." Rhoda enjoyed her newfound attention and wondered whether it had anything to do with her suicide attempt. Tyler too seemed to have a new attitude on life.

Teresa Martinez, dressed in a sexy form-fitting dress the same color as her tanned skin, stopped by to talk with the students and offer her services if required. Rhoda said she would meet with her later. Tyler said he would also consider some counseling.

"I still miss Denise," he said. "I can't believe that idiot Fowler was iKill. I just can't get it through my head."

"But I hate to think of all the deaths that occurred here," Mindy said. Her parents had agreed to let her reside in Edgar Hall now that the case had been solved. She was still a little worse for wear and tear, like Rhoda, but very relieved to return to some sort of normal life.

George didn't want to think about what iKill had done. He would have killed Jerry Fowler if the creep were standing right in front of him now. He could still see Jerry's spoiled, demented face. It reeked of foul play, and George wished he had realized this sooner. But he cringed at the thought of Jenny, Denise, and Sheila dying at the hands of such a merciless killer.

Charlie, standing between Malkin and Teresa, said, "I think a big party to celebrate a new beginning is a great idea. It might also help to erase the past and represent a new start."

"That's right," George said. "Not only a brand new start, but I think to honor the memories of three great women—Jenny, Denise, and Sheila—and the bravery of all of us, but most of all, for Mindy and Rhoda."

Rhoda smiled. Her wrist was beginning to heal, and there were dark circles under her eyes.

"We love you, girl," Jackie said, giving Rhoda a big hug.

The students agreed to plan a party as a memorial to the victims and their families, as a celebration for a move forward, and as a tribute to the bravery of the residents of Edgar Hall. George, Jackie, and Mindy spearheaded the plans and received help from other students and Teresa Martinez, who had served as the calm within the storm during the past week's violent murders.

Malkin returned to his hotel room to avoid all the platitudes and to think. He grabbed a drink and leaned back in his chair to relax prior to considering all the evidence.

"Jerry Fowler, another suicide, wrote up a confession," Malkin thought. That could be that. Perhaps . . .

Not Malcolm, Malkin thought. Doesn't fit the psychological profile. But who did?

Malkin reached for another drink and put his mind to work. "I've been reacting instead of being proactive." As for Gull, Morgan, Tanner and Foster, they meant well but Malkin doubted they could crack an Encyclopedia Brown case.

Malkin had all the evidence in front of him and had asked all the right questions. Gottlieb? No, Malkin thought. Malcolm, no way. George, Mindy, Rhoda, impossible.

Branford? Sneaky sort of fellow, but doesn't have the guts to carry out gruesome murders. He wasn't iKill.

Jerry was probable. Chip was possible. Charlie was possible. Abby couldn't hurt a fly. Neither could Teresa. Chainsaw was probable.

In truth, most of these students at Blackwood were good kids. Shaggy was definitely probable; he was the first to find Jenny and, like Charlie and Chip, easy to cast blame on others.

Malkin threw his head back. He pondered the psychology of iKill, considered the suspects, and narrowed them down to three. One, Jerry, was already dead. So two suspects may possibly still be on the loose.

*   *   *

The following evening, the walls of Edgar Hall rocked. They held the party in the reception area in the basement. The students were happy that all this mayhem was past them. More than a hundred friends and guests were in attendance, including some important dignitaries.

President Keyes, Vice President Flanagan, Officer Tanner from OPS, and Sheriff Foster were on hand to officially open the party as a celebration to remember the lessons of the past and welcome a spirit of optimism for the future.

President Keyes offered the following remarks: "Finally, I would like to extend a debt of immense gratitude and personal thanks to a man who has had a pretty rough week. Thomas Malkin, who came back to his alma mater to give a speech on international terrorism and foreign policy last week, and who works as a consultant for the Department of Homeland Security as well as a private investigator in the Washington DC metropolitan area, offered to stick around and assist local law-enforcement officials working on the iKill case.

"I think we can consider ourselves fortunate to have never before experienced serial killings to the extent of those perpetrated by iKill, and I hope we never do again; I know that Mr. Malkin and Sheriff Foster, Mr. Tanner, and officers Gull and Morgan would all agree with me on that count."

Malkin nodded thanks and shook hands with President Keyes. Malkin said, "Thank you very much. It's slightly ironic that during my speech last week I did refer to the fact that we not only have to be diligent in fighting international terrorism—which must entail going after the enemy on his territory before he brings his trouble to our homeland—but also in combating domestic terror as well. When I made those remarks, of course, I couldn't fathom the week we would have ahead of us.

"In spite of the tragic events that took place, it was a pleasure working with Sheriff Foster and officers Morgan, Tanner, and Gull. This area is well served. And I think that if we learned one lesson from all this, it's that we should take nothing for granted. Evil lurks in every corner of the globe, and decent citizens everywhere must stand on the side of good. As Edmund Burke once said, 'the only thing that is necessary for evil to succeed is for good people to do nothing.'"

Everyone applauded, and Rhoda's parents offered a few appreciative words to Malkin. Afterward, everyone ate snacks and drank a variety of beverages. Malkin was acting the part while playing cool.

Gottlieb joked, "Make sure that's not actual finger food." Chip overheard him and felt like punching the spineless Nazi bastard out, but considering the mood of the evening, he decided against such a move. For once he chose to be conciliatory. Jenny would have appreciated that.

Branford walked up to Malkin and asked, "Didn't you ever think it was me? I was convinced you were planning on arresting me."

Malkin laughed. "Well, I was sure it wasn't you. Wrong personality type. But I'm still uncertain as to how Fowler pulled off everything. I'm sure once we get more information, we'll be able to explain in more detail."

Branford said he was happy everything was behind them. "It was getting maddening just to walk the corridors of this building. Something scary about it. You know, the name Edgar Hall and all—like Edgar Allen Poe or something."

Malkin laughed. "I think you might have something there."

Branford shook Malkin's hand and wished him best of luck in fighting crime and terrorism.

Jackie and Teresa were having a friendly conversation, and Malkin decided to join them. He grabbed some more snacks and jumped into the dialogue.

"I don't think most of the students had any idea how scary it was," Teresa said. "I had never been through anything of this sort. I'm just glad it's over. What a relief not to have to look over my shoulder every time I turn a corner."

Jackie agreed. "I feel much better now, but I think we still need to be careful. They say that Jerry Fowler might have been the James River Killer from a few years ago. But they're still looking into that. It might not fit age-wise, but Jerry Fowler could have done it to have some fun during his high school years. So who knows?"

Malkin said, "No different really than the suicide bombers we keep going after. No respect for innocent life."

Mindy gave Malkin a big hug and introduced her parents to him. Her parents were ecstatic to meet him, particularly her father, Colin. Malkin could tell Mindy had gotten her height, welcoming nature, and genial smile from him.

"Colin Adams," he said, introducing himself. "I've followed what you've been doing fighting terrorism in other countries and in the US— particularly that anthrax scandal that rocked the capital for a good two months. Keep up the good work. We need more dependable individuals like you."

"That's very nice of you," Malkin said. "But the truth is, I couldn't succeed without the help of not only professionals in our field but also the heroic courage showed by many Americans every day of their life— such as what your daughter Mindy showed last week."

"We're just happy to have her safe and sound now," her father said. They spoke for a few more moments before Malkin ran into Head Case Stacy.

"Good to see you," he said. "I guess you were right. Maybe there is something to that black-magic stuff you do after all." Malkin enjoyed humoring her, and he saw that she craved the flattery.

"I know you don't trust what I do, but it makes sense," Stacy said. "I knew all along it was him. I told you two times that Jerry Fowler had to be iKill, but you wouldn't believe me. Like all the cops, they got something against good old-fashioned black magic. But it works, I tell you, it works."

"Good for you," Malkin said, thoroughly unconvinced.

The other students exchanged stories about the events of the week as well as theories advanced by some of the residents. They were subdued and relieved.

"I was so damn stupid," Zach said, staring up at the ceiling.

"Focus on your classes, Zach," Malkin suggested. "You seem somewhat depressed. Are you all right?"

"Yeah," Zach said, somewhat tired of talking about his mistakes. He had made too many mistakes. "I still plan on killing myself."

Malkin pulled Zach aside, grasping his flaccid bicep with his right
hand and squeezing it till Zach winced and pulled it back in pain.
"What the hell are you doing?"

"In case you forgot, this is a party to honor not only the memories
of three of your fellow students, not to mention hall mates, but also to
celebrate the victory of justice and the opportunity for tomorrow. If you
can't handle that, I suggest you leave. In which case," Malkin said, "I'd
be happy to kick your stupid ass out the door in front of everyone in no
time."

Zach moved back somewhat, surprised at Malkin's anger. "So what's
the big deal?"

"Everyone knows Rhoda is back dealing with her own suicide
attempt," he said. "I don't think it helps her much to hear whining
spoiled bastards like you talk about doing the same damn thing. I've had
it with brats like you."

Zach felt uncomfortable and wasn't in the mood to be lectured. He
said, "Maybe Rhoda's problem is that she didn't succeed."

Malkin felt like delivering a right hook but thought twice. Instead
he said, "Or maybe your problem is you don't have the guts to go for
what you really want."

"It's not that easy."

"Nothing is easy. At least, nothing worth doing is easy. I'll see you
around. Try and enjoy this party, this moment. And I'll leave you with
something to consider . . ." Malkin glanced around the large room and
asked Zach to do the same. "See what I see?"

Zach said that he did not. Malkin was not surprised.

"Over there," he said, pointing in the direction of Rhoda, who at the
time was smiling at Jackie and Teresa.

"What about it?" Zach asked.

"She's laughing. She's having a good time. Her wrist is all mangled
up, but she's doing it."

Zach thought of saying "So what?" but didn't pronounce his
thoughts.

"And look again," Malkin said. "Who's with her?"

"That's Jackie Lowell and Teresa Martinez. So what?"

"Who's not with her?"

Zach thought first of himself, then of Jenny. His mind darted from
pictures of dead bodies to guitar chords and back to Jenny.

"But you're here," Malkin said. "And now, I'm going to hang out with someone else who is happy to be on this Earth." Zach watched as Malkin approached Mindy Adams and gave her another big hug. Zach felt jealous and alone, as if his shelter suddenly disappeared. And Jenny would never reappear, only her memory . . .

Malkin was taking advantage of Mindy's standing by herself for a few moments; her folks were busy talking with President Keyes in front of an old picture of Jefferson Hall, the first building at Blackwood College.

"You look beautiful," Malkin said to Mindy, noting that her shoulder was still wrapped up beneath her modest pink dress.

"I'll be good as new in a couple weeks," she said. "The important thing is that this campus is good as new—this building is good as new—thanks to you, Mr. Malkin."

"You're one of the lucky ones," Malkin said. "I don't think iKill's daily planner had you surviving his attempt."

Mindy sighed. "You have no idea how often I've thrown that around in my mind. I should be dead, but here I am. I'll never forget it. I'll never let another day go by without giving it my all."

"If you have time," Malkin said, "go over to that young man over there and tell him what you just told me."

Mindy looked at a sulking Zach and smiled at Malkin. "You got it. No problem."

Malkin wished he felt better, but something still bothered him. He couldn't pin it down. In numerous previous cases, he'd noted that he always felt uneasy toward the end of a criminal investigation. For some reason, he felt even more so today. Perhaps it was due to the extent of the crimes and how they were committed.

Mindy spoke with a despondent Zach and a joyful Rhoda for a few minutes before rejoining Malkin next to the food table. Rhoda stayed with Zach.

"Are you all right?" Mindy asked. "You look like you just left the planet for a few minutes!"

"I think I did," Malkin laughed, "but I rebounded."

"Think I'm going to head up and work on my paper."

"Now?" Malkin asked. "You mean it can't wait till morning?"

"It could, but I hate to waste time. Got it from my father—always use your time wisely. Besides, it looks like the party is winding down.

I'll just say good-bye to my parents and then thank Teresa, then go finish that paper."

"What's the topic?"

"Free trade—though Obama says there's no such thing."

Malkin said, "Maybe he got it from being a stellar community-engager in Chicago."

Mindy laughed. "Can I quote you? I'll put that in my paper and reference it as an interview source. That should get me an 'A'."

Malkin laughed. His mind searched the room and heard a din of voices and shuffling shoes. He watched everyone walk from one social circle to another. Christmas was just around the corner, but tonight it felt like a distant star so far away that one could only admire it from afar with the realization that it would be impossible to ever get there in the end.

A cold chill rocketed down his spine. Malkin's mind raced from crime scene to crime scene. The end. The balance hung in the air. Jerry Fowler's suicide had sealed everything. It signaled the end, he hoped.

Jerry Fowler. He had been iKill and couldn't stomach the fact that he would one day get caught. Malkin liked to think that he always got his man.

Jerry Fowler as iKill. Malkin tried to fit all the jigsaw pieces together.

Chip approached Malkin and thanked him for coming to Blackwood. "I miss Jenny," he said, "but life goes on." Charlie was standing behind Chip and said, "Indeed, life goes on. This is over. Done. Finished. Live for the present and plan for the future, with a positive spirit."

"Well put," Malkin said. "And what about you, Charlie? What are you going to do with your positive spirit?"

"Same as always . . . feels good to be needed, and to have helped with finding Jerry. I guess I'll be the front desk manager till I retire."

Malkin thought that was a curious statement. "Think you'll finish working here at Blackwood?"

"I'm sure, I don't see any other options," Charlie said. "It's back to normal now, that's what counts."

"Guess so," Malkin said, looking around for Shaggy and a couple students.

* * *

Malkin mingled among the crowd for a few more minutes. He realized that this past week at his alma mater had been much different from what he'd expected when he drove down from DC. He thought about the digital murderer named iKill and all the havoc wreaked upon Blackwood College and the surrounding areas. Life is unfair, if anything.

Suddenly Teresa elbowed him from behind and smiled. So much for life being unfair. Malkin loved everything about her; each time he looked at her steamy brown eyes and luscious smile, he had to remind himself of his wife and family back home. He realized at once both the fragile power of fidelity and the burning temptation of pleasure. Malkin fit both extremes into an equation in his head and surmised it was the devil's formula for disaster. Such logic kept him in line every time he felt he was being befriended by one of Satan's kith dressed as light, and Teresa's tight tan dress and sweet red lips perfectly matched the devil he had in mind.

"A job well done," she said with a sexy smile. Malkin thought he heard her purring.

"Thanks," he said. "But I'm afraid you'll be spending many hours with students. Is it post-traumatic stress disorder?"

"Indeed, but not to worry, we'll do everything to help them recover," Teresa said. "These kids—it's not like when we were in college, is it, Tom?"

Malkin shot her an inquisitive glance.

Teresa explained, "I've been walking around campus quite a bit, and I'm amazed at how many students—usually girls, but a lot of the guys too—get out of class and get on the cell phone. But are they calling about something important? Could be, but you should hear the conversations I hear—not that I'm eavesdropping or anything, it's just that they walk right past you saying the most monotonous things. I'm afraid we're raising spoiled time—and money-wasters, and I'm not sure what kind of generation it's going to produce. Certainly one that won't be used to anything but instant gratification."

"I'm with you there," Malkin said. "I'll buy a semiautomatic for my kids before I give them a cell phone." His comment drew a guffaw from Teresa.

There was an awkward moment of silence between the two. Then Teresa noticed Chainsaw staring at the floor. She pointed in his direction and gave a thumbs-up gesture. "It's not going to be easy, but that boy will be all right," she said.

Malkin looked at his watch and decided he should head back to his hotel. Teresa gave him a prolonged hug and a small peck on the cheek. Malkin made sure he moved back before the Sultan of Temptation preyed upon his senses.

"Next time you're in the DC area, give us a call," Malkin said. "I'll make sure my wife prepares a first-rate dinner for us, and you'll be able to meet the kids."

Teresa thanked him for the invitation and hugged and kissed him again.

*   *   *

As Malkin drove back to his hotel, he had that same uneasy feeling eating away at his mind. He felt overwhelming anxiety and saw visions of knife wounds, stabbings, and axes descending into torsos. He watched ghosts parading through forests, eating the flesh of dead squirrels and human beings. He couldn't stop his mind from racing, so he turned on the radio.

Only two decent stations, he thought. It was a wonder anyone lived there.

Malkin walked into his hotel room and took off his shoes. He looked at the time and realized that in about twelve hours, he's see Roxanne and the kids again. Finally.

"Peace and quiet in DC—not exactly synonymous," he laughed.

He turned on the television and packed a few remaining items in his suitcase. Ever since he could remember, it had been his habit to place the clothes he intended to wear the next day aside. That way he never had to think too hard about what to wear after showering in the morning.

Malkin set aside a sweater and other clothing and packed everything but his bathroom items away. The television showed nothing interesting, and he surfed through most of the stations three times. It was the same old same old, he thought—the more things change, the more they stay the same. And he figured that Blackwood was never going to change all that much.

Malkin rolled around in bed for a good twenty minutes and then decided to call his wife. She could always help him sleep, whether he was sleeping right next to her or a few thousand miles away.

Roxanne was in bed fast asleep. It was about one in the morning. They talked for a few minutes before Malkin let her get back to bed.

Sleep. He wondered if he was going to get any this evening. Thoughts of Teresa passed through his mind. Stop! The devil . . . Malkin got up and did a few push-ups.

For a minute, Malkin reviewed the facts. Jenny. Denise. Mindy. Rhoda. Sheila. Might as well have been Halloween week at Blackwood. Something still bothered him, and he knew he had to put on a friendly face at the party. But he reconsidered whether all the pieces completed the jigsaw puzzle.

Malkin thought he might as well do something productive as long as he was awake and went to check his e-mail. He typed in his password and waited for the page to load. He'd probably have to pay for the extra night even if he didn't stay, he thought, still considering whether or not to leave early. Finally his page loaded, and he clicked on "Inbox."

The page took a few moments to load. "Slow server. Probably another five years before this place wakes up to hi-speed wireless," he said, laughing out loud. He thought about getting a drink at the bar and decided against that idea. It would only keep him awake.

There was this e-mail . . . from iKill. The subject was, "Jerry's Last Stand." This was exactly what he was waiting for. He clicked on the message, clenching his fists, and read the e-mail:

Mr. Malkin,

This was Jerry's Last Stand. I had to leave him hanging.
Not very pretty. Not like Jenny or Denise or Mindy or Sheila.
I bet you're wondering how Jerry managed to hang himself and then take these pictures.
I'm wondering that myself. Quite a trick.
Fooling the police and getting away with it is getting boring.
Won't you play along?
Or why don't you just give up . . .
You thought you were so smart.
Think again.
Guess who's next . . .

Best, iKill

Malkin froze at the keyboard. He managed to unclench his right fist long enough to click on the attachments. He pounded his fist three times into the weak compressed wood of the desk while the attachments opened. He knew, and now he was certain.

"Guess who's next . . ." iKill had written. Was it Malkin? This iKill did not know with whom he was dealing. He checked around his room but noticed no abnormalities. He also looked out the window but didn't see any suspicious activity. Malkin returned to his thinking that technology facilitated paranoia.

There were three pictures of Jerry Fowler hanging by that same heavy-duty metal wiring on a plant hook from the ceiling of his room. Each picture was taken from a different angle.

"I'll be damned," Malkin said to himself. He'd had a feeling . . .

He picked up the phone and rang 911. "Get me Sheriff Foster immediately. This is Tom Malkin from Homeland Security, and this is an emergency."

Foster had been sleeping. "What in God's name is the matter, Tom?"

"iKill is still out there, Foster. Meet me at Edgar Hall as soon as possible. I had a hunch."

Malkin next called the hospital and requested an autopsy be performed on the body of Jerry Fowler. While this kind of request would normally have to go through numerous bureaucratic hurdles, Malkin's reputation was enough to ensure the autopsy would be performed as soon as possible. No ticket needed to be submitted for an immediate autopsy, damn it all to hell, he thought.

Malkin was about to leave his room when he decided to make one more call. He asked information for the front desk of Edgar Hall. The midnight operator took what seemed like an inordinate amount of time looking up the number. He finally put Malkin through. Abby answered the phone.

"Seen Charlie around tonight?"

"Not since this afternoon. I haven't seen Shaggy around either. Charlie's not supposed to be in to work till tomorrow morning," she said. "And it was strange, Mr. Malkin, that Shaggy wasn't at the party."

Malkin tried one more time. "And have you seen Chip?"

Abby laughed. "I think he's still at the party."

Malkin said that would be a good idea. He added, "Listen carefully, Abby. I'll contact Frank Tanner and get OPS to keep someone on guard at all the entrances. Meanwhile, just stay put. I'll be there in a few seconds. We may have an emergency on our hands."

Before hanging up, he asked, "Can you give me Mindy's phone number?"

Abby gave him the number to Mindy's room, and Malkin called her. The phone rang several times before an answering machine picked up. Malkin pleaded into the machine: "Mindy, are you sleeping? If so, get up! Please pick up the phone. Pick up the phone now! If you get home and hear this message, lock your door and don't open it for anyone. Call me on my cell at 202-493-3910."

Malkin suddenly realized why he hadn't been able to come close to sleeping. He would have missed one hell of a nightmare, and it wasn't like him to miss nightmares, especially when far away from home, as Roxanne would often remind him.

Roxanne . . . Malkin grabbed his coat and ran to his car.

"iKill . . . Fowler . . ." he thought, maybe not. Strange week.

* * *

Malkin met Frank Tanner and Sheriff Foster at Edgar Hall shortly after he arrived. Tanner had a large cup of hot coffee in his hand.

"What the hell is going on?" he asked.

Malkin explained the e-mail and pictures courtesy of iKill. Tanner and Foster were speechless. Tanner's hand shook so hard from fatigue and desperation that he spilled some of his coffee. He had to sit down.

"This means we better act fast." Malkin asked Abby to call up to Mindy's room again. There was still no answer.

"See anyone suspicious?" Foster asked.

"Not that I can say," Abby said again, a little bit flustered at the sudden commotion and heightened tension.

"Apparently that was one hell of a hoax," Tanner said, as if reading Abby's mind. She began to understand why the officers were so agitated.

"Call up to everyone's room," Malkin said. "We're going up now."

Tanner called OPS for additional officers and then took on the unenviable task of informing President Keyes and Joe Flanagan about the continuing emergency. Foster agreed to check out the fourth-floor lounge, where by now the party was dwindling down to a few hard-core partygoers. Some in rooms, some in alcohol. Some were indulging in both.

Malkin and Officer Sampson, newly arrived, checked on the tenants of Edgar Hall. Malkin first ran to Mindy's door and pounded a few times. There was no answer. They went door to door and checked in with everyone.

Thirty minutes later, Malkin and Sampson met up with Foster in the lobby of Edgar Hall.

"Everyone except Mindy, Chainsaw, and Chip is upstairs," Sampson said.

"Damnit!" Malkin yelled.

"Branford was playing video games and talking to some girl on the phone. Malcolm was asleep with his wife; I felt bad about waking them up. And let's see . . . Gottlieb and George and Jackie Lowell were eating leftover pizza and chatting in George's room. And Stacy was reading with a friend—something about voodoo—in her room." Sampson went over the list of residents and figured that all the students were present except for the aforementioned three.

"This isn't good at all," Malkin said. The other officers wondered why he was in such a panic. Malkin thought he had no time to waste. He ordered Abby not to leave the reception area and to stay by the phone. Malkin asked her to call up to the computer lab; they had checked there but saw no one. Abby called but there was no answer.

"Is there another computer lab on campus?" he asked.

"The only one that is open twenty-four hours is the one in Strong Hall, on the fifth floor. It's just a five-minute walk from here. Lots of students use that one during finals week. All the other labs would be closed by now."

Sampson spoke up. "Say, Malkin, why all the fuss about finding a computer lab? Need to e-mail the wife or something?"

Malkin scowled. "About an hour ago, Mindy left the party early. She said she was going to try and finish a paper."

"Don't see the harm in that," Sampson said.

"Still," Malkin said, "I don't like the idea of it when iKill's out there. You realize this means Fowler was probably killed. Can you guess by whom?"

Foster and Sampson stared at one another in disbelief. "I see your point," Foster said. "But I wouldn't rule out suicide. This iKill weirdo could have just found him and taken pictures just to be the deviant that he is."

"Doubt it," Malkin said.

"You're forgetting, Tom, that the door to Fowler's room was locked. It had to be suicide."

"Those old locks haven't been changed for years," Malkin said as if explaining a simple concept to a child. "It could have been slammed lock and you know that. Now that's of crucial significance." Malkin could not rest until he knew Mindy was all right. He swore he would look for her till he found her and invited Sampson and Foster to do the same. They appeared confused. "Crucial significance?" Foster asked. "How?"

Malkin said he'd explain later. There was no time to waste now.

"I'll stand guard, and you patrol around campus. Look around and see what you can find. Five will get you ten that Mindy's typing away at her paper in that lab Abby mentioned in Strong Hall."

Strong Hall—iKill's favorite computer haunt. Malkin looked exhausted from worry. "I hope not," he said. Then he suddenly realized that whenever he hoped, he feared, and the thing he feared sometimes became a reality. Hope was useless, just a stupid word.

He imagined his fear frame by frame and could think of nothing else. Hope had solved nothing during this week of electronic murder.

* * *

Mindy Adams sat at the second computer in the front row farthest from the door in the computer lab in Strong Hall. She figured she would be able to get more work done in the peace and quiet of this computer lab; working in the lab in Edgar Hall would only invite distractions, conversations, and questions about her shoulder and emotional condition. She wanted to avoid all those topics for as long as possible.

Mindy was working on page seven of a ten-page paper and making good progress. Coming to this computer lab had been a good idea. But she was ready for a break. It was barely past midnight, and the computer-lab monitor had just left. He always stayed till midnight; the lab remained open for use but unattended till 8:00 a.m. Two other students who had been working on senior honors theses had just left as well. Mindy was happy to have the lab to herself. She could have worked in her room, but she had to look up online sources for her paper and the Internet connection was much speedier in this lab.

She decided to take a break and see if anyone was online. She logged on to her e-mail and clicked on chat. She noticed that Greg, an old flame from high school, was online. Mindy hadn't heard from Greg since last June's high-school graduation and was hoping he would remember her and chat with her. She remembered he was a freshman at George Mason and studying economics. She was excited and, with a big smile on her face, initiated a chat:

Mindy: Hello, Greg!

Greg: Mindy! Long time no speak.

Mindy: How's everything at Mason?

Greg: Awful. I'm failing all my classes.

Mindy: Right! I'm sure that's not true.

Greg: So how are u?

Mindy: I've been better.

Greg: Classes tough?

Mindy: Not really. There has been other stuff.

Greg: Too many guys hitting on u?

Mindy: Not that either.

Greg: U been breaking a lot of hearts?

Mindy: I wouldn't do that . . .

Greg: U broke mine.

Mindy: Let's not get into that. We were young.

Greg: U sound like ur about to retire!

Mindy: We had some murders on campus here lately.

Greg: I read about it—it was all over the news.

Mindy: U won't believe this, but I got attacked.

Greg: What?

Mindy: In the shower.

Greg: What happened?

Mindy: I was just taking a shower, around 2 in the morning—I couldn't sleep—and suddenly got attacked.

Greg: Are u okay?

Mindy: Yeah. They caught the guy, finally.

Greg: Was he a student?

Mindy: Yeah, a little psychotic. Some kind of weird pervert who killed girls and had women's shoes in his closet and was mixed up with drugs.

Greg: Sounds like a real winner.

Mindy: He hanged himself in his room. He lived just a few rooms away from me. It was scary.

Greg: Take care of yourself. Don't go out at night.

Mindy: I'm fine. They took good care of me and set my parents and me up in a nice house off-campus till the guy killed himself.

Greg: He was the iKill murderer, right?

Mindy: That's the one. His real name was Jerry Fowler. He was really quiet and mysterious—sort of demented. Never talked much with people.

Greg: How many did he end up killing?

Mindy: I hate to think of it. He killed three girls who lived on my floor. Jenny, Denise, and Sheila.

Greg: But u got away.

Mindy: I feel guilty about it. I got away, but they didn't. So I'm alive.

Greg: Someone up there is looking out for u.

Mindy: Don't I know it!

Greg: Well, I hope things improve.

Mindy: They will. I'm working on a paper right now.

Greg: Any plans for Christmas break?

Mindy: None, just spending time with the family.

Greg: Same here. Will I get a chance to see u?

Mindy: Is that a casual or a serious question?

Greg: Girls always have to complicate things . . .

Mindy: Yes.

Greg: How about dinner at that Chinese restaurant u like so much?

Mindy: You remembered!

Greg: Call or e-mail me when u get in town, and we'll do dinner and a movie.

Mindy: Thanks.

Greg: Anything to please u, Mindy.

Mindy: But it's not an official date, just dinner.

Greg:	Complicated, complicated.
Mindy:	I need some time.
Greg:	U been through hell. I know.
Mindy:	I don't want to think about that anymore. It's all in the past.
Greg:	There you go.
Mindy:	Time to think about the future.
Greg:	That's the attitude I want to hear.
Mindy:	I can't wait to see u, Greg.
Greg:	Me too. I'll let you get back to your paper.
Mindy:	Good luck with finals.
Greg:	Same to u. And be careful!
Mindy:	It's all over now.
Greg:	Still, be careful. I wish I were there to protect u.
Mindy:	I'll be just fine. See you next week.

Mindy sat for a few minutes and thought back to her days with Greg. They hadn't dated long in high school, but she remembered liking him. He was the simple, studious sort she could depend on. Nothing flashy—he would never be the star quarterback or center on a sports team, but he was always on time, and he had brought her flowers on several occasions.

But they broke up after high school, realizing they would be four hours apart and busy with school. Mindy was happy that Greg had remembered her and that he wanted to see her again. It made her feel special—especially after this week's events, during which she felt only like a victim and a target.

Mindy felt a warm glow rise from her heart to her head. She wouldn't mind dating Greg again. Even a long-distance relationship would be better than none at all. She recalled again the times Greg had brought flowers to her—one time for homecoming, once before finals last June, and once for no reason whatsoever. He had them delivered and then waited hiding behind a bush on her parents' front lawn as she accepted them from the delivery boy. Greg knew how to be spontaneous. He might be a simple guy, but he was special. Mindy couldn't wait to see him next week; she wished he were here right now. Actually, he was an economics major, so maybe Greg would be willing to proofread it for her.

Mindy's thoughts turned from Greg to her childhood. She remembered playing with her sisters and other girlfriends and blowing dandelions. All the girls looked so cute in their summer dresses and ponytails. Mindy remembered that her mom would always dress her up like a queen, and she felt so proud, wearing long pink dresses with red and blue ribbons in her long blonde hair. She used to like singing songs with her friends and playing hopscotch and other games. Childhood was a place of safety for her, and she was grateful for that.

Mindy also remembered how her parents would always throw the biggest and best birthday parties for her. For her ninth birthday party, they all went to the zoo and then to the botanical gardens to see all the flowers and animals. Mindy always got to bring her best friends along. Even though her parents weren't exactly rich, they would rent a van just to take her friends with them. She would always get to eat her favorite food on her birthday: donuts, cake, and pizza.

Come to think of it, a donut would taste good right now. She considered going down to the vending machine on the first floor to get a snack when suddenly she thought she heard a soft sound outside the computer lab.

She turned to look but saw nothing. It was probably just the wind blowing a window open.

Mindy returned to her thoughts of Greg. She wondered if he had a girlfriend at George Mason. Probably not, she thought, since he'd never mentioned any. Not that a guy would do that, since all they really wanted was . . .

Mindy's mind stopped in mid-thought. She heard a louder sound outside the room this time. It sounded like a door closing: the elevator door. She heard footsteps, too—slow, steady footsteps. She started to feel nervous.

"Get a hold of yourself," she said. "It's probably just the cleaning staff. They usually come around at this time."

Suddenly the footsteps stopped. She logged off the chat program and returned to her paper. Mindy figured focusing on that would help her turn away from her imagination, which had expanded to include every disastrous possibility since her attack a few days before.

Attack—she had been attacked in the shower of all places. Mindy still couldn't believe it. It was all too horrible to be true, and yet it had happened. She was sure it had happened; she had the scars to prove it.

But some days when her mind was racing around at two hundred miles per hour, she doubted that she was ever attacked. She thought it had all been a terrible nightmare from which she had awakened only yesterday, when she was allowed to return to Edgar Hall.

Edgar Hall—the place where three of her friends had lived and then died. She wondered if the building was haunted. She wondered if the campus was haunted. Mindy even wondered if the city was somewhat haunted.

Not a chance, she told herself—in part to quell her increasing anxiety and in part to shift her endless catastrophic thoughts from imaginary to factual.

Mindy turned quickly to look at the door of the computer lab, which was kept open. She wanted to close it to shut out whoever was walking in the hallway.

If someone is walking in the corridor, that is. She felt as if her mind was so fevered with fear that she could not trust it 100 percent yet. Mindy wondered if she would ever be able to trust herself again.

Two weeks earlier, Mindy and Jenny had discussed Christmas-break plans. Mindy felt like crying; she wondered where Jenny was now and what she was doing and thinking.

Mindy read a few sentences from her paper and turned to look at the door again. She still heard faint footsteps in the hallway, and they sounded as if they were approaching the lab.

It was probably the cleaning staff, she reminded herself. She had to calm down—there was nothing to worry about.

But still, her mind wandered into dangerous territory. Mindy realized that every time she felt a rush of anxiety, she heard water running in her ears. She thought of how Sheila had been killed the day after she had offered to stay in the bathroom while Mindy showered. What a disaster that turned out to be. Mindy had refused Sheila's offer. But had she accepted, Mindy might not have been attacked, and Sheila might still be alive. Mindy was frozen in an iceberg of immense guilt and—

"Shut up!" Mindy said to quiet her thoughts. She knew where this inner dialogue was leading—to madness. She wished she could take some scissors and simply cut the past week from her memory. She began to fear it would torment her forever.

Mindy shivered. It seemed like a cold breeze had blown in through the south windows of the computer lab. She turned and saw that the windows were closed. She took out her sweater from her book bag and put it on. She looked about the room nervously and glanced at the door. There was nothing. Nobody was there. Just stay calm.

She decided to go online again—maybe Greg is still there. He could offer her comfort. But could he be a good boyfriend again? Mindy wasn't sure if she wanted to commit herself to anyone right now. Being a pre-med student and worrying about grades in chemistry and biology was enough of a challenge.

Mindy logged on to her chat program and had an invitation message. It said, "iKill has invited you to join his chat list and would like to be a part of yours. Do you accept?"

Cold blood stopped flowing through her repaired right arm. Her palms vibrated at half the speed of her racing mind. Mindy began to feel nauseated and looked around the room. It was empty. There were no sounds except for the wind beating against the windows of the computer lab. This felt just like that night she couldn't sleep. Was it really only a few days ago?

Jerry Fowler was iKill. He was dead. That meant iKill was no longer on campus. Mindy thought this was most likely some sort of joke. She felt a sudden sensation of relief that calmed her pounding fears as her hands trembled above the keyboard.

She accepted the invitation. She knew she was crazy. What was she getting herself into? If iKill was dead, she had nothing to worry about. He hanged himself in his own room, four doors away from hers. That was that. This had to be a joke.

Suddenly, a chat window opened with a message from iKill. Mindy was convinced this must be some sort of prank. Who would pull a prank like this so late at night? Was someone trying to find her? It wouldn't be Rhoda, she thought. Maybe Greg wanted her attention more than she thought and had created a user name in the last five minutes. But he wasn't cunning and devious like Jerry had been.

Jerry had attacked her. It sounded incredible. Till now, she had always thought of her assailant as some regular guy, the kind you wouldn't notice as being a killer. Mindy's heart rate increased and she put her hand on her chest right between her breasts to calm herself down.

Mindy decided to get to the bottom of this iKill mystery. No one was going to play mind games with her. She had to protect her mind, she thought, because no one else would do that for her. She read iKill's chat message: i**Kill**: Hi, Mindy.

> **Mindy**: Who are u? i**Kill**: So we meet again . . .
> **Mindy**: He's dead. Jerry's dead. Who are u? Is this a joke? i**Kill**: Only if u want it to be.
> **Mindy**: What do u want from me? i**Kill**: Your body.
> **Mindy**: Is that you, Greg? i**Kill**: I could be Greg if it would get you in bed.
> **Mindy**: You're sick. Who are u? i**Kill**: You know me . . .
> **Mindy**: Chainsaw? i**Kill**: No.
> **Mindy**: Tyler? i**Kill**: Strike two.
> **Mindy**: Branford? i**Kill**: Three strikes and you're out. My turn.
> **Mindy**: You're scaring me. i**Kill**: No need to be afraid. What are you wearing?
> **Mindy**: Oh my God—is that u, Zach? i**Kill**: Tell me what ur wearing first.
> **Mindy**: A pink dress with black shoes. i**Kill**: How about underneath the dress?
> **Mindy**: Stop! Better tell me who u r or I'll log out. i**Kill**: Aw, u should know by now . . .
> **Mindy**: I know it's you, Zach. Stop playing around. i**Kill**: U make me laugh, Mindy. I love u.
> **Mindy**: It's over—iKill is dead. Jerry hanged himself. i**Kill**: No he didn't . . .
> **Mindy**: What? i**Kill**: Am I making you paranoid?
> **Mindy**: Zach, shut up. Where are u? i**Kill**: In heaven . . .
> **Mindy**: I swear I'll log off if you don't tell me who and where you are. i**Kill**: Actually, I'm right behind you . . .

Mindy wheeled round to look and saw no one. Her nerves were tattered.

> **Mindy**: No ur not. i**Kill**: Can't u see me?

Mindy: Stop! i**Kill**: Maybe I'm a ghost . . . then u couldn't
see me.

Mindy: Ghosts don't exist. i**Kill**: Well this one does. The
ghost of Jerry Fowler . . .

Mindy: Get real. Why r u doing this? i**Kill**: Don't believe in
ghosts, do u?

Mindy: Nope. i**Kill**: I have a butcher's knife with me . . .

Mindy: Why don't u shove it. i**Kill**: I like that feistiness . . .
shove it down ur throat?

Mindy: Jerry Fowler is dead and ur playing some kind of
sick game, Zach. i**Kill**: It's not a game.

Mindy: Then I'm logging off. i**Kill**: Afraid of ghosts?

Mindy: I told u, I don't believe in them. Good night,
asshole!

Suddenly a door slammed shut. Mindy turned around, but the door near her was open and she heard no other noises. She felt like crying. She felt her shoulder ache and wondered what she had gotten herself into. She wanted to log off and walk home, but even the thought of walking downstairs and back home for five minutes alone scared her to death.

Mindy was sure no one was around. It was probably the cleaning people. And whoever she was chatting with was more of a practical joker than a killer. Jerry Fowler was dead—she had to keep saying that. Jerry was dead.

Jerry was dead. It was probably Zach, because he was going through drug withdrawal, and besides, Jerry was . . .

Her train of thought was abruptly derailed by another message:

iKill: Did you hear that door slam? It scared me too.

Mindy turned around again and realized she might be in trouble. Her heart was booming like a bass drum, as loud as it was that night the lights went out in the shower. Mindy bit all her nails in nervous anticipation of impending doom and decided to continue the chat. i**Kill**: Don't run away. It's cold outside, but it's warm here in Strong Hall.

> **Mindy**: How did u know I'm here? **iKill**: I told u, I'm clairvoyant and I am right behind u, pretty thing . . .
> **Mindy**: No one is here. Stop scaring me or I'll call the police. **iKill**: I wouldn't do that if I were u.

Mindy got out her cell phone and was about to dial 911 when she read another message:

> **iKill**: Use that cell phone and I'll hack u into a dozen pieces, just like I beat the living hell out of Jenny Curtis, your friend. Remember her?

Mindy sat frozen for a minute. She began to hyperventilate and wished she had never left Edgar Hall. Every building had a killer. Someone was stalking her. She remembered once reading an article about copycat killers, and how when a psychotic murderer is caught, sometimes a double will appear on the scene and pick up where the original killer left off.

A door closed. She was sure of it. She heard footsteps coming closer, and someone was whistling. It was the same whistling she heard that night when she was in the shower and the lights suddenly went out.

Mindy gasped and took a deep breath. She saved her paper to her flash drive and hurried to log out of the Internet and her word-processing program. She decided to return to Edgar Hall and get some sleep. In her troubled mind, she still wasn't sure if she really was hearing whistling and footsteps or if it was all mere imagination.

Mindy put her handouts and sources and notebook into her book bag and turned to walk out of the room. She walked fast to beat the demons pounding away in her mind. She neared the doorway, turned right . . . and suddenly felt a spike drive through her heart as she saw a tall man wearing a padded red and black plaid shirt with extra long sleeves and a black mask. She could not tell who he was. She barely looked at him because she didn't want to know. Chainsaw? Zach?

Mindy shrieked and began to run toward the elevator. The man followed her and kept up with her. Mindy slammed on both buttons, but the elevator would not open. She ran and screamed "Help!" several times, but no one came to her rescue.

She looked back and realized that the man had just produced a long steel butcher's knife from his sleeve. Its blade shone in the fluorescent lights of the hallway. Mindy regretted ever having come to this computer lab and wished she were in bed safely asleep.

But safe was the last thing Mindy was. And then a voice from behind sent shockwaves through her chest and fireworks of black dots blazing across her brain and in front of her eyes.

"Come here, Mindy," iKill said. "I got a little something for you."

"Go away, you creep!" she shouted. iKill kept up the chase as Mindy got to the end of the hallway. There were some stairs directly ahead, and she opened the door to run down them. iKill followed.

"Don't run away, little girl," iKill said. "Didn't you get my e-mail? I sent pictures of Jerry and Sheila to you. Thought you might like a tasty midnight snack before going to bed."

Mindy raced down the stairs, turning left three times and hurtling two or three sets of steps at the same time to outrun her assailant.

"I want you, Mindy," iKill said. "I want your love blood."

Mindy began crying and running faster than before. She raced down the flight of stairs—fourth . . . third . . . second . . . running out of breath—and finally got down to the main floor of the building and looked for an exit. She didn't see one.

The man was about twenty feet behind her, and Mindy thought she could outrun him if she tried. Her shoulder ached and her legs were getting tired. But she had to run to save her life. She didn't want that butcher's knife to slice into her skin a second time. He had already gotten her good once.

Who was he? Mindy couldn't identify him even though he had only a padded shirt, black jeans, and a black mask on that concealed his face. She continued to run down the east hallway, looking back to see if she could tell who iKill was. She had no luck. Judging from his size—what little she could see because she was dashing down the corridor—Mindy thought of Zach, Chainsaw, Charlie, Shaggy, Gottlieb?

She thought it might be Chainsaw. He was a big guy, and so was the man chasing after her. It could also be Gottlieb, she thought, but she didn't think it was either Branford or Tyler. They were both too skinny and . . .

Mindy realized she was slowing down while iKill was in hot pursuit, only about fifteen feet behind her but not slowing down one bit. Mindy turned right under an exit sign and exulted that she could run free outside.

But the door was locked. Mindy pounded on the door and screamed for help as iKill laughed.

"Might as well stop running and give up," he said. "I have you beat, and you won't get away from me this time . . ."

"Who the hell are you?" Mindy asked.

"They call me iKill."

"But *who are you?*" She figured that whoever he was, he wasn't all that fast a runner.

Mindy shrieked one more time and pounded on some office door. Nobody was around. She thought surely one lone professor might be around preparing a final or grading, but all the office lights were out.

Mindy turned left to round the corner and noticed a small closet that was half open. She darted inside and held her breath. She was sure that iKill, still running in the east hallway but close to the corner, hadn't seen her sneak inside. If he could pass her, she could go back the same way and leave by an exit next to the stairs they had come down. She should have taken that exit but forgot about it in the panic of trying to outsprint this madman.

Mindy felt like crying but repressed it. Every emotion was tinged with the inevitability of becoming a victim. She wanted to live, she wanted to see Greg, and she wanted to survive long enough to marry and have a family.

"Funny the thoughts that come to mind when you're running for your life," she thought. She buried her face in her hands and felt a few tears roll down onto the palms of her hand. She was certain she wanted to marry Greg. He was right for her.

She took out her cell while shuddering in the small closet space, wondering what iKill was doing.

She heard no noises. That was weird. He had stopped running and was walking somewhere. This was creepy. She didn't want to call and let him hear her voice and then drive the butcher's knife into her head. She decided to wait.

Suddenly, the door of the closet flew open, and iKill looked her in the eyes and smiled. At least she imagined it was some sort of demonic smile behind that mask that shielded his identity. The mask was black with small holes and covered his hooded head, face, and neck, making it even harder to determine the person behind the mask.

"Why don't we make love right here and make some memories before you join the other girls?"

Mindy screamed and pushed him away from her. He raised his butcher's knife to stab her but missed, hitting the wall behind her instead. She felt a slight twinge above her left shoulder blade but thought nothing of it. She ran as fast as she could. iKill followed her toward the east hallway of Strong Hall. She thought for a moment that it must be Chainsaw—he wasn't all that coordinated, but he was solid and slow, just like this idiot.

Mindy ran for her life. She was outside—that was much better than being trapped in the building. She looked around and saw no one. She bolted for Edgar Hall, and iKill ran even faster. Within a couple minutes, he overtook her and tackled her to the ground.

Mindy shrieked loudly to try to get someone's attention. She heard a dog bark. She couldn't believe there weren't any officers on site—where was everyone? She couldn't believe that no one was walking outside. She felt her knees scrape against the pavement. She looked down at her legs and noticed two large red patches of blood.

She felt iKill get on top of her and screamed. He shoved his gloved hand into her mouth and punched her in the face.

"Now you listen to me, you bitch," he said. The mask distorted his voice and Mindy dared not open her eyes, so she had no idea who was on top of her. She couldn't place the voice no matter how hard she tried. "You got away from me once, in the bathroom, but you aren't going to get away again . . ."

Mindy suddenly kicked him in the groin, and iKill winced and fell over. She punched him twice in the face as he let his guard down and set his knife on the ground in order to grab his aching crotch. She hit the target, and he was in excruciating pain. She kicked him in the groin two more times and decided to make a break for it.

Mindy got up and ran toward Edgar Hall. iKill also rose and caught up with her again. Mindy took a different turn and tried to lose iKill, but he kept up his pursuit.

Mindy waited behind a large SUV and caught her breath. She didn't see or hear anyone, so she thought the coast was clear. But fear was pulsing though her veins at around 180 beats per minute, and she was paralyzed. She didn't want to move. She wanted to live. How she wished she could have some help at this moment.

Mindy decided to call Charlie at the front desk. Abby answered and said that Tom Malkin and Officer Sampson were looking for her, but it was difficult to communicate; Mindy was hysterical. Malkin had just returned from searching around campus and was awaiting word from Sampson and Foster. Abby turned the phone over to him.

Mindy talked to Malkin, who wasted no time in slamming down the phone and running out to where she was hiding. He found her cowering behind a bush adjacent to a parking lot on Marshall Avenue, just south of Edgar Hall.

"Are you all right?" he asked.

"I've been attacked . . . in the computer lab . . . in Strong Hall over there . . . it was iKill . . . it wasn't Jerry . . . I don't know what is going on. Tell me . . ."

Malkin brought her into Edgar Hall and put a blanket around her to help minimize her trembling. Abby brought some rum for her. After a few minutes, Malkin asked her to describe everything that had happened to her since she left the party early.

Mindy was still trying to catch her breath. All had been going well with her paper, working on the fifth floor of Strong Hall, till iKill suddenly showed up, first online and then in person. It shook her up badly, and Mindy requested some Kleenex. She was crying like mad at this point. The worlds spinning around her mental disintegration formed imaginary tools of torture that looked all too real.

Malkin gave her more time to collect her breath, emotions, and thoughts before he asked for a description. Mindy described iKill as she remembered him, with that plaid shirt and jeans and knife and black mask. She said she thought it was one of the students.

Mindy begged Malkin to take her to the hotel where her parents were staying. She was afraid that iKill would try to get her.

"Don't worry," he said, "we'll get you there."

Mindy was adamant—she would settle for anything but her old room. She felt her body to make sure she didn't get sliced up when he took a few jabs at her while she was hiding in the hallway closet.

"I know everything, I have for a while," Malkin said.

"Who is it then? Who tried to kill me twice?"

Malkin walked Mindy to his car and said, "I'm glad you're safe. I was worried about you when I got that e-mail tonight. But the whole day I'd thought something was wrong . . ."

"What e-mail?"

"An e-mail from iKill," Malkin said. "I was wondering how he'd gotten my e-mail address of all things, but of course he got it from the handouts given around campus in case anyone had any information to lend to the police."

"What did the e-mail say?"

"It was just a short note saying something twisted—that he had killed Jerry Fowler. He sent a picture of Fowler hanging in his room. That was a real shocker to everyone, but my mind was going in another direction. That celebration was my chance to observe everyone, especially iKill."

Mindy shivered. She was cold with fear and trembling from head to toe.

"Let's get you set up in your folks' hotel," he said. "You'll be safe there. I won't let you get in harm's way . . ."

Suddenly a tall figure ran was seen dashing about 100 feet away, across the street. Though it was dark, his silhouette matched that of the person who had just attacked her—damn bastard.

"Look, over there!" Mindy said. "That's him! That's him!" Mindy scrambled behind Malkin and peered around his left side to see where the dark figure in the distance was running.

"All right," Malkin said, "just calm down. My car is right here. Let's get in and see what he does."

Mindy was happy after she entered Malkin's car. He let her in first, keeping an eye on the tall figure at the opposite end of the parking lot. The man appeared to be limping and got into a car. They watched as he started his car and turned on the headlights.

Malkin thought it was a medium-sized sedan. It was difficult to tell in the dark, but he guessed it was a Taurus or a Camry. He couldn't make out the license plate from so far away, but it appeared to be from Virginia.

"Are you sure that was the same man that just followed you?" Malkin asked. "Are you sure that's iKill?"

"I just know that black and red plaid shirt and that black mask. That's him! I am sure!"

Malkin started the car. "Let's go for it then!"

Chapter Twelve

I Kill pulled out of the parking lot and turned left onto Marshall
Avenue at about thirty miles per hour. Malkin was in hot pursuit of
him and remained a steady two hundred feet behind. He still had
no opportunity to catch the license plates, but he was sure the man was
driving a white car.

Mindy said, "I'm scared. I can't believe this is happening."

Malkin grabbed his cell phone. "Don't worry, we've got him."

"Got who?" Mindy asked.

Just a minute. He called Foster. "Malkin here," he said, using the
police radio since he was speeding up. "Listen, Mindy Adams was
attacked by iKill about an hour ago. She got away from him, and he
followed her back to Edgar. Right when we got into my car to take her
to her parents' hotel room, this iKill fellow—we couldn't make out who
it was, but he's tall and thin and wearing a plaid black and red shirt
with jeans and some sort of weird long black mask, looks like some sort
of Halloween mask, nothing Freddy would wear—got into my car and
we're chasing him down. We're about two hundred feet behind him.
He's headed north on Marshall. He just turned right and is going about
sixty miles per hour east on Broad. We're heading to a traffic light."

Foster said, "Roger. We'll send reinforcements. Let me know if he
heads toward the highway."

"You got it. He blew the red light and knows we're about a hundred
and fifty feet behind him going around seventy miles per hour up Van
Buren Street. He's pushed it to eighty and is heading directly east."

Foster said, "I'll head out that way and contact police in the next
town to set up a roadblock. Stay on the line and make sure he doesn't

make any strange turns. The next town is Grantville, about five miles away."

Malkin put the pedal to the metal and kept up with iKill. He looked over at Mindy, whose face was as white as the moonlight piercing through the wispy clouds above.

"Nice night for a car chase," he said. "Sure you don't want to change your major to LEJA? You'd deserve about twelve hours of independent study just for surviving this bloody mess."

Mindy had other ideas. "Nice night to imagine none of this is happening."

"But this is good," Malkin said. "In a few minutes, we'll have captured the worst serial killer this area has ever known: Mr. Charlie White."

Mindy froze. "What? You know and didn't tell anyone? That's rotten!"

Malkin explained, "There is a time and place for everything. In this case, it's a car chase. Don't worry, we'll get him."

"But how do you know for sure?"

"Everyone was focusing on the students. They were the likely suspects. But I began suspecting others, including Charlie and Shaggy, and let everyone believe it was a Blackwood student. Charlie didn't know he was suspected, so he made a few bad turns, pun intended."

Following a few minutes of contemplation while staying about a hundred and fifty feet behind iKill's vehicle, Malkin laughed. "I should have known earlier. What a damn fool I've been."

Mindy turned to him, the blanket still wrapped around her and her shoulder still bleeding. She stuck her right forefinger into the wound above her left shoulder and saw red blood slivering down her nail as if it were red nail polish.

"At least we know it's Charlie. God, and he seemed so nice. He's just a regular guy who liked helping students. Who'd think it could be him, he's so soft-spoken."

"Exactly. That was his agenda, that no one should suspect him."

"Then why didn't you just arrest him tonight before he came to get me again in Strong Hall?"

"Evidence, since we'd never get a confession out of him. And motive, that was the hardest aspect of the case to attain. Why should he want to kill you or Jenny or Denise or Sheila for that matter?" Malkin laughed.

"Didn't make any sense. And from a psychological angle, it now makes sense."

This Charlie sure knows how to drive. And by the way, he was also the James River Killer.

Foster's voice came back on the phone. "All right—we've got an EMT unit and three vehicles blocking Van Buren just south of Grantville, right before the train tracks. Make sure you slow down just before heading into that intersection. It will come up right after a big billboard on the right for some restaurant."

"Didn't know there were any restaurants in Grantville," Malkin laughed. "Will do. Thanks for the blockade. That should make our job easier. Meet you out there. And by the way, Charlie White is the one we're chasing. He's iKill."

"What?" Foster was befuddled. "Been keeping a secret from us? You mean Mr. Nice, Charlie White? How did you know?"

"I'll explain everything later, for now let's catch the son of a bitch."

Malkin kept up the chase as iKill sped up to ninety miles per hour. The highway curved to the left and again to the right as a slight drizzle began to descend upon them.

"With any luck, this will turn into ice relatively soon," Malkin said. "And then we'll have lots of fun."

The car iKill was driving began to slow down. Malkin slowed down but got close enough to see that he was driving a Ford Taurus; looked like the 2002 model. The roads were getting icy so Malkin called Foster.

"Got the car identified—it's a 2002 white Ford Taurus. Know anyone with that kind of car?"

"Charlie White," Mindy said.

Malkin realized why Charlie was slowing down. About five hundred feet in front of them, beneath the red glare of traffic lights, there were three police cars with their sirens blaring.

Charlie was out of his mind. He made a daring right-hand turn just before that intersection onto a narrow rural road. Malkin followed in hot pursuit and also turned right, gunning it to eighty miles per hour. The rain was falling harder, and he was sure it would turn to sleet. Mindy was clutching her seat and felt like jumping into the back.

"Don't be afraid," he told her. "I've done this a million times."

Mindy sighed. She looked at him but had nothing to say. She got a headache just trying to believe the impossible and how Charlie could have killed so many . . ."

The car accelerated to a hundred miles per hour and tore along the curvy narrow road that split through corner fences surrounding small yards.

Malkin called in to Foster: "We're on a rural road. He saw your roadblock and split right. Don't know which road—about five hundred feet from that Highway 16 and Highway 39 intersection where you guys are waiting."

"We'll follow you on 39 and try to cut him off where the two join just before Jackson City," Foster said.

"Sounds good. Barely remember any of these places. We're going about ninety, so you'll have to gun it."

They pursued iKill for about ten more minutes before a bridge suddenly appeared. Malkin thought about passing him up, but the road was too narrow. Had Mindy not been in the car with him, he would have pulled up next to the car and sideswiped it. Malkin was an excellent driver and enjoyed combat driving.

Suddenly, iKill sped up, and his car jumped up as it tried to cross the bridge. He lost control of the vehicle and it spun out of control on the bridge. It swerved to the left, then to the right, and then to the left again before barely making it across.

"That might be the ice," Malkin said, "or else our friend isn't that great a driver."

"Charlie! Stop already!" Mindy shouted.

"A demented man," Malkin said. "He should have been caught years ago."

"What do you mean?"

Before Malkin had a chance to answer, iKill swerved again and his car hit the side of the road. It spun out of control and sparks flew as the rear bumper scraped against the slick pavement at ninety miles per hour.

"I think he's starting to lose it," Malkin said. "Give him another minute or so and he'll be—"

Suddenly Charlie turned sharply to the right at breakneck speed—must have been at least seventy miles per hour. The car turned on its two left wheels only, and Mindy almost passed out—the two right wheels were a foot above the ground for at least five seconds.

"Nothing compared to killing three women," he said. "And he would have kept on killing if he could have. I am sure of that."

Malkin turned right to follow the vehicle; it accelerated again, and iKill was now headed south on a dirt road.

Malkin called in to Foster. "Apparently he knows our game plan," he said. "He pulled up before reaching Grantville, and now he pulled up and turned right before reaching Hampton. We're on some unidentified dirt road in the middle of nowhere, but we're on him."

"There are five squad cars headed your way—two from Blackwood and two from Grantville. Another one is headed east in case he changes his mind and heads toward Jackson City. So we've got him covered. Stay on him, and we should have our man soon enough."

Malkin told Mindy what Foster had just said, and she covered her eyes. *Anything but this*, she thought. She wanted to jump out of the car because she was sure they were going to have a fatal accident.

The car Charlie was driving accelerated to over a hundred miles per hour. He pulled away from Malkin for a few seconds, but he caught up. Malkin was going over a hundred and ten and thought it was about time to challenge Mr. White.

"Let's see what this serial killer is made of," Malkin said. He took out his Smith & Wesson and opened the window. He fired two shots at Charlie's car—it was the first time he was within shooting distance of the vehicle—and missed.

"What are you doing?" Mindy screamed.

"What do you mean, 'what am I doing'?" He fired two more shots, and this time one of them hit the back window, shattering it into concentric glass fragments. Though he had the high beams on, Malkin still was not close enough to make out the license plate. iKill's vehicle made a sharp turn to the right and hit a few rocks on the side of the road. His bumper scraped the pavement again, sending sparks into the cold night air. Malkin picked up the speed and was within fifty feet of iKill's car when it suddenly turned left onto another small rural road.

"This nut has got this place memorized," Malkin said. "How could anyone know where all these little roads are? There isn't a single light within a mile of here."

Mindy felt scared. This was a nightmare she was living.

Suddenly, Charlie made a sharp left turn and swerved to avoid missing a deer. Malkin barely missed the deer too, which darted back into the field.

"Close call," Malkin said. "Leave it to a deer to help a killer get away."

Mr. iKill spun to the left and then to the right, crossing a major highway without stopping.

"I'll be damned," Malkin yelled. "We just crossed 16 again. I think I know where we are. Our friend just turned west onto National Road."

Mindy recognized the name and realized they were back close to Blackwood again. Malkin kept chase at seventy miles per hour, and then slowed down because he knew there were a few turns ahead.

Charlie made the first turn as the road suddenly veered left around the president's house. There was a steep slope downward, and iKill was clearly trying to make his getaway at this time. Malkin accelerated to push Charlie the iKill to drive even faster. iKill almost lost control of the car when it hit the side of a small hill to the right. He avoided the ditch and continued downhill at nearly a hundred miles per hour.

They approached a small bridge at the bottom of the hill over the James River. Malkin slowed down, but Charlie pushed it to over a hundred miles per hour. His car made a sudden turn to the right and nailed the bridge post on the side of the road. The left side of iKill's vehicle crashed into the cement post, but he continued driving into the dark forest. He collided with a few trees before the car came to a grinding halt. The right headlight stared into the distance as Malkin pulled up on the bridge and called Foster to say Charlie had crashed.

The tall, dark figure got out of the car slowly and tried to make a run for it. Malkin chased him down, and once within fifteen feet fired a shot. Malkin hit his target right where he'd aimed—in the thigh of the left leg—and ran toward the captured killer quivering in the dirt.

Malkin and Mindy ran toward iKill. He tried crawling away and still had his black mask on. All Mindy could think was this was the worst week of her life, all due to this miscreant that everyone trusted.

"The game is up, Charlie White," Malkin said. "You're going to get a lethal dose if I have anything to say about your sentence." Malkin tore off the mask, and Mindy gasped as she found herself staring at the man who had greeted her almost every morning for fifteen weeks with a friendly smile, her mail, and sometimes even a doughnut or some coffee. She couldn't believe her eyes.

"It was you?" she yelled. "What the hell were you thinking?"

Charlie was lying cramped in pain. "My leg . . . you shot me, damn you!"

Malkin laughed. "You're lucky. I wanted you alive, you sick bastard. And now I declare you charged with the first-degree murders of Jenny Curtis, Denise Lansing, Jerry Fowler—that was a clever one—and Sheila Underwood. For all the hell you've put this fine Blackwood community through, I can only wish that same hell upon you."

Other police officers arrived at the scene and hauled Charlie White away. Foster congratulated Malkin on a well-done car chase.

"I've had my fair share of practice," Malkin said. "But never in the backwoods of rural Virginia."

Mindy walked back to the car crying. "I need to call my parents," she said. Malkin thought that was a good idea. He called Edgar Hall, and Abby answered the phone. He told Abby to make sure all the residents of Edgar Hall were assembled together in the lounge by 9:00 a.m. the next morning.

"I have some good news for all of them," Malkin said. "We've caught up with and captured iKill and charged him with four counts of first-degree murder. This time," he added, "we're certain we've got our killer. Mr. Charlie 'iKill' White is in custody."

* * *

Malkin eyed the group of students from Edgar Hall as they collected various foods from the cafeteria. He waited for everyone to be seated before speaking. He looked around at Chainsaw, Gottlieb, Chip, Tyler, Branford, Zach, Rhoda, Mindy, Stacy, Malcolm and his wife, Jackie, and George.

"I just wanted to let you know that this has been a devastating week for all of you, a week filled with unfortunate, senseless murders. But I have some good news for you. Last night, around one a.m., we apprehended the killer known as iKill and charged him with the murders of Jenny, Denise, Sheila, and Jerry."

All the students were in shock. They had not heard any news yet—the story was just breaking but they had yet to hear about it—and Mindy had said nothing to them, since she stayed with her parents.

"And I just wanted to let you know that the murderer known as iKill was in fact Charlie White."

All the students gasped. They couldn't believe what they heard.

"Are you sure? That's impossible!" Abby was incredulous.

"Almost impossible, but not quite impossible," Malkin said. "In my line of work, that's a huge difference."

The students threw question after question at Malkin. He explained what he considered the finer points of the case and told them that he had realized Fowler's suicide could not have really been that since he received an e-mail with pictures of Fowler hanging. That was his first real clue that only Charlie could have access to a key to enter the room—or many rooms any time a student was not at home. It seemed quite simple, and yet the whole time Charlie's temperament—quiet and agreeable—contradicted that possibility and instead led everyone to believe that one of the students must have been the culprit.

Another mistake Charlie made, Malkin explained, was that there was no clear motive—at least at first. A few students asked Malkin about this, and he said he had reached the conclusion that only a deeply disturbed and angry man could have committed the murders of the girls and Fowler. He then saw the only common thread among the various deeds: that someone held deep resentment against the students and that Charlie's motive could be none other than cold-blooded revenge. Let's just say he lost his temper in a very evil way.

Charlie was vengeful for many reasons, but he was particularly angry with female students because he had never married. Presumably he had met a few women who snubbed him, and over the years this resentment increased to unhealthy levels. Think about Charlie's background, Malkin told the students. He never had the opportunity to go to college, and with only a high-school diploma was stuck in the same dead-end job for more than twenty years. He had come to hate students whose parents had given them everything—new computers, cell phones, cars, and spending money for beer and food and all the luxuries they could afford. He mostly resented students who drove fancy cars, and thus he must have particularly enjoyed killing Sheila Underwood in hers following the sorority party.

Malkin explained further that Charlie kept odd hours at Edgar Hall. Sometimes he worked days and other times he worked nights or second shift. He seemed to enjoy being around students because he was a loner; however, at the same time, he was a bitter loner who hated students benefiting with opportunities he would never have. He was not only a dangerous killer but also a fairly good actor. He played the role of sympathetic elder figure rather well.

"One more thing," Malkin said, "Charlie was a very good whistler. We had that from Mindy when she was attacked in the bathroom and again in Strong Hall, but that stood out as significant evidence. It was not the same as Shaggy's or Zach's whistling."

Furthermore, pouring salt into a weeklong wound, Malkin informed the students that Charlie in fact was the James River Killer of a few years ago. "He was the one that Foster described as killing women in the forest and getting away with it. No one was caught for those killings. He was a clever killer, and the most cunning thing about him was that he realized that if police could not come up with a motive, they would have to find another link to deviant behavior—such as Malcolm's drug ring—and connect the murders to drugs. That was part of the killer genius of iKill. He was able to deflect attention away from a seemingly invisible motive. As such, Malcolm almost hanged for what Charlie did, and I'm sure our loyal front-desk manager wouldn't have felt the least bit remorseful."

"Amazing," George said. "And all along I think we all suspected it must have been one of us—I mean, one of the students."

Malkin laughed. "The police were certainly leaning that way. But Charlie was too slick. Sending people e-mails with digital pictures he had taken was just his way of proving he could outsmart a more technologically advanced younger generation he loathed. And therein lies the second big motive for his murders: in general, with each successive murder, he felt he was a little too smart for everyone else. Thus he overcame a huge inferiority complex by murdering and doing so in a technologically advanced, intelligent manner.

"It was all in front of our eyes: motive of resentment and revenge, pure and simple. Fortunately, Charlie is now in custody, and I've been informed he's cooperating with law enforcement in between fits of rage.

"Another smooth move—cunning for someone who didn't appear cunning—was murdering Jerry Fowler and making it out to be suicide.

That was easy enough for Charlie. See, we found out from Malcolm that his drug ring included several students on campus, but mainly Zach, Jerry, and numerous others in Webster Hall. Well, guess what: Charlie was in on it too—not as a user, but as a distributor like Malcolm. It was Charlie who protected many of the students in Edgar. Following Malcolm's bust, Jerry was left without dope and in severe withdrawal. Malcolm cooperated with law enforcement officials but did not divulge information leading to Charlie; instead he mentioned some students' names."

Malcolm nodded.

Malkin continued, "So then Jerry must have confronted Charlie and said he would seek treatment and tell the police everything. Charlie must have agreed to supply Jerry with some dope, and they did some in Jerry's room late at night. But Charlie gave Jerry an overdose to knock him out and then hanged him in such a way as to make it look like a successful suicide attempt.

"Only one thing went wrong. This morning, I received a call from the hospital confirming that a large amount of heroin was found in Jerry's body. Now, if he were going to kill himself by hanging, there would be no point in taking heroin first. Another key point is that people on dope like heroin usually don't care enough to carry out something like a hanging. So Charlie was in on that, and he set everything up quite well—the chair, the computer with confession typed up, the works." Pretty damn smart, and Jerry had everyone fooled despite his suspicious behavior. He came very close to fitting the extremely intelligent profile of iKill, but instead it was Charlie who was behind the Blackwood butchering—like I said, he had guts and a talent for acting. A very dangerous type."

The students of Edgar Hall and Teresa Martinez proposed a toast to Tom Malkin, who realized that he had arrived at Blackwood a week ago to give a speech about terrorism and would leave today having given his second speech on terrorism of a different sort.

"So what's going to happen to Charlie?" Jackie asked.

Malkin looked at her sternly and said, "That's for the courts to decide, assuming they actually go by the Constitution rather than some sort of cosmic, liberal notion like repressed feelings. If I have anything to say about it, I hope he gets the needle. He deserves it. Some crimes, such as the ones he committed, are too ghastly not to be given the ultimate punishment."

"Amen to that," George said, putting his arm around Jackie. Rhoda gave Tyler a big hug.

"From now on, everything is going to be all right." He kissed her on the cheek and Rhoda blushed.